STEEPED
IN
LOVE

JULIE EVELYN JOYCE

Steeped in Love Copyright © 2018 by Julie Evelyn Joyce Doner

All rights reserved. No part of this book may be reproduced in any form or by any electronic or mechanical means including information storage and retrieval systems, without permission in writing from the author. The only exception is by a reviewer, who may quote short excerpts in a review.

Cover design and E-book formatting by Margaret Ethridge
Edits by Sarah Pesce of Lopt & Cropt editing services

This book is a work of fiction. Names, characters, places, and incidents either are products of the author's imagination or are used fictitiously. Any resemblance to actual persons, living or dead, events, or locales is entirely coincidental.

Julie Evelyn Joyce
Visit my website at julieevelynjoyce.com

Printed in the United States of America

First Printing: Oct. 2018

ISBN: 978-1-7239-9434-0

This book is dedicated to my beautiful mother. I started writing Steeped in Love a couple months before she passed away suddenly. It was meant to be a gift to her, and I'm still treating it as such. So, here you go, Mom. I hope it makes you proud.

Addie Mitchell is a pie-on-the-fly entrepreneur who's finally ready to settle down in the big, empty house her late great-aunt Edna left to her. Frustrated with her lack of success in romance, Addie turns to another gift her great-aunt passed on to her—the art of reading tea leaves—to aid her in her search for the ideal mate.

Novelist Ethan Holtz is having a hard time sinking his teeth into his next project, but he finds Addie fascinating. Mainly for her ability to make her dates disappear in fifteen minutes or less. He can't help but eavesdrop on her dates in the local coffee shop, his writing haven, and soon finds himself taking pointers on what not to do from her failed suitors.

Though her methods seem nothing short of mad, he falls fast and hard for the pixie-haired pie-pusher. She thinks they're all wrong for each other, but Ethan teams up with the tea leaves to prove they're so right.

Contents

1	2
2	19
3	31
4	44
5	52
6	64
7	73
8	88
9	98
10	111
11	121
12	136
13	145
14	157
15	171
16	185
17	199
18	214
Epilogue	233

1

Coffee creamed and stirred. Laptop fired up. Knuckles cracked.

Ethan Holtz took a deep breath and waited for inspiration to strike.

And waited.

And waited.

He swigged some coffee, hoping a sudden jolt of caffeine might awaken the creative juices.

Nope. Though it was a particularly good cup of joe this morning. Not wanting to let the discovery go unappreciated, he raised his mug in salute to Gwen, the talented barista and shop owner. Someone around here should be appreciated for their work.

She smiled as she whirled past him, her hands loaded with empty mugs and crumb-filled plates. Lord, he wanted a cherry danish. But not yet. Not until he cranked out the first thousand words.

Ethan had been living in Kendal for months, but even he had to admit he hadn't done much to make an impression. More an observer than participant, he knew who his neighbors were, but he didn't feel the need to engage in meaningless chit-chat with them. Unless you counted Mrs. McCallister and her three grandchildren. They often crossed paths at the public swimming pool.

Typical introvert, at least according to multiple Facebook quizzes, he liked his books and television shows and felt comfortable only in a few particular spots, like the Cup-A-Cabana coffee shop.

He'd been writing there for several weeks now, hoping the change of scenery and the colorful mix of people he observed would help his writer's block. Sure beat staring at the bland walls of the apartment he rented. But until recently, the writing wasn't the problem. It was the fact that the books he worked so hard on weren't selling. A demoralizing reality, but a reality nonetheless.

He knew he was good. His psychological thrillers were deep and thought-provoking, not only according to him but to several critics. When *Thrilled About Thrillers* gave him a Top Pick, he was sure he'd made it. His agent had gushed on and on about the esteemed acknowledgement, yet somehow his critical acclaim hadn't translated to commercial success.

Lowering his gaze to the screen, the blank page glared back and the cursor taunted him.

Oh, to hell with it.

Ethan flagged down Gwen and ordered the damn danish. On her return with the pastry, she topped up his mug. He lifted his head to acknowledge the gesture, but an entirely different woman caught his eye outside the door. She was bent over, locking her bike to a lamppost, unmindful of every man who gawked at her obvious assets on display, including himself. When she righted herself again, recognition dawned.

Adelaide Mitchell, owner and operator of the one and only Pie-Cycle.

He couldn't help but watch as she entered the café, a pixie-haired woman with wide brown eyes, pink lips, and short shorts that hugged her so tightly he felt envious of spandex.

He rarely got to see Addie up close. Gwen called her that, and the short form suited her. They'd never properly met, but he'd noticed her. Even when she'd whiz by in a blur on her bike, oh, he'd notice her. The writer in him enjoyed the mystique about her, had fun contemplating her personality . . . among other things. She always appeared to be in such a hurry, selling her freshly baked hand pies at all the hubs in this town and the neighboring ones. He'd never tried one, being that he was partial to danishes. But a girl like Addie, well, she might tempt a guy to give pie a try.

Did she make a living at it? His cooking skills ranked somewhere between novice and non-existent, and he'd never baked in his life, but people had to eat. No one *needed* to read, as disturbing as that seemed. Writing, he'd admit, was a pie-in-the-sky career choice, but hers was actually pie.

Addie ordered at the counter, speaking animatedly to Gwen who gave an occasional nod while filling orders for other customers. He sat too far away to hear her chatting over the competing noise, but the kaleidoscope of emotions that played across her face kept him spellbound. If the pie thing didn't work out, she could be a mime. Except something told him she'd never be able to hold her tongue.

Addie took a seat a couple of tables over, her back to him. She pulled a tube of lipstick from her pocket and used an old bicycle side mirror from her bag to apply it. Her short hairstyle emphasized the long, slim column of her neck. Her aquamarine bike shoes slapped anxiously against the floor, like it pained her to sit still for too long. He glanced down to find his own foot tapping in sync with hers.

Gwen delivered a steaming mug to Addie's table. "Here's your tea," she said. "Good luck. Hope you find what you're looking for."

Well, that's an odd thing to say. What's she looking for? The meaning of life? The perfect ratio of honey to lemon in her tea—

"How's the writing going, Ethan?"

He flinched, startled to find Gwen hovering over him with a knowing smile on her face. "Fine," he muttered.

Her soft hum proved she'd seen the blank page he failed to minimize fast enough. "Hope your hands don't cramp up," she teased, then sauntered back behind the counter to cash someone out.

Ethan missed those days—when his fingers could barely keep pace with the words flowing from his brain. It was hell to find inspiration when you knew what you were writing would tank before it even hit the shelves. Releasing a heavy sigh, he rubbed his temples. He could be bitter and cynical all he wanted, but the truth was that he needed to rebrand himself if he had a hope in Hades of selling anything. He'd still be a thriller author, but his stories were about to take on a different spin. According to his research, every successful book nowadays had "girl" in the title: *Gone Girl*, *The Good Girl*, *The Girl on the Train*, *The Girl with the Dragon Tattoo* . . .

He looked up, suddenly curious beyond all reason if Addie had any tattoos, another detail he could add to his mental rolodex. But something else stole his attention. She wasn't sitting alone anymore.

A man sat at her table. So that must have been what Gwen meant. This was a date. Addie Mitchell was looking for a man.

Unwritten story forgotten, Ethan pushed his laptop toward the center of the table so he could lean forward. If he propped his elbow on the table and twisted just a little to the right, he had a much better position for eavesdropping.

"I was so glad you contacted me," the guy said.

He was almost a full head taller than Addie while seated. Ethan hated him for that alone. The guy wore a faded grey T-shirt, his hair slicked back like he'd just gone for a run and this meeting was the next item on his to-do list. The biceps bulging beneath the stretched-out fabric probably earned him back whatever points he lost, if any, for his less than impressive first date attire.

But maybe this wasn't a date.

"I love morning dates," Addie replied.

Okay, scratch that theory.

"If it's good, it can run right through to the afternoon and turn into lunch, even dinner if you play your cards right. If it's bad, you still have the rest of the day to make up for it. I'm sure it won't be bad, though, because you seem great, and this place is great, and the food is . . . well, great, so we're definitely on the right track."

Her date blinked, clearly trying to catch up to the woman who talked a mile a minute. "We'll see how breakfast goes first, but I make a mean sandwich."

He couldn't see Addie's reaction, but he could somehow sense she was smiling. She fiddled with her hoop earring and he spotted a tiny green leaf inked just behind her lobe. *Ahh, so she does have a tatt.* He sort of liked that she'd hidden it. She made you work for it. Ethan cocked his head, fascinated that she'd been able to sit still long enough for someone to mark that perfect porcelain skin. Why a leaf, though? And what kind of leaf was it, exactly? Maybe she had a green thumb. Or perhaps she was a pothead. He'd smoked a joint once or twice in his life, but he wasn't about to advertise it to the world.

"More coffee, Ethan?" Gwen asked.

"Thanks," he murmured distractedly.

Gwen ducked down until she was in his direct line of sight. "How's he doing?" she whispered.

"Huh?"

"The guy." She nodded over her shoulder. "Bachelor number one."

Ethan coughed. "I wouldn't know."

Gwen looked pointedly at his idling laptop. "She's been trying the online dating thing. In fact, she has another date lined up later this week. Here again. I guess she figures a public place is best."

"I see. Do you plan on charging admission? I may need to rob my piggy bank."

Gwen shrugged. "Just making conversation."

"I'll be sure to add it to my calendar," he deadpanned. Gwen wasn't usually so chatty with him, and she'd never been gossipy before. Glancing up, he was surprised to still find her hovering. Was it that obvious he'd been eavesdropping on Addie's date?

"She even answered some singles ads in *The Daily Dispatch*," Gwen carried on. "That's where she found this guy."

Ethan rarely paid attention to the local newspaper. It was such rubbish. But if Addie found it interesting . . . "Is that safe?"

Gwen laughed. "I'd say so. We're not known for harboring criminals in Kendal, unless eating too much pie is a crime. I'd happily do time for that."

He knew many people were trying the online dating thing these days, but Addie was looking for love in a newspaper, too. Could it really be that simple? Ethan pulled his laptop closer and wiggled his mouse to wake it, an unexpected wave of inspiration hitting him full force. "He seems to be doing well so far," he grudgingly admitted.

"Keep me posted," Gwen said.

He barely heard her over his fingers tapping frantically against the keys. *The Girl Who Made Headlines. Chapter One.*

Addie absentmindedly stirred her tea as Jonathan prattled on about . . . God only knows what. His chiseled muscles were too distracting for her to care. Based on appearance alone, this guy had it going on. But she doubted her great-aunt Edna would have approved. She had instinctive insight about the opposite sex and always used to say that pumped-up men don't make good husbands. Something about them having too much testosterone and not enough brain power to know when to keep it in their pants.

Her mother, on the other hand, still hadn't forgiven her for not marrying Steve, the guy she went to prom with, and liked to point out how Boring Steve had gone on to become a physician. A man who could provide well meant a comfortable and safe life—her mother's mantra. She didn't have to look beyond her own upbringing for proof of that, but she'd never seen her parents embrace. Her business-comes-first father hardly spent enough time at home to warrant such warmth.

Edna had taken one glance at their carefully posed prom photo and commented that Steve looked like he had fallen arches and wouldn't age well. The elder woman craved spark more than safety but stood by her assertion that the best men could give you both. Addie wondered if Dr. Steve ever found a cure for his own insufferable halitosis.

All her life, Addie'd found it so much easier to connect with her great-aunt than with her own parents. As a child, she'd been enchanted by her, and as an adult, she admired Edna's steadfast commitment to her beliefs.

Which is kind of how she wound up here in the first place, searching for Mr. Right and using a tried-and-true formula passed down from the woman who'd already changed her life by leaps and bounds. She'd inherited her great-aunt's house, along with a tidy sum of money, after she'd died close to a year ago. She never expected to be a homeowner until she got married and had kids, but she was no closer to getting hitched at thirty-two than she'd been at twenty.

Dating sucked. She'd tried it all—blind dating, double dating, randomly-meeting-a-guy-at-a-bar dating, and she'd even played the damsel in distress at the hardware store, having heard it described as the hotspot for handy homeowners. A drill, a handsaw, and four new hammers later, and she still hadn't reeled one in.

So now she was trying Edna's method. Edna believed fully in seeking love by the leaf. The practiced tasseographer met and married her husband all because the tea leaves told her he was the one. Of course, Addie thought the idea ludicrous at first, but Edna had proven time and again how reliable the leaves were. Eventually, she'd given in and let the dear old woman teach her how to read her own leaves.

Not that she'd done much with the skill, but it was becoming harder and harder to ignore. Indeed, one night, about a week ago, as she sipped her tea at the kitchen table, the unrelenting hiss of the wind through the un-weatherproofed windows sounded suspiciously like Edna whispering to her, mocking her pathetic love life. The next morning, she vowed to stop enhancing her tea with valerian root to help her sleep. She also found herself flipping through the singles ads in *The Daily Dispatch*, and registering for an online dating site.

So far, two bachelors had agreed to her request for a meeting. Well, the only two with any real potential, that is. She'd been inundated by cheesy pick-up lines and pictures of appendages—because that was a thing now—and eagerly dismissed the lewd dudes. Duds.

Addie lifted her gaze to find Jonathan, bachelor number one, staring at her intently, like he awaited some kind of response. "Uh . . . yes?" When in doubt, "yes" was the best answer.

He beamed. "Sweet! We'll have to try it sometime."

Oh, Christ. What had she agreed to? "Right, sure. It's . . . the perfect weather for . . . that."

"I know, right? I'm so stoked you're game."

In all honesty, it didn't really matter what he proposed. The guy was gorgeous. If he'd asked her to go streaking in a cemetery, she would have agreed just to see him in his birthday suit.

"You seem like you're up for anything. What other kinds of adventurous stuff do you like to do?" While the question sounded innocent enough, the borderline-lecherous look in his eyes indicated his direction of thinking.

Maybe she *had* just agreed to go streaking in a cemetery. Her mind raced as she tugged nervously at the clingy fabric of her tank top. "Oh, I'm a regular Bear Grylls," she lied. "Name a mountain, I've climbed it. Sandboarding? Done it. Whitewater rafting? Child's play." Fibs, fables, and fictions so ridiculous even she had to stifle a smile, but at least she'd pulled a grin from him, too.

He chuckled, leaning in closer, lowering his voice so only she could hear him. "I meant . . . bedroom activities."

She nodded like a bobble-head doll because that's the only thing she could think to do. Her brain screamed, "Panic! Code red! Danger, Will Robinson!" Her blood pressure spiked to Mount Everest heights.

But outwardly she was totally calm and cool and collected and . . . *Holy moly, when did it get so hot in here?*

"What's your favorite position?" he murmured.

Okay, she hadn't dated in a while, but from her experience, dates usually passed the thirty-minute mark before they took a decidedly sexual turn. And in those cases, maybe a bit of teasing innuendo was thrown into the conversation, then brushed aside as appetizers arrived or drinks were served. Ten minutes with this guy, and he already wanted to know if she preferred missionary or doggy-style. It was one thing to talk about sex, and a whole other thing to fully expect it to happen at the drop of a hat. Jonathan's hungry gaze suggested he'd be ready and willing to take her on the table if she gave the green light.

She'd never felt comfortable rushing into intimacy, but maybe she'd wasted too much time warming up. She wasn't getting any younger. Plus, he was really—like, *really*—hot. And it had been a long time since she'd been . . . serviced by such an attractive man.

Needing a shot of courage, she drained her mug and folded her arms on the table, but a disturbing pattern in the leaves caught her eye. *Oh, no. No, no, no. Not a snake. Anything but a snake.* Just when she'd begun to dream of seeing another snake entirely.

"You okay? Need more tea?"

Addie met his gaze, sighing mournfully. He was so sexy. So buff. Edna had warned her against snakes. They were a sign that someone was unworthy of your trust. But, then again, she was a healthy, unattached woman. An adult who could make adult decisions. Who said she couldn't entertain something purely physical with this guy? A little fling on the side while she searched for the real deal. But what if he was already seeing someone, or worse, married?

She groaned. "I may give up tea altogether after this. It's too depressing."

"How about sex?"

"Pardon me?"

He leered at her. "You're not giving that up, too, are you?"

Frowning, she rewound their conversation, trying to remember what he'd said before she lost the thread. "I'm not sure how the two are related."

"You never answered my question, about your favorite position."

"Oh! Oh . . . well, I'm, um . . . ."

"Ever tried the plough?"

Feeling a little constricted by the intensity of his gaze and the ever-increasing heat level of his questions, Addie stared into the depths of her mug once more. She could have him if she wanted him—he'd made that abundantly clear—but some men weren't worth having. Or worthy of having her. Edna had never failed to remind her of that, either. "Jonathan, I don't think this is gonna work out, but I wish you all the best."

"What?"

The poor guy. He had no idea she knew he was a two-timing, double-crossing serpent. "I hope you find someone who's right for you. Really appreciate you meeting me. Have a nice life." She stretched her arm across the table to shake hands.

Jonathan's jaw hung so low it almost scraped the floor. His wide eyes blinked rapidly. He probably wasn't on the receiving end of rejection very often. "Hey, look, sorry if I said something to scare you off—"

"Not just you. My dead great-aunt won't shut up."

"Your dead aunt won't *what*?"

"*Great*-aunt." She pressed her fingers and thumb together repeatedly to simulate someone yapping in her ear.

He blinked several more times. "I thought we were having a good time."

"Yeah, well, unfortunately, I'm like Indiana Jones. Me and snakes don't mix well."

The confusion on his face soon turned to anger. "Whatever. Shoulda known trying to find a chick in this lame town's newspaper would fail spectacularly." He didn't bother shaking her hand. Instead, he plucked a few bills from his wallet, dropped them to the table, and stomped toward the door.

Damn, he had a nice ass. Props on covering the tab, too. Ahh, well. She could start fresh with her next date and attempt to avoid men who were overly aggressive with their sexual advances. Tea leaves or no tea leaves, she refused to be charmed by a snake.

She rose to her feet, turning toward the counter to say goodbye to Gwen. She wouldn't call herself a Cup-A-Cabana regular, but her occasional visits, along with the weekly yoga class the two attended, and their failed attempt at Paint Nite, allowed them to form a tight bond. And, despite her less-than-frequent stop-ins, on every recent visit she'd noticed the man at the corner table next to the window.

The writer guy was more than a touch mysterious. He was so quiet, so focused, even with all the goings-on around him.

Her frank perusal must have pulled him from whatever world he was creating. He lifted his gaze from his computer screen, turned around, then swiveled to face her once more, as if to confirm that she was, absolutely, looking at him.

She took a step closer, admiring the half-eaten pastry on the plate next to his laptop. "How are the danishes here?"

"I never eat anything else."

A feeling akin to jealousy fluttered inside her. *What have you got against pies, buddy?* She might have asked him, too, if she weren't distracted by the impossibly long, thick eyelashes that swept down over his hazel eyes, or the dusting of freckles on his forehead and cheeks.

She reached out her hand to shake his, hoping one man would meet the gesture. He wiped his palms on his pants and accepted her offering. The warmth from his hand radiated into her own. "I'm Adelaide Mitchell, or Addie for short."

"Ethan Holtz."

They held on a little bit longer than was probably right for almost-strangers. "So, you're a writer, I take it," she said, dropping her hand to her side. "Blogger? Travel and adventure? Self-help?"

"Thrillers."

"I don't have the patience for writing. Don't have much time to read, either, but there's hardly anything worth reading anymore. Everyone's an author now that self-publishing is a thing. That Save-Mart cashier over in Smith's Falls who organizes the floats in the Christmas parade every year? She wrote a book. Sexy one, or so she says. It's like everyone thinks they have this big story to share, ya know? I mean, to be perfectly honest, most people just aren't that interesting—" She caught herself mid-tangent, realizing she'd insulted the man at least twice in the span of ten seconds.

Instead of telling her off or defending himself, which she fully expected, Ethan nodded to her abandoned table. "Was that the guy's problem?"

"I'm sorry?"

"The guy you were sitting with. Wasn't he interesting enough for you? Read too many books, maybe?"

She struggled to find the right words. How could she tell him the real reason she ditched her date was because her tea leaves told her to? There were some things you couldn't share with strangers. "He was just a ssss . . . um, selfish. Too into himself. You know those types. The muscle-bound gym rats. Vain, party of one." Addie forced a chuckle.

"But you agreed to go bungee jumping with him."

"What? Jesus. *That's* what he asked me?"

The smirk on his face would've pissed her off if it wasn't accompanied by a pair of dimples that completely threw her off-guard.

"Weren't you listening?"

"Not as much as you were, apparently," she shot back. "Aren't you here to write?" Like she had every right in the world, she grabbed the notebook next to his laptop and casually flipped through it.

"Aren't you trying to find 'the one'?" Her head jerked up. "Give the guy a chance."

"You seem to know an awful lot about me." Addie returned the barely broken-in notebook to the table and he immediately repositioned it a fraction of an inch. An act of stubbornness, rebellion, or just one of the many peculiar behaviors of the author in his natural habitat, she couldn't tell.

"I'm observant," he said. "We author types tend to notice things. People, places. Social interactions. I guess our own lives are far too mundane."

She ignored the obvious jab, suppressing the urge to point out that he'd failed to notice the cherry filling clinging to the corner of his mouth. Because if she pointed that out, she'd have to admit she'd been staring at his mouth. "I have another date on Thursday," she blurted.

"Hope he's thick-skinned."

Rolling her eyes, she said, "I'll be sure to not ask for your opinion about it."

"I'll pretend to care."

Addie turned on her heel, biting her lip to keep the grin that threatened from breaking free. She already looked forward to Thursday, and the possibility of sparring with Ethan again had nothing to do with it. Much.

I'll pretend to care? What am I, twelve?

Ethan sighed as he flipped through his very own copy of *The Daily Dispatch*. He'd slipped out to purchase the local paper approximately sixty seconds after Addie left, then returned to his still-warm seat in the coffee shop. He skimmed over the wacky town events and sped through the story of some guy named Martin who'd started a GoFundMe campaign to have his bunions removed. Shuddering, he turned to the sports section, happy to read about the Kendal High Knuckleballers baseball team capturing another big win in their division. They had a tournament coming up. He would try to catch a game or two. As a kid, he'd taken up the sport more as a way to curb the questions that plagued him when asked what his interests were. Writing never seemed to satisfy his critics. Still didn't.

He never expected he'd actually enjoy playing the game, though. And he was good. Ethan'd skinned his knees more than once to stop a ball from entering the outfield. Shortstop. Sounded more like a punctuation mark than a fielding position. He played all through high school until he learned about the creative writing club. Then, his interest in playing shortstop stopped short. So too did the support from his parents.

Swallowing down the bitterness such memories always produced, he turned to the classifieds section, his gaze settling on the singles ads. "Just a Tinder fella looking for his Tinderella," one ad read. "Seriously, dude?" he muttered. "You ganked your own Tinder bio for a newspaper ad?"

Of course, Gwen happened by right then, her ears perked up. "Got yourself a copy of *The Dispatch*, huh?"

He raised one shoulder indifferently. "I like to, uh . . . stay informed."

"I see," she said with a smug grin. "And I suppose you're in the classifieds section to read more about that lawnmower Mr. Turcott has for sale, right?"

"Exactly."

"Ya know, you're kinda cute when you blush."

Ethan groaned in response. It wasn't the first time Gwen had made a flirtatious remark, and he never usually minded. After all, it was common knowledge that she was very much off the market. Her boyfriend sometimes showed up during her shifts decked out in his security guard uniform, and the two would disappear into the kitchen for several minutes. He couldn't help but envy the guy's guilty smiles when Gwen would return to the dining area with her lipstick smeared. Guess when you worked the hours she did, you couldn't be too picky about your pecking locations.

"Can I top you up?" she asked.

"No, but I'll take another danish. Please."

She cocked an eyebrow. "Two danishes before noon? You're hitting the hard stuff early, Ethan."

Her parting wink disarmed him. Gwen was pretty. He'd made that observation the first day he'd entered the Cup-A-Cabana. And she'd always been easy to talk to, no matter how little they talked. She felt like a friend, the first real friend he'd made in the town.

Addie and Gwen were friends, too. Addie . . . the woman who'd known him all of three seconds before insulting him six ways from Sunday. The woman he hadn't been able to stop thinking about since she left. She'd already burrowed under his skin too much for him to pretend otherwise, but he couldn't deny his disappointment in discovering her shallowness. *There's hardly anything worth reading anymore*, she'd callously said. Whether it was an accusation or a challenge, he wasn't sure. Self-publishing made the path to becoming published a bit easier, sure, but writing a book wasn't easy. Anyone who'd ever tried and failed could attest to that.

He would take it as his civic duty to correct her misconceptions about writing. Not everything in print was a joke. There *were* interesting books out there, tons of 'em! If she spent less time judging a book by its author and more time reading them, she might realize it.

But, man, he'd gotten a kick out of their bantering. And if the grin on her face as she'd spun around and headed for the door was any indication, she had, too.

2

Addie strode into the crowded coffee shop for date number two with renewed determination. She'd met Simon online. They'd successfully made it through three sessions of getting-to-know-you questions and exchanged a few emails, but her immediate draw to Simon were his cobalt-blue eyes and curly brown hair. What woman alive didn't want curly-haired babies?

The rich scent of freshly made coffee and pastries filled her lungs. The shop glowed with its bright yellow walls and burnt-orange accents. Though the color scheme might have been jarring to some, to her it felt lively. Energetic. Like the opposite of a dark, smoky coffee house.

Her gaze traveled around the room, searching for Simon, but she spotted Ethan instead. He quickly ducked behind his laptop, and she grinned. Feigning nonchalance, she took a seat at an empty table right next to his, facing him this time.

"How's the writing going, Hemingway?"

He looked up, gave her an eyeroll, and resumed typing.

"What pretentious drivel will you share with the world today?" She only said it to get a rise out of him, but the bastard wasn't taking the bait.

She drummed her fingers on the table, searching for something clever or witty to say to snare his attention. Her eyes lit up when she landed on the perfect ploy. "How many thriller authors does it take to change a light bulb?"

Ethan huffed but otherwise ignored her.

"Two. One to screw the bulb almost all the way in, and one to give a surprising twist at the end."

Finally, his eyes met hers. She would swear she saw a hint of mirth hidden in his features. "Come up with that one yourself?"

"I might have heard it somewhere. I thought it was funny. I'll have to run it past Simon to see what he says." She laughed when the unintended joke registered. "Simon Says. Oh, wow, that brings back memories."

"Why are we discussing someone named Simon?"

"Oh." She smiled sheepishly. "He's my date."

Long seconds ticked by without a response, amplifying her self-consciousness, then he quietly muttered, "Simon Says, quit bugging me and let me do some writing."

Addie scoffed at his insulting tone. "Simon Says, get a sense of humor." A chorus of giggles sounded from the counter. She twisted in that direction to find Gwen and another woman huddled together, practically shaking with pure delight. At least some people in this joint knew how to laugh.

When their heads popped up, Addie instantly recognized the other woman. Hannah Barker, the owner of The Barkery down the street, specializing in treats to fulfill every furry four-legged friend's desire. Addie had seen Hannah in passing, but they'd never met. Unsurprising, given that Addie wasn't an animal owner, nor would she likely ever be after what happened to Gus, her goldfish. Yeah, she was five at the time, but some wounds ran deep.

As if sensing her inner animal turmoil, Hannah headed for her table, with Gwen close in tow.

"Is this the famous Addie who's taking the dating world by storm?" Hannah said by way of greeting.

"She's the bravest woman I know," Gwen chimed in.

Addie chuckled. "I wouldn't call it a storm, exactly. More like a soft summer shower. Some mild precipitation at best."

Hannah barked out a laugh. "I'm Hannah," she said, reaching for Addie's hand and shaking it firmly. "Just wanted to wish you luck. I find the best guys are the ones who have dogs. Patient, nurturing, and damn good in the sack from my experience!"

"I'll keep that in mind," Addie said, grinning. "You know, Gwen used to be my wingwoman, but then—"

"But then Shawn," Hannah cooed in a mocking tone.

Gwen rolled her eyes. "What? Oh, don't look at me like that. I'm not that smitten."

"Yeah, and I'm not up to my eyeballs in kibble," Hannah shot back. "It's always the way. When one of the girls gets herself a guy, she leaves the other friends to fend for themselves."

"Preach," Addie said. "Blinded by her own romantic triumph, she ignores her poor, defenseless sisters . . . ."

" . . . As they struggle their way through the cruel, unforgiving world of dating, like little lambs being led to the slaughter," Hannah finished in dramatic fashion, placing the back of her hand across her forehead.

Addie could definitely see them being friends.

The bells jingled, giving Gwen a temporary reprieve from the gang-up, and in walked Simon. All five-foot-nothing of him.

"That him?" Gwen whispered.

Addie sighed, then nodded.

"Well, height doesn't matter when you're horizontal," Hannah was quick to point out.

Addie cringed. "Let's not get ahead of ourselves."

Gwen laughed and squeezed Addie's shoulder affectionately. "Knock him dead, sweets."

Then her two cheerleaders returned to the counter, and Simon took their place. She was glad to be sitting. Even barefoot she would have towered over him.

"Addie?" he asked. When she nodded, he broke into a wide grin. "I'm Simon."

They shook hands and she gestured for him to sit. The usual first date pleasantries were exchanged as they perused the menu. She noticed right away that Simon talked with his hands, but they were really nice hands. Well-manicured. Remarkably large. She wondered if he was similarly proportioned in other areas, too.

Gwen took their orders, mouthing "He's cute!" as she backed away. He *was* cute, but there was something . . . off about him. She couldn't put her finger on exactly what, though. "You said you work in real estate?"

"That's right. Not the field where I thought I'd end up, being a philosophy major and all. I mean, at first I felt really out of place, and so naïve. Like I was the sole Aristotle in a world full of Socrateses and Platos."

She blinked. "Uh, no doubt."

"But once I got the hang of it, it was just like riding a bike."

"Well, since you've given me the perfect segue, my job is just like riding a bike, too. Literally. I own a business called the Pie-Cycle.

I bake and sell hand pies from the back of my bike."

His eyes widened with interest. "So you travel with them by bike?"

"Yep. I'm still trying to find a foolproof way of transporting the pies without squishing a few during my rounds. Potholes are pie killers."

"It should be easy as pie," he joked. "But seriously, that sounds like a dream job. I do most of my work in the city, so I haven't had the pleasure of tasting one of your pies yet, but I'd sure like to."

She cocked her head, trying to gauge whether pie was a euphemism for . . . not pie. After her last date, she almost expected every conversation to go south a little sooner.

At that moment, Gwen delivered their order, sliding Addie her cup of tea. As she took a fortifying sip, she caught Ethan's stare before he lowered his gaze back to his screen. *Gotcha!* He could pretend to be indifferent all he wanted, but she knew he was tuned in to the action at her table. She convinced herself that the flutter in her stomach was satisfaction, nothing more.

"It's definitely an enjoyable job," she said, returning her attention to Simon. "I love baking. I get to be active, visit the neighboring towns, meet a lot of people . . . ."

He smiled. "That's one of the things that appealed most to me about the real estate business. The people part. I'm drawn to people like bees to honey."

"Umm. I think you mean flies. Bees *make* honey. I don't think they actually eat it. That's like . . . cannibalism or something."

"Right." Simon laughed. "That's what I meant, of course."

"Of course," she repeated, drinking more tea.

He took a healthy bite of his scone, his white teeth slicing through the dense biscuit. That's when she noticed his left front tooth was twisted sideways. Or *his* right, *her* left. Whatever. But it wasn't unappealing. Nor was the scar above his eyebrow. His decision to wear a striped shirt with gingham shorts gave her pause, however. "What brought you to the world of online dating?"

Reaching for a napkin, he brushed the crumbs from his mouth and sat up taller, like he only just now realized she was several inches above him. "I guess I'm guilty of letting my career take over. I figured there'd be plenty of time to date once I got the rest of my life sorted out. But . . . wow. Meeting people is so hard."

Laughing, she nodded. "You aren't kidding."

"I've attended one too many events without a plus-one. That's when I knew I had to wake up and smell the writing on the wall. So I started being more proactive about dating and searching for that special someone."

Wake up and smell the writing on the wall? He has to be doing this on purpose. And have his eyes been asymmetrical this whole time? The left one looks lower. Or the right higher.

"I tried speed dating once. Boy, that was awkward. Everyone else there seemed so relaxed and at ease, like they'd done it a thousand times. I could barely string sentences together. I'm sure I made an absolute fool of myself, but I guess it gets easier with time and practice. Putting yourself out there. Risk earns reward."

"Right." Out of the corner of her eye, she spotted Gwen and Hannah giving her the thumbs up. Hannah's advice popped into her head. "Simon, just out of curiosity, do you have a dog?"

"No. As I said, I stay pretty busy with my career. I don't really think I'd have time to care for a dog, especially now that I've added dating to the mix. In the real estate business, you have to work hard to stay on top. It's a dog-eat-bone world."

"Dog," she blurted. "Dog-eat-*dog*."

He laughed. "Now *that's* cannibalism."

Oh, Jesus. There was no way this could work. How could she possibly belong with a man who mixed his metaphors, wore mismatched clothing, had lopsided eyes, and, and . . . well, the crooked tooth alone wasn't a deal-breaker, but it helped to tip the scale toward no-way, nuh-uh, never-gonna-happen.

But just to be sure, she drank the rest of her tea. The still-hot liquid burned as it trickled down her throat. A sacrifice she was willing to make to spare her ears the trauma of hearing another butchered analogy.

Blowing out a deep breath, she dropped her empty mug to the table and studied the leaves that pooled at the bottom. Though a bit hazy, she could make out the shape of an anchor. Anchors symbolized instability, or, in some cases, an unpleasant situation you should sail away from. Time to set a course for . . . far, far away from here.

She heard a faint buzzing sound, wondering if it was her conscience calling. Jerking her head up, she determined the culprit to be Simon's cell phone.

He glanced from the screen to her, his mouth drawn in a straight line. "I hate to do this," he said, "but there's a couple who just put in an offer on a house I've been trying to sell for months." She waved off his concern and he took the call, turning his back to her.

Sighing, Addie fought the temptation to run her fingers through the chocolate-colored curls on his head. Some lucky lady out there would have curly-haired babies with this man. Likely one who couldn't tell the difference between a cliché and a clinch.

Simon swiveled to face her once more, his crooked tooth on display as he beamed a smile. "Sounds like we're close to a deal. I'll head over to coordinate things once we're done here."

Addie perked up at the possibility of cutting the painful date short. Anchors aweigh! "Well, uh, there's no need to delay on my account. Seems like this is a very important transaction . . . ."

"Oh. Are you sure? I mean, this can wait. I'm having a great ti—"

Addie patted his hand. "I insist. We'll reschedule for another time." A little white lie or two never hurt anyone.

"Wonderful. I look forward to it. I'll take care of the bill at the counter," he said, rising to his feet. "Thank you so much for meeting me."

She nodded and had the good grace to meet him in an awkward hug. "Hope you get your sale."

"Oh, I'll sell it, by hook or by ladder."

"Crook," she muttered.

His head snapped back as if she'd slapped him. "What? Why would you say that?"

"Say what?"

"I'm not a crook!"

He spoke so emphatically, Addie had to bite her lip to keep from laughing as images of Richard Nixon flashed through her mind.

"Many owners start at an asking price above market value," he pressed on, his voice getting louder. "If the buyer isn't savvy enough to do their homework—"

"Book!" she cried. "I said book, not crook. You have a live one ready to buy, so you'd better book it!"

That knocked the wind right out of his sails. He blinked, blushed, then stuttered out an apology. "Oh. S-sorry. I'm sorry. Uh, thanks again for the date, and I guess I'll . . . see you, then." Darting toward the counter, he dropped an absurd amount of cash into Gwen's open palm, then made a beeline for the door. The bells signaled his departure.

Her gaze zoomed back in on Gwen's palm. There had to be enough dough to cover their tab and six other tables. *Well, shoot. I could have been a trophy wife.*

Ethan couldn't help but marvel when Addie chased off yet another man in under fifteen minutes. Who was this woman? She certainly didn't like to waste time, which he supposed was admirable in a way, but how could anyone make such a judgement call in mere minutes? From his perspective, neither bachelor one or two had anything overtly wrong with them.

She'd very clearly caught him staring halfway through the date, despite his best efforts to remain undetected. And the writing wasn't happening. At all. He'd written and re-written the opening chapter so many times his head spun. There was no use acting like he was in the middle of a breakthrough.

So this time, when she looked his way, he didn't try to hide behind his screen. She took that as an invitation to invade his space and claimed the seat opposite him.

"What was this guy's problem, Seinfeld? Too vertically challenged?"

She gaped at him. "Seinfeld?"

"You're as judgmental as Jerry. Did this guy have woman-hands? Was he less attractive in dark lighting? Did his belly button talk to you?"

Planting her elbows on the table, she leaned in closer and glared at him. "I'd think you, of all people, would understand my aversion to someone who mixes their metaphors. Is that not a deal-breaker for you, Shakespeare?"

A smile twitched the corner of his mouth. "Things might get a bit sketchy if it's a serious case of malapropism, but I'm more likely to ditch someone who has difficulty with possessiveness."

"Do your women like to keep you tied down?"

"It has more to do with the correct forms of 'your,' 'you're,' and 'yore.' Mixed metaphors are just a minor inconvenience."

"Did you *hear* the dog one?"

"Guess you can't teach an old dog new tricks."

"Or a Simple Simon how to put together a proper metaphor," she shot back.

"Poor Simple Simon, just wanting to meet a pie-woman." He mirrored her position and lowered his voice. "Date him again. I double-dog dare you."

She shook her head, her eyes crinkling at the corners. "You are one sick puppy."

"I won't deny that."

Addie arched an inquisitive eyebrow, then reached for one of the balled-up pages of his notebook. He didn't bother trying to keep her from attaining her prize. *Someone* should be aware of his efforts in this coffee shop, since his on-screen word count was currently 2317. In the red.

She silently read his haphazard handwriting, chewing on her lower lip as her eyes scanned the mangled page. He waited for the expected scathing remarks, even took a long pull of air to brace himself.

But they never came.

"You sure you wanna trash this, Tolstoy?"

"Why?" he asked warily. "You need some kindling?"

She frowned, returning the scrap of paper to its crumpled comrades "Are all you author types this vulnerable? I was just paying you a compliment."

A jolt of pleasure rippled through him. Praise. Not from an agent or an editor or anyone who had a hope of helping him get on a bestseller list, but that didn't make a bit of difference. It felt ten times as good. Schooling his features, he said, "Sorry, I must have missed it. Guess I'm not the brightest bulb in the shed."

Her face lit up in a megawatt smile. "Guess not."

He couldn't look at her when she looked like that, with those doe eyes blinking back at him, tempting and taunting all at once. How could he possibly hold it together? His gaze shifted to his screen and he pretended to type something. "Who's on deck next?"

Maybe if he kept fake-typing she'd get the hint and take a hike. Not that he wanted her to. But he needed her to. She was a distraction, plain and simple. Flighty. Footloose and fancy-free. He didn't have time to entertain her if he intended to get any writing done and make some semblance of a living. But then why was he asking her questions and keeping her engaged?

"A single father from Newtonville. He claims to be a magician in his spare time."

"Ahh, perfect for you. He'll be able to disappear before you find a reason to run him off."

She had the good nature to chuckle at the dig. "Maybe he'll magically type words without pressing the keys like you."

His head jerked back at the direct hit. Heat scorched his cheeks. The harder he fought it, the hotter they flared. Dropping his hands to his lap, he met her eyes, but what he found in her gaze wasn't smugness or derision or even amusement. There was curiosity. A touch of empathy. And, if he wasn't mistaken, the tiniest bit of genuine interest.

Their eyes held a fraction too long. She looked away first, nervously fiddling with the waded paper balls that decorated his workspace. "So, the date's next week."

"Okay."

"Probably here again." She raised her chin, as though expecting him to object.

"Coffee shops are the perfect place to meet strangers."

"And eavesdrop on conversations. Er, write, I mean."

He might have taken offense if she hadn't accompanied the insult with a wink. A slow breath escaped his lungs when she stood to leave. Thank goodness. He'd run out of things to say, and type, and think.

"Don't work too hard, Hemingway. You're burning the midnight oil at both ends."

With that parting remark, she spun on her heel and joined the other women at the counter. Things were burning, all right. He grabbed his glass of water and chugged the remainder of it. Then he cracked his knuckles, opened a new document, and started typing.

The Girl Who Created Fire. Chapter One.

3

When she started out on her bike Saturday morning, Addie felt invigorated. Alive. Like a woman with the world at her fingertips. Okay, so her great search for Mr. Right wasn't off to the most promising start, but she'd started. That alone was cause for celebration. And if the dates weren't worthy of reminiscing, the post-date play-by-plays with Ethan definitely had their perks.

She couldn't figure out what drew her to his table. Warm and inviting weren't words she'd use to describe him, yet somehow, anytime she was around him, she felt comfortable. They fell into this effortless give-and-take routine. He was remarkably easy to talk to. Or banter with. Quiet at first, but honest . . . almost to a fault. She wanted to know him better, she just wasn't entirely sure for what purpose.

By eight-thirty, she'd already sold out of her blueberry and banana-hazelnut pies, targeting the sweet-toothed early birds in the neighboring town of Madoc. The batch of the new s'more flavor she'd added to the mix was dwindling fast and getting rave reviews.

She hit up Trenton soon after, still riding high on her success. The sports field outside the community center was littered with tents and tables of all shapes and sizes for their weekly farmers' market. Parking her bike under the shade of a nearby oak tree, she checked her watch. Like clockwork, townspeople and farmers alike paraded over for a hand pie or two.

Once noon rolled around, Addie was back in Kendal with an empty basket and a growling stomach. After baking all night, she felt like letting someone else do the work. The Cup-A-Cabana was the obvious choice. Gwen made quick, tasty food at reasonable prices, and it was close by. And she kept a great tea selection. And Ethan might be there . . .

The bells chimed as she entered the coffee shop and her gaze homed in on Ethan right away. At his usual corner table. Tapping away at his keyboard. Lost in his own creative world.

He glanced up and their eyes met. She smiled and waved like a dork. He nodded to the seat opposite him, and she happily accepted the invitation, plopping down with an excess of enthusiasm. "Hi!"

"Hey," he said, closing his laptop and shoving it into his bag. "What are you so cheerful about?"

"Sitting with you, of course, and preparing for another round of witty repartee."

"You'll have to forgive me. I'm not used to people being so excited to see me, other than the ink suppliers of the world."

"I just finished a pie run and I'm starving. Wanna have lunch with me?"

"Oh. Here?"

"Well, yeah," she said, confused. "We're both here, and it's lunch time . . . You haven't eaten yet, have you?"

"Nope. Let's eat." Ethan signaled Gwen.

When she dropped off the menus and some cutlery, she darted her gaze back and forth between the dining companions, then shot Addie a pointed look. "Are you two on a date?"

Addie's cheeks flamed. "Why would you think that? Can't two people of the opposite sex sit together for a meal without it being termed something other than what it is? Which is lunch. We're eating lunch. I mean, technically, we're not eating it yet, but we will be once we order it . . . ." She trailed off at Gwen's amused expression.

"It was a joke, Addie," she said. "Lighten up."

Ethan chuckled at her stumbling. "Thanks for the menus, Gwen," he said, passing one to Addie as Gwen wandered over to another table.

Grateful for the distraction, she flipped open the cover and reviewed the menu items. She must have sounded like a complete lunatic. No doubt Ethan read more into her steadfast denial of this being a date than if she'd agreed that it was a date. A casual date. Between friends.

Eventually, when she felt brave enough, she lifted her head. "What did you mean by 'here'?"

"Huh?"

"Earlier, when you asked if we'd be having lunch here."

He toyed with the cutlery in front of him, using his napkin to wipe invisible water spots from his knife. "There are just other places I would have taken you for a lunch not-date, that's all."

She smiled and couldn't help but probe a little deeper. "Yeah? Where would you have taken me for our not-date?"

"Hmm . . . The Cat's Caboose for some wings and beer. Or El Camino for some Mexican. Or Zen Kitchen, that new place in Bloomfield that everyone's talking about."

"All this time I've been looking for men, but you think I need to find my zen first?"

"Zen, then men. Zen, then men."

She grinned at his deadpan expression. "I love wings. And beer. And I believe Mexican food should have its own religion."

"I'd worship at the Taco Temple every day."

God, he was fun to talk to. Intelligent. Gave as good as he got. And he made her laugh. Even if the guy was lousy in bed, he had a heck of a lot going for him. But she wasn't thinking about him in bed, or anywhere near a bed. She coughed. "Uh, so if we request tacos, what are the odds that Gwen'll bring us some?"

"Slim to even slimmer," their timely waitress answered without missing a beat. "Last I checked, this was a coffee house, not a taquería."

Frowning, Addie turned to Ethan. "Don't you have an 'in' with her? I hear she sets aside danishes for you on the days when they're especially busy."

Gwen laughed. "I've felt the wrath of Ethan with low blood sugar. Learned my lesson fast."

"You're her BFF," Ethan pointed out to Addie. "Shouldn't you have the 'in'?"

"BFF?" Addie blurted. "Did you just say BFF?"

"I do believe he said BFF, my BFF," Gwen confirmed, grinning.

A blush lit the tips of his ears and reddened his cheeks. "I'll have a turkey and swiss on rye. Pickle on the side."

Still giggling, Addie said, "My darling BFF, I'd like a grilled chicken wrap, hold the tomatoes, and a Diet Coke."

"Comin' right up," she said, then added, "Bestie."

"Regretting that lunch invitation now?" Addie baited once Gwen had disappeared.

"Nah. You're a pretty cheap not-date. You should have at least ordered some chips, too."

Up till now, the tugs had been faint enough that she could ignore them, but this time her heart felt a very distinct vibration. "Does that mean you're buyin'?"

He lifted his mug to take a drink, buying time if nothing else. "She sits at his table, coerces him into eating lunch with her, and he has to pay for it."

"Hey, you're the one who brought up the topic of money. And before we get into what I anticipate would be an epic debate on gender roles and stereotypes, please consider the entertainment value I'm providing here. You have to admit, talking to me is way more exciting than staring at your computer screen."

Gwen appeared then with their meals and a drink for Addie. "Let me know if there's anything else I can get for you two."

"A moderator might be a good idea," Ethan said, his attention fixed on Addie.

Addie smiled—not at the words themselves, but at the fire in his eyes. That kind of passion could, and surely would, transfer to other parts of his life. Other, more intimate parts. "Or a referee."

"Not in the job description, sorry," Gwen said. "Just take the boxing gloves off while you eat and enjoy, okay?"

Addie obediently bit into her wrap as Gwen moved on to the next table. Slurping some Coke through her straw, she swished the liquid around in her mouth to free any bits of food that might be caught in her teeth. "On a more neutral topic, how's the book coming?"

"Authors hate it when people ask that."

Grinning, she said, "Oh? What else do they hate?"

"Having to explain themselves. Being asked how many books they've sold, or how much money they've made. When readers tell them to name a character after them . . . ." And the list went on. She smiled as he warmed to the subject. "Getting emails from fans wondering where your next book is two weeks after you finished the last one. When people tell you what they ate for breakfast and think that's a plot for a book." He paused to take a breath. "You have mayo on the corner of your mouth."

"What?" she asked, even though she heard him perfectly fine.

"Mayo. You're wearing it on your mouth."

He'd only know this if he were staring at her mouth . . . or if the gob was so big he couldn't do anything but stare at Mount Mayo. She reached for a napkin and wiped where he instructed, cringing at the amount she removed. Dropping her crumpled napkin to the table, she pressed her lips together, trying to salvage whatever lipstick remained.

"I've never understood that," Ethan said.

"What?" She took another bite of her wrap, licking the corners of her mouth to avoid a repeat performance.

"Lipstick. I mean, you painstakingly apply it, and it so easily rubs off. On glasses, napkins, a guy's collar. Seems like way too much work for little reward."

She stared at him for a moment, this man who continued to reveal parts of his personality she found both boggling and amusing. "You've thought about this a lot."

He shrugged. "Observations."

She nodded. He'd mentioned before how authors were observant, but she wondered if he spent half as much time observing others the way he did her. Popping the remainder of her wrap into her mouth, she chewed unhurriedly as she took in their surroundings. There were a lot of people in the shop, typical of this time of day. Old, young, and in between. All very observable people. Several lined up to make their selections at the pastry counter, and others waited patiently for a table to open so they could order off the lunch menu.

"What do you observe about them?" She nodded to a young couple who'd snagged a table near their own. The girl couldn't have been more than one-hundred pounds soaking wet, and the guy—her date, by the look of it—was at least double that.

Ethan studied the pair for a minute, then returned his attention to Addie. "Looks like a first date. He ordered water, which tells me he's cheap and probably won't pay the tab. She put on the sweater that was tied at her waist. Strange, given that it's the middle of summer, and yet not so strange, considering they're at the table with the draft. He's too self-involved to notice the draft, however, and won't switch seats with her. Oh, and she has an annoying laugh."

Addie giggled at his freakishly thorough assessment. "Think they'll make it to a second date?" she asked, tracing her index finger along a scar on the table.

"I think he wants to . . . so it all depends on her."

Quiet seconds ticked by until finally she raised her head to find him staring straight at her, his expression hopeful. How did he do that? Take something that wasn't even about them and spin it in such a way that made it sound like it *was* about them. Evil psychological genius. Avoiding further eye contact, she slurped the rest of her soft drink. The longer she stayed here, on her not-date, the easier it would be to forget all about the real dates soon to come. Plus, she had a lot to get done today. Like baking. And . . . other things she'd think of eventually.

Ethan must have sensed her desire to leave. It could have been that she was halfway to her feet. "Guess you'd better split. I'll get the check."

"No, I got it."

He waved her off. "You were right. Talking to you is way more exciting than staring at a computer screen."

Her heart swelled against her ribcage almost stealing her breath. "Thank you."

"Maybe we'll try those tacos sometime?"

"Uh, yeah. Yes! Tacos. Love those tacos." The only thing more idiotic than everything she'd just said was that she patted him on the shoulder afterward. "So, thank you again, and I . . . I'll see you."

He smiled as she made her departure, tripping over the strap of a woman's purse on the floor, only to catch herself before nearly running into an older man at the entrance. The guy reached out to steady her, and Ethan envied him that fleeting moment of being able to hold her.

Well, hey, he got to spend a whole hour in her company. An unexpected hour, too. She'd sought him out, chose him and him alone to dine with. Even if it'd been a spontaneous 'you're here, I'm here' kind of invitation, out of all the tables in the shop, she'd wanted to sit at his table. On a fake date.

Ethan stood and gathered his belongings, settled the bill with Gwen, and grabbed a danish to go.

As he walked along the sidewalk, he passed by the familiar homes—an interesting mix of Victorians, Craftsmans, bungalows, and split-levels. He rented the upper half of a two-story home on Crescent Street from Carmen Deacon, a seventy-five-year-old spitfire of a woman and part-time palmistry practitioner.

They spoke on occasion, but mostly he avoided her. There was something spooky about a woman who claimed she had the ability to discover a person's secrets in the lines of their palm. He'd had more interactions with her cat, MoJo, whom she insisted was going through an identity crisis. Ethan had laughed out loud the first time he saw her put the poor feline on a hot-pink leash and walk him to The Barkery to buy him dog treats. Thankfully, Carmen hardly ever hung around the house. The social butterfly flitted about the town, anxious to be a part of all the goings-on. He preferred to stay holed up in his half of the house, typing his life away.

He'd grown to love the quietness of Kendal, the beauty of the surrounding forest, the history. Mark Twain was said to have resided in the general area during his later years. As a boy, he'd been enthralled by the storyteller. As a man, he yearned to find a writing voice as unique, as captivating to audiences young and old.

Some townspeople, like him, were city transplants. Perhaps they'd grown tired of the rat race, or they chose to commute to their corporate jobs instead of dwelling in the shadows of endless skyscrapers and strip malls. Others, he knew, had been born and raised in Kendal, never wanting to leave the charming hamlet they called home. Carmen fell into that category. Maybe Addie did, too.

If not for the weeks of wordlessness, he'd have happily stayed put in his makeshift home, limiting his interactions with the outside world. But he'd been pummeled by a creative dry spell so powerful that none of his usual tricks seemed to help break through the block. Thinking a change of scenery might inspire him, he'd forced himself to scout the town for another potential venue.

The park was too kid-cluttered. The bookstore seemed ideal, but staring at books written by more successful authors was too depressing.

He thought he'd found the perfect spot inside the bowling alley-slash-pub. A handful of men frequented the place in the daytime and stuck to the bar side since the lanes didn't open till the evening. Ethan could hit his word count well before the night crowd poured in. But then some pinheads petitioned for a daytime bowling league, and Sam, the owner, saw dollar signs in his eyes.

Ethan turned into the driveway of the two-story and climbed the steps to the front door. Wiggling his key in the lock, he felt the tumblers shift and click into place. He pushed the door open and entered into the always-stifling foyer. Carmen kept the house at Tahiti temperatures on the main level. He had his own thermostat upstairs, thank the Lord, but heat had a funny way of rising.

Toeing off his shoes, he dashed up the steps and dropped his messenger bag on his bed, earning him a startled meow from MoJo, who was camped out near his pillow. Stretching back on his hind legs, he glowered at Ethan.

"What are *you* so peeved about? My bed. Mine. We've had this discussion before. Do I need to mark my territory?" Carmen notoriously left her separate entrance open, giving MoJo free rein of the whole house, though he couldn't blame the cat for wanting to escape the heat . . . and his strange human.

MoJo sniffed in response and promptly curled into a ball, his ass facing Ethan.

"Glad your communication skills have improved."

Anxious to get out of the sweltering house, he pulled on some swim trunks and a T-shirt, planning to hit up the public pool.

"You better be gone when I get back," he instructed the aloof ball of fur. "And keep the bathing to a minimum."

While he was searching for a towel in their shared linen closet, Carmen called from behind him, "I've got just what you need, big boy."

He spun around to see her carrying a basket full of towels and bed sheets.

"Fresh and toasty from the dryer."

"Thanks." He cautiously reached for a towel from the top of the pile, then took a big step back.

She looked him up and down. "I really admire your dedication to fitness."

"Thanks," he said again, bracing himself for an inappropriate follow-up, but none came. "Okay, well, I'll see you later."

Carmen stepped aside, allowing him to pass with a saucy smirk on her face. "Buns of steel," she murmured.

Ethan sighed. A burlap sack would do a better job at hiding his form, though he half-suspected the woman had X-ray vision. Yet another reason why he steered clear: she was friskier than her feline. Remembering to snag the bottle of sunscreen he'd left on the hall table, he bolted down the stairs and then he was out the door again, walking in the direction of the public pool.

His mind circled back to his previous train of thought as his feet ate up the pavement. He'd tried for exactly one fitful day to write at the bowling alley-slash-pub, but he had to nix that idea when every crash of the pins gave him a splitting headache.

He resigned himself to writing at home—that is, until his coffee maker raised the white flag. Ethan could live without a lot of things, but caffeine wasn't one of them. He'd made an emergency trip to the Cup-A-Cabana to restore his vital signs. Eventually, he'd bought a new coffee maker, but by then he'd been hooked. He'd found his home away from home. His writing haven.

He could claim it was the coffee, the change of scenery, the heavenly danishes . . . but the truth was, being there, amongst the people, regardless of the fact that most of them ignored him, he sort of felt like he belonged.

Entering the fenced-in area, he spotted Mrs. McCallister herding her three grandchildren out of the pool. The water-logged kids begrudgingly followed orders and stepped foot on dry land again. One by one, they towelled off and waited obediently by the gate for her next command. He had to give the woman credit. She ran a tight ship.

"It's all yours, handsome," she said to Ethan when the last of the children had been gathered.

He smiled, like he always did. And she winked, like she always did. He didn't seem to have any trouble attracting the sixty-and-above crowd.

Dropping his towel on a nearby lounge chair, he nodded in greeting to the pimple-faced teenager serving as lifeguard on duty. The teen barely glanced up from his phone screen to mutter a "Hey." Shrugging off his shirt, he sprayed on some waterproof sunscreen, stretched a little, then headed for the deep end.

Taking a long, cleansing breath, he dove through the glassy surface, kicking his legs till he reached the opposite end where he emerged again. He slicked a hand through his hair as he stood in the shallow end, the water only reaching the top of his trunks.

Was Addie attracted to him? She seemed to enjoy talking to him, so she was at least attracted to his intellect if not his physicality. Oh, God, she was friend-zoning him. She had to be. Why else would she have paled at the thought of them being on a real date? Maybe he gave off a certain 'I don't date' vibe. But he *did* date. Here and there. Once in a while. If he could be dragged out from behind his laptop and force-fed overpriced food in dimly lit restaurants playing 'eclectic' music, that is.

As it happened, most women didn't have the patience for a guy who came across as mildly cranky at the best of times. Or so his last date claimed as she dashed toward the nearest exit following his rant on miniscule portion sizes in upscale French bistros. Too bad. It'd been one of his finest rants.

Dropping back into the water, he pushed off the side and sliced through the surface, barely kicking up a splash. His strokes increased. His long legs propelled him to the shallow end and back again. Over and over. Deep, then shallow. He'd kiss Addie the same way. If he ever got the chance.

She'd agreed to the tacos, but she'd probably qualify that as another not-date. Fake date. Whatever. What if she did finally agree to a date-date with him and pulled the plug in a matter of minutes? He froze mid-stroke and gasped for air.

She could. She might. But he'd never know if he didn't try.

With renewed determination, he plunged through the water again. He deserved a fair shot, too. She might shoot him down afterward—or maybe his advances would trigger an onslaught of affection. Buoyed by the latter thought, he swam another fifteen laps. He wasn't a romance novelist, but for once, he was hoping for a happy ending.

4

Addie breezed into the Cup-A-Cabana on Wednesday afternoon, fresh from an impromptu breakfast date and in need of a post-date dissection. She'd needled Ethan for eavesdropping on her previous dates, but she'd grown accustomed to their discussions. His snappy comebacks. His smiles and frowns. His face.

Because of him, she was turning into a Cup-A-Cabana regular.

Her gaze landed on him at his usual table, unpacking all his writing supplies. He bent down to dig for something else in his bag, and when he sat up, he startled at Addie sitting in the seat across from him.

"You're very high-maintenance, Hemingway. It must be hell to travel with you."

"Please, have a seat. Make yourself comfortable."

She smiled. "I'm in need of a good mocking partner, so I hope you're feeling especially cynical and snarky today."

"I've got the cynical part down, but I may need a danish to help me reach my full snark potential."

Another smile lit her face as she signaled Gwen and ordered a cherry danish for him and a blueberry muffin for herself. Both arrived within moments. "There you go. Chew fast."

He took a big bite and swallowed it down before asking, "So who, or what, are we mocking on this occasion?"

"I'll take 'The worst date I've ever been on' for five-hundred, Alex."

"It's Ethan, but you're getting closer. It should actually be six-hundred, though."

"I'm sorry?"

"Or even a thousand." When she continued to stare at him in bewilderment, he kindly elaborated. "The point values on the *Jeopardy!* series changed to two-hundred-dollar increments over a decade ago. Asking for a 'five-hundred' is so 2001. You need to up your game."

"Right. Can I continue my story now?"

He waved for her to proceed. "Carry on. So it was a bad date?"

"Horrible. And I've been on plenty of bad dates, but this one was the absolute worst. I thought it would never end."

"Really? Worse than Simple Simon?"

She nodded her head vigorously. "Much worse. This guy was a *Jeopardy!* hopeful who worded every response in the form of a question or a clue. Apparently, he's taken the online test seventeen times—with no success, I might add—but this is *his year*."

Ethan pushed his half-eaten danish aside. "What happened to the other guy? Magic Man?" he asked, a tad brusquely.

"We postponed till next week, and his name's Daniel. Anyway, I'd been chatting with this new guy online and we both had a window of opportunity this morning, so we decided to meet for a breakfast date at a place in Madoc."

"I don't know how you can keep them all straight."

"You don't seem to have any trouble with it."

Conceding the point, he pulled back his plate and resumed eating his danish. He'd more than reached his full snark potential. With his mouth otherwise occupied, she continued with her story. "When the waitress asked him how he'd like his eggs, he said, and I quote, 'This egg dish is stirred, beaten, and cooked together typically with milk, butter, and various other ingredients.'"

"What are scrambled eggs?"

She sighed. "You're not helping."

"They should have a rule that you can only fail the online test ten times before you're blacklisted. *Jeopardy!* shamed. Publicly humiliated by Mr. Trebek himself."

"Yeah!" she said. "After each show, before the credits roll, Alex could read a list of names . . . ."

"*Jeopardy!* wannabes who've jeopardized their chances of appearing on *Jeopardy!*"

She laughed, breaking off a piece of her muffin and chewing it thoughtfully. "What's with all the weird, bordering-on-unhinged guys out there, Hemingway?"

"Maybe you're just not looking in the right places."

And there it was. Another subtle hint of flirtation. They'd been playing a game of cat and mouse from the moment they met. Something burned just beneath the surface, waiting for one of them to crack. "You think I've been looking for love in all the wrong places, Johnny Lee?"

"And in too many faces," he muttered. "I hope that ends our tribute to country music because that's the extent of my knowledge."

Tickled by his apparent distaste in the topic, the fiendish side of her couldn't let them skip past it. "I bet you're a closet Kenny Rogers fan. Or is Willie Nelson more your style?"

He said nothing in response, his face expressionless.

"That's a good poker face you got there. I bet you know when to hold 'em."

The barest hint of a smile crossed his features. "Are you finished?"

She huffed, scarfing down what was left of her muffin. "I guess your mamma didn't let her baby grow up to be a cowboy." She would have happily sat there all day and beaten him over the head with country music lyrics until he 'fessed up that he knew more than he let on, but she'd promised Sam down at the bowling alley that she'd make a pie run before the tournament ended, and a glance at her watch told her she needed to skedaddle.

Ethan frowned as she stood. "Where you going?" he asked.

"I know when to walk away, but I ain't runnin'. I'm biking. Duty calls," she explained. "Hey, the danish is on me." She counted out some bills and dropped them to the table.

"You know, uh, you shouldn't count your money when you're sit—er, standing at the table."

Warmth spread all over her body. She appreciated him for not getting the line exactly right but trying anyway. For playing along. For listening. For the snark. "Thank you," she said, hoping he understood it was all-encompassing. "I needed that."

He nodded.

Addie waited a beat, but figuring he'd either used up his words or was saving the rest for his neglected manuscript, she turned on her heel and headed for the door. She unlocked her bike from the lamppost outside the coffee shop, hopped on, and pedaled fast toward home where she'd left her hand pies cooling on the counter.

Ethan, like her pies, was crusty on the outside, but deep down there was a sweetness about him. And when you got to know him, bit by bit, he'd let it show. She'd grown fond of the sugar rush that came from exposing that sweetness. He filled a void in her life, one she never realized existed before now. She'd been lonely, not simply for romance but for male companionship. A partner in crime. Excitement bubbled up inside her at the thought of seeing him again. Perhaps tomorrow.

Once she made it home, she loaded the pies into her bike basket which she'd parked just inside the backdoor to protect the goodies from hungry critters. She had a few minutes to spare and returned to the kitchen. It'd been like pulling teeth to prepare the dough the night before. Her mixer, Maybelline, hadn't been cooperating as of late, and Addie prayed the rebellion was only temporary. Standing on her tiptoes, she reached for the thick, hard-covered, lovingly dog-eared book stuck behind the flour on the shelf above the sink. *The Art of Reading Tea Leaves.* Edna's version of the bible.

After enduring an hourlong breakfast with Arthur, which felt more like a quiz show than a date, she'd seen what most resembled a mouse in the remnants of her tea. She wanted to double check the passage about mice to be sure she'd interpreted it correctly. Turning to the proper section, she located the mouse symbol and read the description. *Money woes. Swindling. Theft.* Ironic that he spent most of the hour proving he was worthy of being a contestant on the popular gameshow with monetary rewards, despite seventeen failed attempts. Maybe his eighteenth attempt would break him. He'd put on a ski mask and rob the nearest convenience store. Or steal money from his mother's purse.

Hmm. She examined the images closer and debated her initial conclusion. The pattern she'd seen along the side of her teacup had a longer torso, and the ears were different. Could have been a rabbit. No, it was a mouse. Probably. Well, it didn't matter either way. He wasn't about to capture a starring role in her love life, and unlike the *Jeopardy!* judges, she wasn't inclined to give him more than one audition.

Carrying the book with her, she sat down at the kitchen table. Memories flowed through her fingertips and seeped into her bones. When she was a little girl, Edna had given her a bike for her birthday and taught her how to ride it. As she grew older, the two would ride their bikes together down by the lake. They'd talk about boys and dreams. She'd tell Addie tales of all her beaus before she found her dear Thomas. And how her tea leaves never led her astray.

"People come into your life for a reason, a season, or a lifetime," she'd say. "You won't always know right away, but when you learn the truth, you'll find endless peace."

In other words, every relationship, even the failed ones, had a purpose.

Days after her twenty-third birthday, following a painful breakup with her then-boyfriend, she had sat down with Edna at this very kitchen table and received a lesson in tasseography.

"My mother, your great-grandmother, taught me how to read my leaves when I was about your age, too." Addie's heart squeezed. Her own mother never touched tea and discouraged her from taking anything Edna said without a grain and a half of salt. But then, they'd never really seen eye to eye, no matter what the subject.

Addie stared into her cup, unable to make out any shapes, let alone something recognizable. She met Edna's eager gaze and shrugged her shoulders. "I don't see anything."

"Look again," the older woman said. "The more you look, the more you see."

Concentrating with all her might, Addie scrutinized the leaves until, suddenly, an image of a dancing woman appeared. She wore a tiara on her head, a puffy skirt, her legs akimbo. "I . . . I think I see a dancing woman."

"You do *see her,"* Edna corrected. *"Commit to what you see. Trust in it."*

"What does it mean?"

Though her tasseography book was well within reach, Edna knew the contents like the back of her hand. "It represents an omen of coming pleasure, of good news. It's a wonderful symbol, sweetheart."

"Does this mean Peter will realize he made a horrible mistake and beg me to be his girlfriend again?"

Edna smiled. She stood up from her chair and came around to the other side of the table, wrapping her arms around Addie from behind. "It means you need to open up your heart to other possibilities, pet. Whenever I see good things reflected in my cup, I do whatever I can to make sure they happen. If you believe in what you see, and you set your mind to it, fate will handle the rest."

Addie gazed at the ceiling, hearing those words of wisdom as surely as she'd felt Edna's embrace. Peter had wanted to ditch life for a while and travel around the world with only the clothes on their backs and a few bucks in their pockets. Addie had a waitressing job, and she couldn't bear the thought of leaving her family and the town she loved for an indeterminate amount of time. He'd called her cowardly, said she'd forever be stuck in that small town.

As much as his words had hurt, they—in combination with the tea leaves—gave her the push she needed to do the most uncowardly thing she'd ever done: start her Pie-Cycle business. Long before she could bike, she learned how to bake. Due to her mother's social commitments, she'd often wind up at her grandmother's house after school where, instead of plopping her down in front of the TV, her grandmother would arm her with a container of flour and a mixing bowl and let her turn the kitchen into an experimental playground.

In the beginning, Pie-Cycle was just a side gig. She continued working at the Country Corner restaurant, with the added bonus of baking some of the items on their dessert menu when she wasn't serving customers. Now, her business was no longer a side gig—but it wasn't an end game, either. She dreamed of opening her own bakery one day.

Releasing a wistful sigh, Addie stood and returned the book to its shelf. She'd finally opened her heart to the possibilities Edna spoke of, now it was only a matter of seeing who'd be joining her on the next big adventure of her life.

5

Ethan took a slug of coffee and sighed. He'd opted for more caffeine today, but nothing short of an IV pump could jumpstart his creativity. Addie would likely be arriving soon, intent on shattering another man's ego.

Was it a defense mechanism? Or did she just not have the whole dating thing down pat? Could be that nerves got the better of her. Whatever her reasons, he had to admit it didn't suck seeing someone else failing at the whole love connection thing. It made his own pathetic love life seem a little less . . . pathetic.

He'd gotten to know her over the last weeks, but she never stayed long enough for him to test the waters. To see if she might be interested in more than clever conversation. What did she see when she looked at him? An intellect she could trade barbs with? A lonely, pitiable, and soon-to-be-broke poser who was anything but marketable?

But the problem wasn't what she saw on the surface. It was the fact that she didn't really see *him*. Not the way he wanted her to.

Waking his laptop, he opened a new document, rolled his shoulders, and typed the first line: *The Girl Who Couldn't See. Chapter One.*

A chorus of whispers and breathy sighs from the female clientele drew his attention. He followed their line of sight to a tall, herculean man clad in plaid who clomped his way toward the counter in work boots more fitting for the back woods than a quaint coffee shop.

"You rang, your majesty?" he said to Gwen.

"Ahh, Matt, my loyal handyman." She laughed, gesturing for him to join her behind the counter. "I've got a stove that won't ignite, and the toaster's out."

"Again?"

"'Fraid so."

He rolled back his sleeves, displaying muscular forearms. "Buy a new toaster," he grumbled.

"But if I did that, I wouldn't get the pleasure of your company."

"Don't you have a boyfriend to fix this stuff for you?"

Gwen sighed. "Shawn can't even fix his gaze long enough to win a staring contest."

The guy shook his head and said, "I'll be finished shortly," then disappeared into the kitchen, much to the disapproval of his obvious admirers.

Ethan gave a moment's thought to the impact the lumberjack look had on the ladies. Maybe he could give the plaid thing a go . . . *No. God, no.* But there was no mistaking Matt's appeal to the fairer sex, and Ethan sort of envied him for that.

The bells jingled again, and he jerked his head sharply toward the door. He'd have one hell of a crick in his neck by the end of the day. But the momentary pain faded to a memory when he saw her. Her spiked hair looked shiny and deceptively soft. Her pink lips were temptingly full. Today's tank top of choice was a baby-blue one that complemented her fair complexion. Right. Because he was staring at her skin tone. Not her breasts. Not how well they filled out the form-fitting fabric. His gaze lowered to the heart-stoppingly short shorts. Possibly the shortest pair on the planet.

If she noticed his blatant ogling, she didn't let on. No, she flashed him a smile as she turned toward the counter to chat with Gwen. Seconds later, Matt emerged from the kitchen, capturing the attention of both women. Ethan couldn't hear their conversation above the rising din, but he could easily read their body language. The laughter, the warm smiles, the handshake between Addie and Matt that lasted too long for Ethan's liking. And, to cap it all off, Matt fished out a notepad from his back pocket and scribbled something down. Probably Addie's number, because why not book another date with another guy before the date you're actually supposed to meet arrives? Made perfect sense.

He watched as she entered the dining area and navigated her way around the tables, plunking into a seat at the one nearest him. This time she sat perpendicular to him. Always something different with her. She was intriguing, in an annoying sort of way, because he couldn't possibly get any work done with her around.

"Are your dates consistently late, or are you just perpetually early?"

She adjusted her position to face him head-on. "Good afternoon to you, too, Hemingway."

Was it afternoon already? He glanced down at the time on his computer. Yes, and he still had nothing to show for half a day's time. This was becoming a vicious cycle. Why hadn't he been able to write? He hadn't written a word since . . . the last time he saw her. *Whoa.* Was she his muse? She certainly had all the makings of a muse. Beautiful, witty, a colorful vocabulary. And those eyes. Lord, the woman could hypnotize a blind man.

"I'm early because I like to be early," Addie continued, probably realizing he wasn't planning on returning the proffered greeting.

"So you can scope out the best table?"

"Yes, the one closest to my favorite eavesdropper."

Ethan scooted to the edge of his seat and met her challenging gaze with one of his own. "I don't think you can call it eavesdropping anymore. You know I'm listening. We're not strangers."

"We're not?"

He took a drink of his coffee, then shook his head. "Nope."

"What are we, then?"

He had to give the woman credit. She didn't even flinch when she fired the loaded question. There was even a glimmer of a smile on her face.

She dangled that carrot far too close for him to resist a nibble or two. "I don't know what we are, but I can tell you what I'd like us to be—"

Before the shock fully registered in her features, the damn bells jingled once more, and in walked Magic Man himself. This had to be the guy she mentioned—the single father/magician from Newtonville. The tyke glued to his hip kind of detracted from the mystique, but maybe the kid was part of his act.

"You must be Daniel," Addie said to the man with the forty-pound growth hanging from his midsection.

The guy beamed a smile and nodded. "Sorry for the intruder. This is Jacob. The sitter canceled at the last minute. Hope you don't mind."

"No, not at all."

Ethan rolled his eyes. *Right. And I'm the next Stephen King.*

Addie stood to shake Houdini's hand, then squatted down to say hello to the kid. And then a rousing game of musical chairs ensued. Daniel went to sit opposite Addie, but Jacob had a fit over it.

Apparently, he'd taken more of a shine to Addie's seat in the twenty seconds it'd been a part of his life. She graciously gave up her spot for the tiny hellion and his father, which put her farther away from Ethan but in his direct line of sight.

Jacob bounced atop his father's lap with a calculating glint in his eye, the clear victor of round one. It didn't take long for the kid to lose interest in the boring adult conversation, which left Ethan with a very unwanted admirer.

Wide blue eyes fixed on him, unblinking. "Who're you?"

Ethan stared right on back and said, "The greatest author in the entire world." A feminine snort alerted him to the fact that Addie was a fellow dabbler in the art of eavesdropping.

The kid's eyes lit up like flashbulbs. "I seened baby otters at the M'rine World show!"

"*Author*, not *otter*," Ethan corrected.

"Can I play on your 'puter?"

Ah, children. Minds whirring at one-hundred-and-fifty-billion miles a minute. Always wanting to touch and grab . . . everything. "No way. I don't want your grubby hands on it."

Jacob's forehead crinkled and his lower lip quivered, but he held strong. "Why not? Daddy says you should always share."

"In that case, I'll share my story with you. It's about a little boy who asks too many questions."

Addie unleashed snort number two at that. He glanced up and caught her gaze before she shifted back to the conversation she was *supposed* to be paying attention to.

His keeper finally contained the kid, giving Ethan a much-needed opportunity to down several gulps of coffee.

"So . . . how'd the magician thing come about?" Addie, the queen of the segue.

"Oh, well, that's an interesting story. I'm a nuclear physicist by day, but even I haven't mastered the science of mollifying a toddler mid-tantrum," he said with a laugh. "One night, about a year ago, Jacob was particularly fussy so I invented a game—hide the nucleus. I've never seen a child respond so positively to a stimulus before. That one trick turned into a second and then a third. I took a course to better hone the craft."

Ethan failed to contain a chortle. *Magic 101? Wizards R Us? The Growing Wand?*

"As it turns out, magic is said to inspire and aid in early development. But, anyway, it's just a hobby."

Addie nodded. "Right."

"I put on my act at the Nuclear Physics for Kids convention each year. The kids gobble it up. It's never too early to start training their brains, you know?"

"Yeah, sure."

The guy planted a kiss on his son's crown. "Everything you do matters. I play Mozart every night while he sleeps. He's enrolled in the 'Inspiring Young Minds' art class taught by a former Julliard student. I bought him his first Faulkner last week. I think we'll start reading that over the summer."

Houdini ran a hand through his wavy blond hair and smiled that revolting Colgate commercial smile. He was well-built, probably from escaping straightjackets, or sawing his assistant in half. Doubtful the extra heft came from tossing around the kid. Hell, he was surprised Junior didn't come equipped with a padded helmet, lest he damage his future-surgeon brain.

Gwen came to take their orders, and Addie requested tea again. Cripes, the woman was obsessed with the stuff. That weird leafy kind, too. He always thought tea tasted like socks. Not just any socks, but the ones that had been fermenting under the bed.

"Well, I'm sure Jacob will reap the benefits. You're obviously doing a great job with him." Addie beamed at the pint-sized prodigy, who promptly stuck out his tongue at her.

His proud papa either missed the diss altogether or ignored it. "I know you don't have any kids yourself, but what are your thoughts on the whole . . . insta-family thing?"

Addie appeared thrown by the direct question. "Uhh. It's, uh, not something I've given a lot of thought to, to be honest. You're the first . . . father I've ever dated. But in this day and age, at *our* age, it's certainly not uncommon."

Ethan wasn't a father to any children, illegitimate or otherwise, but he supposed the laptop and notebook he carted everywhere with him could count as baggage. They didn't spit up or talk back, thankfully.

"So, you'd be willing to give us a chance and see where things end up?" The expectant look on the guy's face would have been more compelling if not for the miniature terror on his lap, picking his nose like it was his job.

Gwen returned with two cups of tea and a chocolate milk for the squirt. Addie lunged for the tea, spending countless seconds gazing into its liquid depths. Slowly, she raised her head and said in a quiet voice, "I'm, uh, just not sure that I'm ready for . . . this kind of a conversation right now. I mean, it's Monday. Seems more like a Thursday kind of topic—"

"It's Monday? Fudge, fudge, double-fudge! What time is it?"

Ethan didn't bother stifling his groan. *Fudge me, just drop an F-bomb. It'll be good for the kid. Give him a taste of the real world.*

Addie jolted at her date's sudden urgency. She glanced at her wristwatch. "Half past one."

"Jacob has a violin lesson in the city at two every Monday. We have no hope of getting there unless we leave right now."

Ethan rolled his eyes. *Violin lesson? Lemme guess, his teacher is another former Julliard student.*

"Well, I'm sure missing one practice won't kill—"

He paused mid-gathering up the kid and the alarming amount of gear required to care for such a small creature. "Missing practice isn't an option. It's critical to Jacob's development." Like it was some sort of consolation prize, he added, "I'll call you and we'll make plans, okay?"

"Um, sure. Okay."

In an impressive sleight of hand, he managed to pluck some cash from his pocket without dropping the kid or any of the kid's crap and place it on the table, then he stooped to kiss Addie goodbye before hustling to the door. Barely more than a glancing blow across her cheek, but well played all the same. In Ethan's opinion, public displays of affection were nothing short of nauseating, but women usually went for that kind of stuff. It showed a guy's . . . sensitive side, or something. The kid looked back as the bells jingled and stuck his tongue out at Ethan this time.

Yeah, well, while you're learning to screech out "Twinkle, Twinkle, Little Star," I'll be here chatting up your daddy's girl.

Addie blew out a deep breath. Talk about divine intervention. Surely, along with harps, they played violins in heaven. She stood and made the short trek to Ethan's table, plopping into the seat across from him.

He clapped his hands. "That was the best disappearing act ever."

"I didn't chase this one off. He left willingly."

"You don't sound too disappointed. Between saving the world one nucleus at a time and pulling rabbits out of his hat, he seemed like the perfect guy."

She shrugged. "It's one thing to sign up to date a guy with a kid on paper, but having it there in front of me, right from the get-go? It was just too much, too soon, ya know?"

"It?" he asked pointedly.

"Him," she said. "The kid."

"Jacob, you mean?"

"Wow, you really do take your eavesdropping seriously, don't you?"

Ethan rubbed a hand against the back of his neck and sighed. Tiny freckles dotted the patch of skin visible above his collared shirt. He wore glasses today, perhaps to look more the part of a good and proper writer. Whatever the case, they looked . . . nice. Attractive, in a distinguished sort of way.

"So Houdini has a kid. Is that his only problem, or was there something else wrong with him?"

She startled at his harsh tone. "I didn't say there was anything wrong with him. I'm just not ready to be saddled with a child at this point in my life."

"You don't want kids?"

"Well, yes . . . I mean, eventually. Maybe. If I find the right person."

Their eyes met and held. When Ethan spoke again, his voice was smoother, gentler. "He could have been the right person. The guy had hair. Nice hair, too. Plenty of it. Of course, you never know if that means he has lots of hair everywhere, but let's not get that far ahead of ourselves. He wasn't a moron. He didn't mix a single metaphor. And, yeah, the kid was annoying, but cute . . . in a semi-psychotic, budding prodigy sort of way."

Addie blinked and cocked her head. "Are you interested, Hemingway? Want me to set you guys up?"

"You know what your problem is?"

For a guy who claimed *she* was judgmental, he sure didn't have any difficulty passing his own judgement on all things concerning her love life. She narrowed her eyes and crossed her arms over her chest. "No. What's my problem?"

"You don't take the time to get to know someone. You make up your mind before you give the guy a chance. How can you decide something like that without digging a little deeper? You only see what's on the surface. You're in such a big hurry, but . . . well, you can't hurry love."

"Seriously?" she scoffed. "You're Diana Ross-ing me?"

Deep shades of crimson crept up his throat and peppered his cheeks. "In my head, it was the Phil Collins version."

"Okay, Dr. Phil, if you're such a big, fat expert on dating, then why don't you prove it?"

"Prove it?"

"I'm asking you out."

"Oh." He looked off to the side, then his eyes shot back to hers. "What?"

She had to bite back a smile at his shell-shocked expression. "Let's try that Zen Kitchen. I think we both need a little more zen in our lives, don't you?"

"Uh, yeah. Y-Yes."

"Good. How about tomorrow night? You free?"

He nodded, still staring at her like she'd grown a second head.

"Good," she repeated. With that, she rose to her feet, turned on her heel, picked up her abandoned cup of tea, and stalked several tables away from him. She sat for a long moment and stared at the wall, unblinking. Bringing the mug to her lips, she tipped her head back and swallowed down a few gulps. The liquid had cooled to room temperature now, but her insides were overheating. Her pulse raced. She felt dizzy and excited. And sick to her stomach. And starving. *Am I dying? When did I eat last? Is there a doctor in the house? Holy hell, did I just ask him out?*

She spun in her seat to see if he could either confirm or deny, but, to her surprise, he was gone. Every trace of him. No writing implements. No empty plates or cups or balled up napkins. All gone. Poof.

Like Houdini.

She drank more tea as she contemplated what life might be like married to Daniel. Nuclear physicist by day, Baby Einstein trainer by night. Poor Jacob would probably grow up to be an emotionally stunted clinical psychologist who preached the benefits of coddling one's children.

She cracked a smile, wishing Ethan had stuck around long enough for her to share that bit of inspiration. She'd only be lying to herself if she pretended not to have noticed him in a romantic sort of way . . . Mr. Know-It-All who couldn't wait to pass judgement on her failed attempts at finding The One. *We'll see how you do.*

Two more gulps emptied her cup, save for the leaves at the bottom. She peered at them closely. There could be no mistaking the formation of leaves in the shape of an arrow. Arrows were an indication of bad news from the direction in which they pointed. Was this one pointing toward Ethan's empty seat or Daniel's? She was with Ethan last, so did that mean the leaves were more heavily influenced by him? She hadn't even tasted her tea while sitting with Daniel, but they *were* on a date. She and Ethan weren't. Yet.

But as of tomorrow, that would be a different story. Rising to her feet, she turned away from the arrow and bounded out the door.

6

A young woman dressed all in white greeted Addie when she arrived at Zen Kitchen. "Welcome to your food awakening. I'm Zelda."

"I'm on a date. I mean, I'm Addie. Sorry, I'm meeting someone and I'm not sure if—"

"Your date is here waiting for you." Zelda smiled. "Let me direct you to your table."

Layers of loose, flowing fabric practically danced against the woman's glowing skin as she led the way. Addie wondered if everyone who worked at Zen Kitchen had to have a Z name. *Zack, Zane, Zoe, Zander, Zeke . . . and I'm out.* Fellow zen-seekers filled almost every table, speaking in hushed tones. In the center of the restaurant, a see-through glass water feature stood from floor to ceiling, and calming music played gently in the background. Everything was blue and white and clear.

"Tranquil, isn't it?" Zelda asked.

"Yeah." Or trippy.

"Here we are." Zelda stopped at a table that appeared to be made of tree bark, painted white. Ethan sat on a chair—also white—with blue roots entwined around the legs. "Enjoy your date," she said. "Awaken your palate and your heart."

It took less than two seconds for Addie and Ethan to share a smile that spoke of the mocking to come. She hopped onto her chair across from him, folded her arms, and dove right in. "I'm terrified they're going to serve our meals on a bed of soil so we can become more in touch with the earth."

"I'm not sure people even eat here." He nodded to the tables surrounding them. "I don't see any food. Maybe you order food and eat it in your mind."

Addie laughed. "How are we supposed to awaken our palates with imaginary food?"

He shrugged. "There's cucumber water."

She noticed the glass in front of her for the first time. "Did tiny woodland creatures deliver this?"

"Shockingly, no. That was our waiter, Zack."

"Ha! I knew it!" At his probing gaze, she explained, "I have this theory that everyone working here has a name that starts with a Z." Easily the least weird thing about the place. She took a drink of her cucumber water, and the reality of the situation washed over her. They were on a date. She and Ethan were on a date. And he looked really good. While he studied the menu of imaginary food, she studied *him*, starting with the white dress shirt he wore that should have made him blend in with the scenery, but instead made him pop out from it. The sharp contrast of the crisp white cotton with his sun-kissed skin held her in thrall.

His hair had this sexily sleep-rumpled look. But the thing she found most compelling about him were his freckles. He wasn't totally covered in them, but there were enough that she could happily spend all day counting them.

He drank some water, then returned his glass to the precise position it'd rested before, using his napkin to mop up the droplets of condensation left behind on the table.

"Hey," she said, drawing his attention. "We're on a date."

His answering smile warmed her clear through. "A date-date?"

"Yeah, one of those."

Another ethereal being floated to their table in his all-white ensemble. Zack, she assumed. "Good evening. How is your Zen experience thus far?"

"Uh. Enlightening," Addie supplied.

He waited as though he were expecting a lengthier review. "Hmm. Would you care for another drink?"

"I'd love a cup of tea." This way she could make certain the arrow had been pointing at Daniel and not Ethan. "It's real, right? Like, you're going to actually bring it to me?"

Zack stared at her in silence.

"I don't have to pretend to drink it?"

"No. It's real." His words came out slow and measured, like he was speaking to a person in a straightjacket.

"Okay, just checking."

"And you, sir?" he asked Ethan.

Ethan picked up his glass of water and swirled it. "I'm good with the cucumber water. It's bringing out my inner zen."

With a forced but blindingly white smile, Zack glided away to pretend-serve other tables.

Addie made sure he was gone before saying, "I don't think he likes us, which is crazy because I think we're adorable."

"Incorrigible, too."

She grinned. "You should totally write about this place in one of your—" Catching herself, she stopped mid-sentence. "I forgot. Authors don't like being told what to write, do they?"

"Beats anything I've got."

"What?"

He sighed and rubbed the pad of his thumb against his chin. "I, uh . . . can't seem to get started. I've hit a wall. I mean, I know what I *should* be writing, but I can't get my brain to cooperate."

Ethan kept his eyes averted as if he'd just disclosed the most humiliating bit of information. For a writer, she suspected it was, and she found it touching that he'd chosen to share his struggles with her. He'd cracked open the door to his private world. "Maybe you just need to write, like, anything. Write something you want to write about."

She hoped the suggestion didn't come across as intrusive or insensitive, but the books she enjoyed most—when she managed to find time to read—were the ones that stood out from the crowd. That didn't fit a particular mold.

"I don't think it really matters what I write. Every time I start a new project, I hit a dead end. It's just . . . I guess it's like a fear of failure or something."

Addie wanted so badly to hug him, but she thought it more important to keep him talking, to help him sort through whatever problems he was dealing with. "Haven't you already been published?"

"Yes, multiple times, but that doesn't make me a success."

"How do you define success, then?"

He appeared a bit stymied by the question at first, dabbing at fresh water droplets on the table with his napkin. "In this business, it means producing and selling books." He folded his napkin back onto his lap and regained eye contact with her before continuing. "I'm not doing a great job of either at the moment, but others are."

"Who was it that said comparison is the thief of joy?" she asked with a teasing grin.

"Roosevelt. But this isn't about comparison," he shot back a tad defensively. "I've studied the trends and figured out what's hot, so I'm going to do that. It's about taking advantage of a proven formula for success."

It sounded more like selling out to her, but she wouldn't risk saying so and setting him off. The gutsier thing to do, in her opinion, would be to push through and persevere, write what you love, and the rest would fall into place. "Never pictured you going along with the crowd. Seems a little too . . . bandwagon-y for you."

He released a sardonic laugh, undoubtedly preparing his rebuttal when Zack happened by with her tea.

"Ooh, it *is* real!" Addie marveled, earning an eyeroll from their server who didn't stay long enough to take their entrée orders.

"What's your obsession with tea?"

Her cheeks flamed. Expecting they'd resume their book chat, she was thrown by the question and debated how to respond. She loved the taste of it—that was true. But not the entire truth. She definitely didn't owe him any truths, but for some reason, out of all the people in her life, she thought that maybe he'd understand and appreciate her unusual approach to finding a partner. He was a creative type, after all. "It's the leaves," she confessed.

"The leaves?"

"I've been trying to find love through tea leaves."

"Excuse me?"

She pushed back from the table and sat up straighter. "This whole . . . search. Looking for the right guy. I've been reading my tea leaves to determine if the relationship will work."

His look of confusion melted away to one of genuine concern, and then, worst of all, mockery. "Tea leaves? You've been dumping guys right, left, and center because of tea leaves?"

The condescension in his tone irked her. "Hey, I haven't been doing all the dumping. And I'll have you know that tasseography is a legitimate practice. In fact, it traces back to medieval times—"

"Wow, there's an actual name for this brand of crazy?"

Addie opened her mouth to snap at him, then thought the better of it. "I admit, it's not the most conventional method of finding 'the one' . . . ."

"Do the Tetley people know about you? I see huge marketing potential here."

"But it's been passed down for generations in my family," she pressed on, undeterred. "My great-aunt Edna taught me all she knew. She swore by it. I guess . . . I thought . . . well, I had nothing to lose."

"Except the last of your sanity. Hang on." He plucked his cell phone from his breast pocket. "I've got my shrink on speed dial."

Mortified by his belittling comments and the attention they were attracting from other diners, she slipped from her giant tree seat and gathered her purse. "I can't believe that I was such a fool to think things would be different with us, but you just turned around and mocked me the way you do everybody."

"Addie," he started, reaching for her arm. "I get that you think this is some deep, predictive way of looking at things, but—"

She pulled away from him. "You don't know what I think. You don't know a damn thing about me."

"You won't let me know you, or anyone else know you, for that matter. What are you so afraid of? That you might meet someone and things will click and then . . . what? You'll actually have to make room for someone else in your life? Isn't that the whole point of dating?"

Tears of humiliation burned behind her eyes but she stubbornly held them at bay. "I guess you'll never have to worry about finding out the answer to that. We're more alike than you think we are, Ethan." She paused then, as stunned as he was that she'd used his real name for the first time. "We're both failing, but I'm the only one who's brave enough to do something about it."

Every Zen enthusiast in the restaurant watched her walk out on him, their mouths agape, then their heads swivelled back to him. What would he do? they likely pondered. Chase after her? Drown his sorrows in cucumber water?

He did neither. Flagging down Zack, who was uncharacteristically responsive, he asked for the check. Moments later it appeared, including charges for the tea she hadn't touched and the cucumber water. A whopping $4.50 for stupid water they didn't order. *Zen, my ass.*

Plucking some bills from his wallet, he threw them on the table and slid from his seat. "Enjoy your food awakening," he muttered to his remaining audience as he trudged toward the door. He'd driven to Bloomfield to meet Addie at the restaurant, but he felt much too agitated to drive and decided to take a walk to cool his jets.

I'm the ass.

The whole thing had been a disaster, starting with that ridiculous sham of a restaurant. They should have gone for Mexican food. Shove enough tacos in his mouth and he'd shut up. He might never open his dumb mouth again at this rate.

A cool breeze shook the trees along the sidewalk. The clouds overhead spoke of an impending storm. Maybe he was paranoid, but it felt like everyone he passed was staring at him. Pitying him. *Guess news travels fast in Bloomfield.* Not too far in the distance, he noticed a sign that was all at once comforting: Bloomfield Public Library.

He hurried his steps as he felt the first fat drops of rain. The lights inside the library shone like a beacon to him. Still open. He reached the door before enduring too much of Mother Nature's wrath. A white dress shirt in a rain storm . . . not a good look for any man, real or fictional.

An older woman at the circulation desk smiled at him as he entered. "Good evening. Is there anything I can help you with?"

"I'm okay for now, thanks."

"We're open for another hour."

He nodded and made his way to the row of touch-screen computers and typed in a few search words. The results page that popped up astonished him. Shaking his head in dazed wonder, he used his phone to take a screenshot of the call numbers, then headed in the direction of the philosophy and psychology section.

A mother and her young daughter sat at a little square table while the girl read a story about a jungle safari. A college-age guy carried an armful of books to the circulation desk, griping all the way about the injustice of summer school and the insanity of having to memorize every bone and muscle in the human body. *Ladies and gentlemen, the next med school dropout.*

Arriving in the appropriate section, he referred to his phone to help him locate the books he sought—*Tea Leaves and Tasseography*, and *The Truth Hidden in the Bottom of Your Teacup*. Before coming there, he would have bet every dime to his name that no such books existed, but oh, how wrong he'd been. Gathering his finds, he carried them to the nearest table and took a seat.

He flipped open the cover of the second book and read a few lines of the preface. *In your palms you hold the secrets to an ancient divination. A world of spiritual illumination is at your fingertips. Tip over your teapot and fill your cup with wisdom and wonder that traces back to medieval times!* Ethan had to stop himself from hurling the book at the wall. Or just hurling in general.

Addie had said something similar, about the medieval roots. Christ, he'd jumped all over her for inviting him into this obviously meaningful part of her life. He doubted many people knew about it. She probably feared their reactions, and he gave credence to that fear by reacting so harshly. Frankly, he'd been a ticking time bomb from the very start of the date—if you could even call it a date. To him, it'd felt more like a dare. He could almost hear her taunting him. *See if you can do better than any of the others, Hemingway. Go ahead, give it your best shot.* He was the next lucky—or unlucky—bachelor in line for her tea leaf trickery.

But he'd hurt her. It wasn't some silly experiment in her eyes. She believed in this stuff.

Rolling back his shoulders, he flipped to the next page and settled in. He couldn't even begin to understand that kind of belief, but he'd try. If she put her trust in tea leaves, if they figured so importantly in her life, then he owed it to her to try.

7

Addie'd been brewing mad ever since she left the restaurant, and not even a warm bath and a cold glass of wine could soothe her tattered nerves. How dare he! How dare he criticize her like he had every right in the world. On a date, no less. She'd been such an idiot to think things would be different with him. She was glad she left before drinking a drop of tea. He'd have put her on the spot and forced her to read the leaves. It'd only have added fuel to his fire.

Smug, self-righteous . . . man. She fumed, wishing she could find the words when she needed them the most. Why did she let him get to her? If she believed so whole-heartedly in tasseography, then why did it matter what Ethan thought? Why did his disbelief cut so deep? Because it wasn't simply that he judged her methods of sifting through suitors. He accused her of using it as a cover because she wasn't ready to commit to someone.

Sighing wearily, she glanced at the clock. Barely eight, and all she wanted to do was slide under the covers and sleep the rest of this awful day away.

Then, of course, someone knocked at her door. Wearing her PJs, complete with fuzzy pink cupcake slippers, she hustled down the stairs and opened the door to find Matt Tully standing on her porch, looking as gloriously rugged as he had when she'd met him the previous afternoon in the coffee shop.

Raking his gaze over her from head to toe, he frowned. "Is this a bad time?"

"Oh. You mean the pajamas? I just . . . I figured I'd slip into something more comfortable. For bed, I mean, not for you. Not that I was going to bed yet, but I tend to wake up early for the baking thing, and I wasn't sure that you were . . . ." She stopped and took a breath. "Would you like to come in?"

Chuckling, he crossed the threshold. "I wish I'd have known we were having a slumber party. I would've dressed the part."

An image of the burly man in a plaid flannel onesie tripped through her thoughts. Trying not to giggle—or purr, for that matter—she led the way to the kitchen, happy to be in her sanctuary. "Thanks for coming by so quickly. As I mentioned, I've been having trouble with my mixer, which is kind of a critical component in the whole pie-making process."

He nodded. "I can imagine. What's the trouble?"

"She's making a weird grinding noise, like the gears need grease, but nothing I've tried seems to work." Addie walked to the counter where the malfunctioning appliance stood. "Matt, this is Maybelline. Maybelline, Matt."

"Do you name all inanimate objects, or just certain ones?"

"The special ones."

"Gotcha. I'll take a look at it . . . *her* and see what I can do."

She smiled gratefully and took at a seat at the table. Resting her cheek in her palm, she watched him pull tools from his belt and tinker with the cherry-red stand mixer.

"So, where you from, Matt?"

"Newtonville," he said, unknowingly triggering memories of the magician, which in turn triggered memories of her fight with Ethan. Like she'd been able to think of anything but that. "My family owns the Tully Tree Farm. You might've heard of it. We run all sorts of events there year-round—Easter egg hunts, strawberry picking, hay bale mazes—but our biggest draw are the Christmas trees."

"Uh-huh," she said distractedly. "People have to make room in their homes for Christmas trees, right? I do that every single year, without fail, but does he think I'm capable of making room for a person in my life? Nope. Pffft. Like he knows me at all."

Matt shot her a questioning look but kept working.

"People take up way less space than trees, anyway. Unless it's a really big person, but I've never dated a person bigger than a tree, so . . . ."

He grunted and mumbled something incoherent in response as he plugged in the mixer. The stubborn girl still made that insufferable grinding noise.

"It's tradition to have a tree," Addie spoke over the racket. "I'm a traditional girl. But just because I decide to take a slightly unconventional route with dating, he thinks I'm the one with the problem. Can you believe that?"

Matt huffed, yanking the plug from the outlet. "This is impossible. I can't fix it. I can't fix it . . . ."

"He says I'm rushing things. I'm not the one who chased those guys off. Okay, admittedly, I spooked Snake Boy on purpose, but that would have ended badly. Come to think of it, he was more tree-size—"

"What is wrong with me?" Matt growled, shocking her into silence.

Concerned, and more than a touch wary, she slowly stood and inched toward the man who currently had her mixer in a headlock. "Hey, you okay?"

His eyes snapped to hers, as if he only now realized she was in the same room. "I just . . . I wanna make things right." His voice cracked on the last word, and it nearly broke her heart in two.

"Let's, um . . . come sit at the table." She tugged on his arm but he wouldn't budge. "You're gonna have to let go of your hostage here first."

He relaxed his death grip on the mixer, and she managed to pry her precious appliance free.

Addie pulled out a chair for him to sit in, plugged in her tea kettle, then returned to her own seat on the opposite side of the table. Best to give the big man some space. "What's going on?"

"I can't fix your mixer."

"Don't worry about the mixer," she said. "Tell me what's really bothering you."

He folded his hands on the table, looked anywhere but at her, and finally, after an eternity, he met her gaze. If he was deciding whether he could trust her or not, she couldn't blame him. They were the next thing to strangers, but sometimes it was easier to pour your heart out to someone who knew nothing about you.

"I screwed up. There was a girl . . . a woman. Amy. God, she's just . . . she's perfect. I've loved her for as long as I can remember, but I was too dumb to ever say so. Until I found out she was leaving town."

Addie leaned forward. "What happened?"

"She got a job offer in the city. Amy's one of those arts and crafts junkies. It was only ever a hobby, but then she started selling some of her creations in the Christmas craft show one year, and people went nuts over them. Baubles and tree toppers and skirts. It got to the point where she'd spend half the year making stuff so she'd be able to keep up with demand. This past Christmas, a purchasing manager from a major department store happened to be in town for the show. He saw her designs and invited her to their head office for an interview. She aced it. They offered to set her up with her own design space, an apartment, the works."

"Wow. Sounds like a fairy tale." When he glared at her, she quickly back-pedaled. "I mean, you know, with the job. Not the moving. I'm guessing she took them up on their offer?"

He nodded, the glare still in place.

Her tea kettle whistled. "You want a drink?" She leapt to her feet, anxious to create some distance. Grabbing two mugs from the cupboard, she fitted the strainers inside and spooned some loose-leaf tea into their centers, pouring hot water over top. Tea was calming. Soothing. Addie breathed a sigh of relief when he started talking again.

"The night before she left, the whole town threw a big party for her. My idea. I figured the ink was dry, her decision was made, I might as well be happy for her, right? Or pretend to be."

"Right."

"I kept trying to get her alone that night, hoping I could talk to her. Didn't have a clue what I'd say. I just knew I needed to say . . . something."

Satisfied she'd let the tea steep long enough, she strained the leaves and joined him at the table again, sliding a mug over. Matt blinked as though it were a foreign object. He peered into its liquid depths, smelled it, and took a cautious sip.

"Good?" she asked just as cautiously.

"Tastes like vanilla."

"Yes. Vanilla almond. It'll help you sleep. Sorry, please continue."

He drank some more and let out a deep breath. "By midnight, most people had left. Only a few stragglers remained. That was my chance."

Addie braced herself for the story to take a turn. His blue eyes were almost black with anguish, and, for the first time, he looked small to her. Like his whole body was curling into itself.

"I told her not to leave. I said that she was making a huge mistake and that the city would eat her alive. I was angry and I hurt her. But what hurts even worse is that she still doesn't know how I feel about her. And now she's there, and I'm . . . an idiot."

"Have you spoken to her since?"

"Nope."

He crossed his arms and dropped his chin to his chest, as if he'd said all he'd wanted to say and that was that.

"Listen, I'm certainly no expert on love and matters of the heart, but maybe she needs this chance." His gaze met hers again, that charming glare back in place. "To find herself, see if she can make it. And . . . I think she does know. She knows how you feel. If you didn't care, you would have let her go and wished her well. We hurt the ones we love more than anyone else because we care about them the most."

Suddenly, she found herself back in that restaurant, blinking away her tears at Ethan's harsh accusations. Shaking off the memory, she reached for her own mug and took a warm, soothing drink.

She was surprised to find him smiling when she lowered the mug again. "I came here to help you, and you're the one doing all the helping," he said.

"Well, you're welcome. I won't even charge you."

Matt laughed, then quickly sobered. "I should go. I've taken up enough of your time." He stood and started for the door.

Addie jumped to her feet to keep pace with him. "Thanks so much for stopping by."

"Thanks for the tea. And sorry again about the mixer."

Waving him off, she said, "I'll get a new one." *Eventually.* If she could ever find it in her heart, or conscience, to replace Maybelline. For now, she'd just deal with the grinding noise. There were bigger problems in the world.

He was halfway out the door before he turned and said, "Don't listen to that guy, whoever he is. Do what you think is right. Go with your gut."

"Oh. Okay," she murmured, stunned that he'd been listening to her ranting. "Thank you."

Addie stood transfixed as Paul Bunyan's body double thumped down her steps and climbed into his truck. She waited for his taillights to disappear, then closed the door and headed back to the kitchen.

"Go with my gut, huh? Yeah, well, right now my gut is tangled up in knots. Think I'll stick to the tea." Speaking of, curiosity got the better of her. It's not like Matt was a taken man . . . exactly. Maybe there was a reason they were brought together by the powers of a faulty mixer. She grabbed hold of her mug and polished off the remainder of her drink. The leaves that remained at the bottom formed the pattern of a fence—a sign that served as a minor setback. A man like Matt would bulldoze through a fence if it meant getting back the girl he truly loved. He wouldn't be controlled by limitations; he'd laugh at them. Too bad the woman he truly loved wasn't standing in this kitchen.

Couldn't blame a girl for wanting a guy who loved that fiercely.

Unable to resist, she brought Matt's mug closer and read his leaves, too. A clump of leaves gathered in the shape of a bow, and the significance brought a relieved smile to her face. Bows symbolized reunions after an absence or estrangement. She knew Matt and Amy would find their way back to each other. They'd get their happily ever after, wrapped up in a neat little bow. A Christmas love story? Maybe Amy would return to Newtonville for the craft show and . . . boom! Insta-romance. Just add snow. Next time she saw Matt, she'd tell him what she'd read. Maybe he'd be more inclined to believe her than some other people.

Her cell phone chirped out a much-too-perky-for-this-late-hour ringtone. "What, you want to share your two cents now, too?" Groaning, she retrieved it from the counter, answering with a tired, "Hello?"

"Addie? It's Hannah. Hannah Barker. Remember, we met at the coffee shop a while back? I got your number from Gwen."

"Hey, Hannah," she said, carrying the phone with her to the couch. "What's up?"

"I think I've found the perfect man for you!"

Considering they'd known each other all of ten seconds, it was hard to take her assertion seriously. "Oh?"

"He came in today with his schnauzer, all tall and sexy and *single*."

"The guy or the schnauzer?"

Hannah's tinkling laughter rang through the line. "The guy, silly! I told him all about you and the pies. He totally knew who you were and seemed really interested. You up for meeting him?"

Well, he had a dog. That was a good start, at least according to Hannah. Her date with Ethan had been a bust. What did she have to lose at this point? "Okay, sure."

"Yay! I'm so excited! You know, I've always fancied myself a matchmaker. His name's Tyler Jameson. I've got all his information right here in front of me, so I'll set everything up. You won't need to worry about a single thing . . . except not being single anymore!"

Addie chuckled, slightly alarmed by the woman's enthusiasm. But then another thought occurred to her. "Hey, if this guy's such a catch, why didn't you pounce?"

"Oh, he's way too clean-cut for me, sweetie. I like my men a little rough around the edges, if ya know what I mean." She could almost picture Hannah winking suggestively.

It sure was nice having another single girl in her corner. Gwen had been off the market for months and was too preoccupied with Shawn, the apparent love of her life. Shawn was fabulous, though. She kind of hated how good they were together, except she couldn't have been happier for them. Hashtag: single woman problems.

"Listen," Hannah continued, "I'll give Tyler a call and find out his schedule, then we'll plan a date. You okay with the coffee shop again? Seems like the ideal location for a casual first date."

That practically guaranteed an encounter with Ethan. She'd hoped to avoid him for as long as possible, but they lived in a small town, and she was a grown woman, and she didn't want him to think his words had that much of an effect on her. "Let's book it."

Three days later, she sat in that very coffee shop, a good ten tables away from Ethan—the nosey, know-it-all, no-goodnik—and was half-tempted to stick her tongue out at him, like his little buddy Jacob had.

Yep, she was a grown woman, all right.

Thankfully, Jacob's daddy never called her back for a second date. Probably too busy carting the kid to his astronaut-in-training classes. It was all for the best, anyway. She knew, deep down, he hadn't been the guy for her.

Addie glanced up and found Ethan's gaze fixed on her. She shot him a glare and waited for him to look away before she did, too. His accusations had been upsetting, more so because there'd been a grain of truth to them. Okay, a few grains. She could admit that her approach to this dating thing had been a bit Seinfeldian in nature, but none of these men were quite what she was looking for. Not really. Perhaps she'd been rushing things a bit, though. But this was new territory for her—dating to find a potential partner. Someone to help fill her big, empty house and make it a home.

In the past, she'd best describe herself as a casual dater. She liked fun, flirty outings with men she'd sometimes see again, and sometimes not. There wasn't any pressure. Just two people out for a good time, talking, teasing, kissing, and occasionally more. Dating for the sake of dating.

Everything was different now. And, yeah, Ethan hit the nail on the head. She feared stepping into the unknown. But, by the same token, she was determined to keep trying. It was impossible to uncover all the qualities a man had to offer in the span of fifteen minutes, especially on a first date. She would concede that point. Jitters, nerves, and idiotic ramblings tended to overshadow their more redeeming virtues. Her tea readings had been premature. She needed to give the men more time.

That settled it. Tyler, the lucky duck, would see a new Addie today. She'd give him the opportunity he deserved, let the idea of him as a permanent fixture in her life percolate, and then—and only then—would she read the leaves.

Of course, the thing Hannah hadn't mentioned in this whole matchmaking process was that she, too, would be in the coffee shop for the date, watching over things from the peanut gallery. Before Addie even saw Tyler, she knew he'd entered the coffee shop based solely on Hannah's squeal.

Addie turned toward the door. A tall man with dark eyes homed in on her. She must have smiled because his answering grin came pretty close to stealing her breath. In fact, she was still trying to recover oxygen when he closed the distance between them. She stuck out her hand but he swept her into a hug instead. Her chin barely reached the top of his shoulder. He smelled so good, like minty toothpaste and leather. The latter probably because he wore a pillowy-soft leather jacket. Oh, hot damn, did he have a motorcycle? She took another whiff of the leather and her gaze zoomed in on Ethan. Just because she could, and maybe a little bit for show, she held the hug for as long as possible.

All too soon, Tyler stepped back and took her in from top to bottom. Her cheeks flushed under his frank perusal. "I'm so excited to meet a woman who bakes pies for a living. And you smell like pie, too. Delicious."

Addie grinned, tickled by the compliment. She'd struggled with what to wear on this date, wondering if her new attitude required a different dress code, too. In the end, she'd gone with a tangerine and white striped summer dress with a form-fitting bodice and swishy skirt that made walking fun but riding a bike hell on wheels. Good thing she'd crammed more bike-appropriate wear into her backpack.

She circled the table to put distance between them because she was afraid she'd jump the guy before their drinks arrived. And she hadn't spoken yet. Not even to utter so much as a hello, and she felt like a complete ninny. Obviously taking his cue from her, he pulled off his jacket, draped it over the back of his seat, and sat across from her. She was sitting too, somehow, though she didn't have even the slightest memory of how and when it happened.

"I really like pie," Addie finally spoke, groaning inwardly at the inanity of her remark. "Actually, I love all kinds of sweets. Cake, chocolate, ice cream, gummy bears, licorice . . . bubble gum." She glanced up at the sound of his laughter. Way up. The guy had to be six-five or more. "Luckily, the biking is good exercise, so—"

"Sure seems to be," he murmured.

She'd never been more grateful for two-wheel transport in her entire life. "Umm, so . . . Hannah said you knew me? You've tried one of my pies before?"

"Oh, man, the apple-cinnamon?" His eyes rolled into the back of his head and his Adam's apple bobbed. She had to tamp down the urge to lick that delectable protrusion. "Awesome."

"Uh-huh." Shaking her head to clear the less than pure thoughts, she said, "I don't remember ever meeting you. You're not the type of person . . . I mean, you're a memorable . . . You're really tall, and tall people stand out . . . ."

Again, he laughed, bringing her moronic babbling to an end. "We haven't met. My sister bought some of your pies for a family gathering. Everyone raved about them. Mom was a bit miffed when Dad said it was the best he ever had."

"Tearing families apart, one pie at a time," Addie said in a solemn tone.

"That could be your new slogan," he teased.

Yeah, or 'My hand pies bring all the hot guys to the yard.'

"I've seen you around and I've been meaning to introduce myself, but," he reached for her hand across the table to still it, because it was as jittery and jumpy as the rest of her, "this is even better."

She nodded. Yes. Better. Much better. Better than pretty much anything in the world. He stroked her fingers, then turned her palm over to trace her life line with the tip of his index finger. "So you have a dog?" she croaked.

Gwen chose that moment to do some snooping, er, serving. Tyler ordered a cappuccino, and Addie went with her usual. Their shameless waitress lingered for an awkward amount of time, straightening things that didn't require any straightening, polishing the already-pristine surface of the table. Addie's not-so-gentle elbow to the ribs spurred the woman into motion, but not before she shot her a "this isn't over" glare.

Unfortunately, the interruption also brought a temporary end to the hand-sex. There was no other way to describe the intense feeling of pleasure ignited by his dexterous digits. Plus, it was the most action she'd had in longer than she'd care to admit, so . . . yeah.

"I have a schnauzer," he said.

She imagined those long, strong fingers on other parts of her body. Stroking, tempting, tracing every curve, leaving a fire in their wake. It took her a full minute to register that he'd spoken. "Hmm?"

He smiled as though he knew exactly where her thoughts had drifted off to. "You asked if I had a dog—"

"Oh! Right, yes. A schnauzer, you said?"

"Yep. His name's Max. He's my best bud, and he's spoiled rotten. The minute I walk through the door, he drops at my feet for a belly rub. I've bought him state-of-the-art dog beds and put 'em in every corner of the house, but he insists on sleeping at the foot of mine." His eyes lit up as he spoke fondly of his four-legged friend, and, God help her, she envied the dog. If only it was socially acceptable to roll onto one's back in a public establishment . . .

Gwen dropped off their drinks—first Tyler's, then Addie's. As she moved around to her side of the table, she stepped hard on Addie's foot. "Ow!"

"Oh, I'm so sorry. I didn't see your foot there." She had to hand it to Gwen. The she-devil almost sounded sincere. In the next breath, she sing-songed, "If there's anything else I can get for you two, just holler."

"We could use a new waitress," Addie grumbled as Gwen twirled away.

"You two know each other?" Tyler asked once they were alone again.

She smiled guiltily. "What gave it away?"

"Just a wild guess." He planted his elbows on the table and leaned in closer. "So, Addie, tell me all about you. Your hopes, your dreams, and how you make your crust so flaky."

It was impossible not to flirt with this man. He commanded flirting of the highest order. She leaned in nice and close, too, batted her eyelashes, and said in a throaty voice, "That last one's a trade secret."

He heaved a dramatic sigh. "Well, at least I tried."

"Who put you up to it? Your sister? Certainly not your mother . . . ."

"I do a little baking in my spare time."

She quirked an eyebrow. "Really?"

"What, I don't look like a baker?"

"You look like a biker. As in, a guy who owns a motorcycle but doesn't have enough piercings or tattoos to belong to a gang."

Tyler chuckled. "Are you a biker gang aficionado?"

Addie raised her mug to her lips and took a drink of tea, her eyes never leaving his. "Maybe." Ugh. Lame response of the year. Making intelligent conversation seemed ten thousand times easier when her heart and hormones weren't wreaking havoc.

"You're right about the motorcycle."

"The leather gave it away."

He smiled a sexy smile, and she wondered if he too was fantasizing about the many other uses for leather. "I don't belong to any gangs, unless my crew counts. I'm a contractor."

Oh, great. The man worked with his hands. Because he wasn't already perfect. "You think you could handle a malfunctioning mixer?"

"I can handle anything you want me to handle."

She was about to list a dozen things he could handle when he signaled for Gwen and ordered a cinnamon bun for them to share. Tall, handsome, smart, sorta-badass who worked hard, liked to share, and knew that cinnamon was the way to her heart. Yep, she was smitten.

8

Christ, the guy was a walking Harley Davidson ad, with the leather jacket and the dark shades and an air of cocky confidence about him that probably drove the ladies hog wild. What was he doing in their small town? Maybe he traveled from town to town trying to pick up women simply to prove he could. Well, Addie would see right through him and send him packing before he even got a chance to read the menu.

Three days had passed since he'd last seen her. Three utterly unproductive days. Oh, he'd written some words. Thousands of words, to be sure, but they were all garbage so he deleted every last one of them. Just when he began to think he'd never see her again, she crossed the threshold of the coffee shop . . . and sat at the very opposite end, as far away from him as she could possibly get.

Then her date arrived.

He almost felt sorry for the poor bastard. That is, until he realized he'd been sitting there, in the seat across from Addie, for more than fifteen minutes. Hell, it was pushing thirty at this point. Ethan tried his hardest not to pay attention, not to read anything into her body language, but it was no use. Things were going well. Every smile she smiled at him felt like a knife being jabbed in his gut. Every laugh dug the blade a little deeper.

He heaved a frustrated sigh and dragged his laptop closer, punching the keys with unsuppressed irritation.

The Girl Who Shoved It in His Face. Chapter One.

Wait. Maybe it was all for show. His head jerked up mid-typing rampage. Yes. She was trying extra hard to like this guy because of what Ethan had said to her, had accused her of—that she'd been too quick to judge and feared stepping into the unknown.

Or did she actually like him?

Jesus. This is why he didn't get tangled up with women. They did things to a man. Made him think nonsensical thoughts. But Addie wasn't just any woman. She had a sense of humor, intellect, a nice face. No, she was beautiful.

And this new guy could clearly see it. He sat there, learning things about her that Ethan would likely never know. As she drank her tea and he sipped his mocha latte whatever, the minutes continued to tick by. *Well, I know things about her, too, like the fact that Addie has a tattoo behind her ear. Bet you don't know that.* He'd determined the green leaf tatt was of the tea variety whilst researching at the library. Made sense. The woman's whole life revolved around tea.

Weird, but Ethan suddenly craved it. When he signaled Gwen and ordered a hot tea, she stared at him like he'd sprouted a horn in the center of his forehead. "What?" he grumbled. "I have a sore throat."

She delivered the drink in a heartbeat and he took his first sip. Not awful. And surprisingly soothing considering he didn't really have a sore throat. He continued to drink as he recalled his last conversation with Addie.

He'd been such an ass. He let her rush out of there, tears in her eyes, and hadn't done a thing to apologize for it. And here she was, taking his advice. With another man. Could he really blame her?

The bells jingled, and what seemed like the entire Kendal High baseball team entered the shop, successfully blocking his view of Addie. The noise level also increased fifteen-fold. *Good. It'll break up the love fest.*

Teenagers took over every spare inch of space near the counter, pointing out the baked goods they desired to cap off their latest tournament victory. Gwen leapt into action, packaging up chocolate chip cookies, brownies, and rice crispy squares for the hungry boys. And then, joy of joys, the health-conscious kid in the mix ordered a fruit smoothie. So the blender joined in the chorus of chaos. Surely that would be enough. No date could survive such commotion.

But then he heard it again. Her laugh.

It floated in the air, rising above every other sound. Was she doing it on purpose? Yes. She was mocking him with that laugh. She had to be. He couldn't bear to sit there any longer. He couldn't write, and he certainly couldn't handle watching her salivate over another guy. Time to pack up his stuff, take a walk, and clear his head of all this craziness.

One by one, the kids vacated the premises, and he made to follow suit. Scraping his chair across the floor, he stood abruptly and knocked over his half-full mug of tea, spilling most of it onto his khakis. Hey, what better way to attract a little notice? Dabbing at his lower half with a wad of napkins, he earned one or two curious stares, but none from Addie.

Rolling his eyes, he shut down his laptop, threw some money on the table, slipped his bag over his shoulder, and stomped toward the exit. He passed within feet of her, but she was too busy to even care.

He went straight home and changed into his running gear, then he took off down the stairs. Right as he reached the entryway, Carmen came in the door. She perked up at the sight of him in his workout clothes. "Going on another run, Ethan?" she purred.

"Yep," he said, still moving toward the door, hoping she'd let him go without further comment.

"You sure do keep that body of yours in tip-top shape. There must be a special lady in your life."

Why he responded, he would never know. But then again, there was no one else he could talk to, or vent to, and Carmen had the proximity thing going for her. "She's special, but she's not mine. Not now, maybe not ever."

"Listen, I'm no spring chicken, but I know a thing or two about romance. Don't buy her flowers," she said. "It's common, expected, and expensive."

"Not to mention totally cliché."

"That too," she agreed. "Now, this might sound a bit unconventional to you, but hear me out. Sometimes the best way to summon love is through the spirits."

Oh, Lord.

"Do you have a Ouija board?"

"No."

"Not to worry. I have one you can borrow."

Great. Kill me now.

"You and your special friend will place your fingers on the planchette—that's the heart-shaped piece you move about the board to spell out words—and the very nearness of your hands practically conjures love even before the spiritual realm becomes involved!" She laughed with glee, obviously quite pleased with herself. "The spirit will lead you through 'Yes' and 'No' questions about your potential partner."

"Wow, it's like Tinder for ghosts," he said blankly.

"Yes! And if that doesn't work, I've got a copy of *The Kama Sutra* in my—"

"I think I'm good," Ethan blurted, cutting her off. There wasn't enough bleach in the word to wash that unfinished sentence from his brain. Hopefully he could sweat it out. "Thanks for the, uh . . . just thanks."

"Anytime, sugar."

Once safely outside, Ethan took a cleansing breath. Sometimes, a long, hard run was the only way to clear his head. He preferred to run without music, to hear the sound of his breathing and the soles of his shoes slapping against the asphalt. Turning in the direction of the town's center, he set off at a vigorous clip.

His pace slowed as he neared the coffee shop, where Addie'd been making googly eyes at . . . whoever the lucky schmuck was. He threw back his shoulders and kept his head forward. He didn't need to know if they were still in there. Didn't matter one single bit to him. Nope. Okay, one quick look. He gave himself a split second to scan the interior.

Still there. *Christ.*

Clenching his jaw, he increased his tempo, punishing himself for looking, as if that weren't punishment enough.

Somehow, he needed to make amends with her. Some kind of friendly gesture or peace offering. If he was honest with himself, he hadn't felt a moment's peace since their argument. No, since she'd first spoken to him in that coffee shop. She drove him crazy in every possible way, and he couldn't get enough of her. He craved interactions with her as badly as he craved his daily jolt of java.

Rounding the corner, he ran smack into a guy carrying a stack of posters that scattered in every direction. Ethan shook it off, bending down to help retrieve as many as he could before the wind swept them away. The other man crawled on all fours, which wouldn't have struck him as amusing if he hadn't glanced at one of his precious posters. Front and center was a picture of a dog with a leash in its mouth. Beneath it, the caption read, 'Dogs need leashes. Let's 'paws' for the cause. A campaign for concerned citizens.'

Cheesy pun aside, the guy had a point. Last week on his run, he'd nearly trampled over one of those rat-sized dogs who'd leapt from its owner's purse in search of freedom. Funny thing was, he'd gotten more of a lecture than the yappy escape artist.

The other man finally stood, gratefully accepting the posters Ethan had collected. "Thanks a lot, man. I appreciate it."

"I had to *paws* for a good cause," he joked.

"You got a dog?"

"Nope," Ethan said. "But I'm forced to cohabitate with a cat who, oddly enough, has a leash."

"Now *there's* an owner with their head on straight."

Not hardly. "Well, keep fighting the good fight," he said in parting as he took off again toward the town square. Ethan hadn't been one of those kids who begged their parents for a dog. He was quite content in his solitude, which made it all the more surprising when he came home from school one day to find a Border Collie parked in the middle of the living room, his teeth clamped around Ethan's paperback copy of *Moby-Dick*. Needless to say, the two hadn't bonded right away.

But, no matter how hard he tried to remain indifferent to the pesky pooch, Buddy got under his skin . . . in the best possible way. He was the reason Ethan developed a love of running. He read to escape from the world, and he ran to reconnect with it again. Buddy ran simply because it'd been bred into him. But no matter how long or how far they ran, it was never enough for his furry friend. Their backyard was too confined, and he'd chewed through too many pairs of his mother's expensive shoes to be given free rein in their home.

Five months into their mutual admiration society, Buddy leapt over the backyard fence and ran so far and so fast, it took them two full days to track him down again. After a tear-filled reunion, his parents sat him down and delivered an even more painful blow. They'd decided to give the dog to another family who owned a farm and had the land Buddy needed to roam free. In his heart, he knew it was the right thing to do, but it cut him to the bone. He'd curled up next to Buddy on the floor that night and cried himself to sleep. A boy and his dog.

Every time he ran, he thought of Buddy. They weren't really all that different. He'd run away in a sense, too. Circumstances, and a little bit of luck, had brought him to this town, where cats walked on leashes and pies were delivered by bicycle. Wacky but wonderful.

Had he ever told Addie how wonderful she was? He would. He'd make things right again . . . Or better.

She never intended to stay there so long. In truth, she hoped to be out within an hour and still have ample time for a second round of pie-pushing. But three hours later, two empty mugs, and a crumb-filled plate between them, they were only just getting around to saying their goodbyes.

Addie stood and met him in another delicious hug. She peered over his shoulder at the other patrons in the coffee shop, looking for one in particular. Ethan's chair was empty. Well, the guy obviously didn't live there. He had a life and other things to tend to. He wasn't required to check in with her before he left. So why did she feel a twinge in her stomach?

Tyler leaned down and kissed her cheek. Warm tingles replaced the twinge. "Addie, I really hope to see you again soon."

Play it cool, Addie. Play it cool. "Well, you know, I've got that mixer that needs fixing . . . ." And then she giggled like a loon.

He offered to walk her out, but she respectfully declined, saying she needed to catch up with Gwen and Hannah. With a promise to call her later, he turned and headed for the door. Eyes glued to his ass, she watched him walk away until he disappeared from sight.

She liked this guy. Pure and simple. He was incredibly attractive. Confident without being cocky. Kind and gentle with his words, but his arms felt so sure and strong wrapped around her. And, Lord, the man knew how to flirt.

There was absolutely no reason not to see him again, unless . . .

She couldn't put it off any longer. Dropping back into her seat, she pulled her empty mug closer and analyzed the pattern of leaves in the bottom. There were a few distorted clusters and shapes, but one clear form stood out above all others: a bed.

The symbol indicated it was best to sleep on it before establishing a close love or business relationship. Did that mean she could sleep on *him*, too? That was something she'd been missing. The physical closeness. Sleeping with another warm body next to hers. Spooning.

As if reading the racy direction of her thoughts, Gwen and Hannah barrelled over to her, grabbed two chairs, and sandwiched her between them.

"Spill!" Hannah demanded.

Gwen eagerly nodded, then raised her eyebrows at Addie. "Starting with the hug that never ended."

She laughed, recalling said hug in vivid detail. "He just . . . felt really good. And smelled really good. And looked really, *really* good."

Hannah let loose another squeal. "Did you *see* his leather jacket?"

"I'd say so. She's the one who was pressed against it for two minutes straight," Gwen supplied with a smirk.

"He must own a motorcycle," Hannah said, a far-off dreamy look in her eyes. "Unless he's taken to wearing leather all year round, which, for him, totally works. But let's be real. *Anything* works for that man."

"Yes, he owns a motorcycle," Addie confirmed. "And he's a contractor. And he *bakes*."

Gwen gasped. "Shut up! He does not!"

"He was trying to find out the secret to how I get my crust so flaky."

Hannah held up both hands. "Okay, okay. Let's pause here, take a deep breath, and reflect on how fabulous I am for finding this perfect man." Both women laughed at that. "Are we good? All right, now walk us through the entire date, and don't skip any details!"

Addie was happy to oblige, but part of her—a tiny, infinitesimal part—wished it were Ethan giving her the third degree. She missed his snark, his dry wit, the banter they so effortlessly fell into. She missed . . . him.

9

On Monday afternoon, with her to-do list done, Addie took a break to pop over to Schnitzel Fritz's. The restaurant Frank and Fritz had run for two decades had been empty since they decided to retire a few months before. Many residents were still shaking off the remnants of their hangovers from the retirement party the town's social committee had organized for the pair. Addie was having a hard time living down the sloppy karaoke rendition of "Livin' on a Prayer" she'd dedicated to the retirees.

Nearly every day, during her loops around the town, she passed by Schnitzel Fritz's, her heart thrumming whenever she saw the 'For Sale or Lease' sign in the window. And on each occasion, she'd successfully pushed the thought to the back of her mind, but today, something inside her told her it was time.

Propping her bike on its kickstand, she slowly walked toward the front windows, peeking around the edges of the paper coverings. From what she could tell, much of the décor remained untouched, leading her to believe Fritz and Frank were hoping for someone to pick up where they'd left off. She'd finally worked up the nerve and she was here now, so she might as well get a look at the interior from the perspective of a potential business owner and not merely a patron.

She unzipped her shoulder bag and pulled out her cell phone, tapping in the numbers on the sign.

"Hello?" a jovial voice answered on the second ring. She could tell it was Fritz because Frank was a gruff baritone.

"Hi, Fritz, this is Addie Mitchell."

"Of course it is, you lovely girl. Are you calling about the restaurant?"

She smiled at the warmth in his tone. "I am, actually. I'm here right now and wondered if I might be able to see the inside . . . I mean, if you're not busy."

"Who is it?" she heard Frank's voice break through the background.

"Addie Mitchell. She's asking to see the restaurant," Fritz whispered back, obviously forgetting to cover the receiver.

"Oh, I love that girl. And those pies of hers!"

"I know. You ate three of the pecan praline last week."

Addie chuckled at their back and forth, wondering when Fritz would remember she was on the other end of the line.

"Addie? Are you still there?" Fritz asked.

She grinned. "Yep, still here."

"I'll be there momentarily, dear," he told her. "The lock box number is 8-6-9-5, and the key's inside. Go ahead and let yourself in."

"Thanks so much! See you soon."

Disconnecting the call, she dropped her phone back into her bag and entered the combination Fritz had given her. Another joy of living in a small town. People trusted one another. It likely wouldn't be long before Fritz arrived as they only lived just down the street, but she greatly appreciated his gesture of kindness all the same.

The location was perfect. Not on the main street of town, but close enough to be noticed. Unlocking the door, she stepped inside, soaking in every detail of the interior—from the flags hanging from the ceiling, to the shelves lined with beer steins and other German accoutrements. If she could look past the kitschy décor to the bare bones, it really had everything she needed. Her eyes were drawn to the counter with the big glass display cases. Three of them connected in a row. She'd tried almost every cake they'd sold: apple cider, crumb, buttercream, and black forest, to name a few.

Closing her eyes, she imagined the interior with her own personal decorative touches. She envisioned herself walking out of the kitchen with a tray full of baked goodies as a crowd of people looked on with wide eyes, licking their lips, jockeying for position at the front of the line.

"It's a good space, isn't it?"

Addie nearly jumped out of her skin, pressing her hand to her heart while Fritz sputtered out a dozen apologies. "I didn't hear you come in," she panted.

"I can go right back out again if you'd like."

"No, no." She laughed. "I was just . . . dreaming what it might be like, owning this place."

He took her hand and gave it a squeeze. "It doesn't have to stay a dream."

Now in her direct line of vision, she spotted a dollop of shaving cream on the side of his neck, which made him all the more endearing to her. She'd never once seen the man with a rogue whisker on his face. His shirts were always freshly pressed, never a tail untucked. "No, it doesn't," she agreed.

"Come on, then. I'll give you a quick tour."

He showed her the kitchen first, boasting about the state-of-the-art appliances that were aching to be used again. Part of her expected a candelabra to burst on the scene and sing about the good old days when they were useful. It was a large kitchen with room to add another oven if she needed to. Plenty of counter space. Room for baking racks and mixing bowls and a multitude of mixers, too.

"Frank and I are delighted you're thinking of expanding your business," he told her as they took a right out of the kitchen and headed behind the bar, which could easily be transformed into an additional display area.

Fritz and Frank often purchased pies from her, always tipping her an extra dollar or two, so she knew their delight was genuine. "That's so sweet of you."

"I just wish it wasn't so close by. It'll be too easy for us to get our fix every day. You know, hypothetically speaking."

Grinning, she listened as he detailed the purpose and functionality of each nook and cranny of the establishment, all the while relishing the idea that there was so little need for renovation. She could do this. This could actually happen.

"So, my dear, it's here, and we're here, if you'd like to see the place again," Fritz said as they came to a stop near the entrance. "We've had a few bites but no takers yet."

"Thank you so much for showing me. For making my dream feel a little more possible."

"Anything is possible," he insisted. "I'm married to a man who doesn't know how to use an iron and leaves wet towels on the floor, so, truly, anything is possible."

Laughing, she waved goodbye, telling him to pop by the town square later on as she planned on making another pie run.

"You can count on it," he promised. "Oh, and Addie?"

"Yes?"

"Frank and I would be very willing to provide a lease-to-own option as well, if that makes any difference."

Addie smiled gratefully. "I appreciate that, and both of you, very much. I'll keep in touch."

Feeling lighter than a feather, she climbed onto her bike and practically floated all the way home to box up the pies and get them ready for transport. Just for kicks, she pressed the power button on Maybelline, wondering if her mixer miraculously healed itself while she'd been running errands. Sadly, that was not the case, as proven by the God-awful screeching and grinding noises.

The chime of her cell phone broke through the cacophony of unpleasant sounds. She lunged for the phone on the island counter, too elated by the distraction to even check the call display.

"Hello?"

"Addie. It's your mother."

Point taken, universe. Always check the call display. "Yes, Mom, I recognize your voice."

"Hmm," she replied in that oh-so-unaffected tone she'd perfected over thirty-two years. "How are things?"

"Things are . . . pretty great, actually. Other than my mixer dying a slow and painful death."

"Buy a new mixer."

Bluntness—another skill her mother had perfected. "Not really in the budget at the moment, Mom. I'll try to get along with Maybelline for a little while longer."

"You're still doing that?"

"Doing what?"

"Naming inanimate objects?"

Addie ran a hand through her hair and slumped into a chair at the kitchen table. "Is there a reason you're calling?" Cringing at the bitterness in her voice, she added, "I mean, um, I need to do another pie run and don't have a lot of time for small talk . . . unless there's something specific you wanted—"

"Tell me about the other things," her mother cut in. "The pretty great things."

"Oh." Her lips twitched. "There's a guy." She paused, expecting some kind of caustic remark, but none came. "His name is . . . Tyler." She'd nearly said "Ethan" out of reflex and quickly steamrolled right over that thought. "A friend set me up with him, and those usually never work, but he seems really amazing. He's tall, attractive, and he loves my pies." If she'd seen herself in a mirror, she'd probably be embarrassed by the wattage of her smile, but, man, it was nice being excited over a guy.

"Good, as he should. You've always been a great baker, like your grandmother. It's a wonderful side hobby. Not a profitable living."

Smile officially neutralized, she sucked in a breath and counted to five, unwilling to be goaded into a fight. "Anyway, the great thing is that the tea leaves are feeling favorable toward him, too."

"Oh, good grief, Adelaide. Please tell me you haven't taken up that foolishness."

She stood, suddenly too stirred up to sit still. "It worked for Edna."

Her mother's sigh vibrated through the phone. "Your great-aunt Edna was as crazy as they come, and you'd be just as crazy if you think there's any truth behind that silly tasseography book of hers."

"Crazy or not, I believe in it, and she believed in me. Quite a concept, isn't it? I have to go."

"Addie, wait—"

"Goodbye, Mother." She ended the call, almost shaking with suppressed hurt. A wayward tear trickled down her cheek, and she angrily swiped it away. She and her mother never had what she'd describe as a warm relationship, but they respected one another. This was the way things always went with them. Two steps forward and five steps back. Lately, though, it seemed like every choice she made was met with glaring disapproval. Well past the age of adulthood or not, she couldn't deny the disappointment she felt deep down in her belly when her would-be career was brushed off as a hobby, and her method of finding the right guy was ridiculed and belittled.

Returning her phone to the counter, she pressed her palms against the cool granite as a memory drifted through her mind.

"Did I ever tell you the story of how your great-uncle Thomas and I met?"

Addie shook her head, even though she'd heard it twenty times before, but this was their bit. One of many. "No, tell me." She folded her hands on the kitchen table and watched as Edna flitted about the kitchen, still spry at the ripe old age of eighty-five.

"I worked part-time at the general store, and one evening, as I walked home from work, I got caught in the rain. I hurried my steps, hoping to get home before I was soaked through, but then, suddenly, the rain stopped."

Addie loved this part of the story and leaned forward anxiously.

"I was befuddled. You see, it was still raining just as strongly as ever, pelting the street and sidewalk, but I didn't feel a drop. I looked up to see an umbrella over my head, my eyes then finding the handsome

stranger who gripped the handle in his fist. We never spoke a word to each other as we walked side by side in the darkness. And when the rain slowed, he slipped the handle into my grip, gave me a smile that made my insides melt, and disappeared into the night."

Addie gratefully accepted the cup of tea Edna prepared for her, and the older woman sat across from her at the table with her own mug, a serene expression on her face.

"That night, I had a hot cup of tea to help me warm up. Do you know what the leaves showed me?"

"No, what?" Addie asked, playing along.

"An angel. Good news for a girl looking for love." She reached out and squeezed Addie's hand.

"What happened next?"

"I wasn't sure how or when our paths would cross again, but two days later, wouldn't you know it, I got caught in the rain a second time. I waited and waited for my handsome stranger to swoop in. I must have wandered about aimlessly for half an hour, till I was soaked to the skin and chilled to the bone. Just as I had given up and started home, I heard a voice call to me, 'Hey, wait up!' I turned to find my handsome stranger splashing through the puddles. He was drenched, too. Turns out, I'd taken his only umbrella the day we met."

Addie grinned. She always did at that part.

"He couldn't offer me an umbrella this time, so he offered to buy me a hot drink instead."

"And you ordered tea," Addie supplied.

"Of course. I took precious sips, trying to prolong our time together, but when my cup was empty, I spotted it right away. A ring of leaves on the side."

"A symbol of marriage."

"That's right, my love. I pointed it out to Thomas. He smiled at me and said, 'Let's have an indoor wedding.' I knew then and there I'd found the man for me. Even thinking about it now makes my head spin with happiness." She squeezed Addie's hand again. "I want that for you, baby girl. For you to be so happy you feel dizzy from it."

"I want that, too. Like, any day now would be great."

Edna nodded in understanding. "You're still young."

"I'm almost thirty."

"I didn't meet Thomas till I was twenty-six. It'll happen when it's meant to happen. But until then . . . have lots of sex."

They'd laughed until they were breathless.

There was no doubt in Edna's mind that the leaves played an instrumental role in bringing her and Thomas together. She believed in their power, and Addie believed in her.

Ethan spent most of Monday in the coffee shop, hoping Addie would make an appearance, but as the hours rolled on, it became more and more apparent she had other important things to do. Or people to see. Her world didn't revolve around him. He stretched his arms over his head and rolled his neck, stiff from yet another day of hunching over his laptop, typing and deleting hundreds of words.

His stomach growled, belatedly objecting to the fact that he'd skipped lunch. He could see an extra-large deluxe pizza in his future, but not until he worked for it. If he tacked on another mile to his run, he could pick up the pie on his way back home again and dig in guilt-free. That settled, he grabbed his gear and headed home long enough to change into his running clothes and don a pair of sunglasses, then he hit the pavement. Fast.

The sun beat down on him, still blazing an uncomfortable temperature. Ten minutes in, he stripped off his shirt to wipe the sweat from his face and tossed it over his shoulder. He usually circled around the gazebo and ran the scenic route back home, but as he neared the town square, an entirely different view drew him up short.

Addie. She had on another pair of short shorts, which he was growing very, very fond of, and a white tank top with glittering red lips all over it. A sign from above? He'd sure as hell take it as one.

She was dealing with a customer. Ethan slowed to a walk, dabbing at his face with the T-shirt slung over his shoulder as he casually checked out the pies she had on display in the basket attached to the rear of her bike. Down to three: cherry, blueberry, and salted caramel apple, according to the tags. The older gentleman had a single pie wrapped in wax paper in his hand, already chomping into it. If Ethan bought the three remaining, she would be sold out. That's what he'd do. Then, he'd walk her home.

With one last wave, the other man left, and Addie turned her full attention to Ethan. Her lips parted as she took in his bare, sweat-streaked torso. She swallowed noticeably. "H-hello there. How can I, uh, help you, sir?"

She didn't have a clue it was him. He almost laughed, but there was no sense setting her off any more than he already had. Removing his sunglasses, he rested them on top of his head and rocked back on his heels, waiting for recognition to dawn.

Addie blinked, releasing an audible gasp. "Hemingway. I . . . you . . . You're sweaty."

This time, he did laugh. "Uh, thanks?"

"Sorry," she said, shaking her head self-consciously. "And you're tall. I don't think I've ever seen you at your full height. You're always sitting."

"Six-foot-two according to my driver's—"

"And I've never seen you in shorts," she blurted at the same time.

Yep, he was tall and sweaty and wearing shorts. And she'd noticed.

Why did he care so much what Addie noticed? He enjoyed running and his daily exercise routine as much for the health benefits as the physical rewards, but she had a way of making him feel vulnerable. It was unsettling, to say the least. "So I'm just a pants guy to you? I'll have you know, my closet is full of shorts. Cargos, board shorts, Bermuda shorts, running shorts . . . I mean, mine don't get quite as short as yours, but there are probably laws against that kind of exposure."

She planted her hands on her hips and glared at him. Not a good sign. He needed to stay focused. Be charming. Buy some hand pies, and maybe, by the end of it, she'd be eating out of *his* hand.

Clearing his throat, he said, "Listen, there were some things I said the other night—and just now, apparently—that, in hindsight, might have been a bit out of line—"

"Might have? A bit?"

Ignoring the interruption, he pressed on. "I regret what I said. I mean, not everything I said, but more the way I said it. I guess what I'm trying to say is, let's let bygones be bygones." He looked straight at her, eager for a nod or a smile.

Her face softened into a curious frown. "Was that you apologizing? 'Cause you suck at it."

"And pie," he quickly added. "I'm buying the last of your pies. Because nothing says I'm sorry like tasty, flaky pastry."

That finally won him a smile. "Are you buying them for me or for yourself?"

"For you, of course."

"Liar."

As she wrapped up his pies, Ethan felt in his pocket for his wallet. *Oh, shit.* He checked the other pocket, knowing it was a futile effort, and there was a very good reason for that. He'd forgotten to take his wallet out of his other pants when he'd changed. So much for a friendly gesture.

Glancing up, he found Addie's inquiring gaze fixed on him. "Uh, hi," he choked out.

"That'll be twelve dollars even, please." She stretched out her hand, palm up.

"Right, sure. Um, just out of curiosity, where approximately do you live?"

"Why?"

He shuffled his feet nervously. "Any chance you're near Crescent Street?"

"I'm on Oak. But what does that have to do with anything?"

Ethan huffed out a breath and his shoulders sagged in defeat. Might as well confess and deal with the fallout like a man. "I left my wallet at home."

"Oh." She sighed, withdrawing her hand. "Forget it. Just take the pies."

Addie thrust the paper bag at him, but he held up a hand to stop her. "Addie, no. I can't."

"It's on the house," she said. "An end-of-the-day blowout sale."

He continued to shake his head, even took a step back when she tried again to pass him the bag. "Addie, this is your business. Please let me pay for them. I'll run home and get the cash right now."

"Ethan, stop."

Every time she spoke his real name, he felt a slight tremor course through his entire body.

"Or I could walk you home, and we could stop by my place to get the money . . . ."

She rounded the bike so nothing separated them anymore, and the urge to touch her was overwhelming. "Take the pies. They're good pies," she insisted as she forced the bag on him once more, successfully this time. "So I consider this an investment because I know you'll be back for more."

He wanted more, all right. "Let me walk you home anyway."

"No, thanks. I—"

"I can push the bike." He waggled his eyebrows temptingly.

Rolling her eyes, she plucked the bag from his grip and plunked it in the basket. "Fine, Hemingway. Let's walk."

He'd caught the smile on her lips when she turned her back to him. Good thing his hands were on the bike. Lord knows he'd have a hard time not pulling her into his arms and kissing the bejesus out of her before their walk was through.

Hey, he still might.

"Ready to go?" she asked him.

"Lead the way."

10

She couldn't remember the last time a guy walked her home. Certainly one had never offered to push her bike before. With good reason, of course, because she usually rode it. But this was nice. Different. A little old-fashioned, but in a good way. As afternoon approached evening, the streets grew empty of townspeople and a calmness enveloped them.

Ethan drew to a halt when they reached the first of several tree streets, propped the bike on its kickstand, and dove for the bag of pies. "Sorry," he said at her pointed look. "I'm starving. I missed lunch." He took an enormous bite from his pie of choice. She would have guessed cherry, even if part of the filling hadn't dribbled down his chin. "Want some?" he mumbled around the monster-sized mouthful.

"Nah, I'm good," she said, biting back a smile. "There're napkins in the basket."

"Thanks."

"You, uh . . . must have left the coffee shop fairly early last Friday."

He nodded as he wiped his mouth and chin, then tucked a few napkins into his pocket. "Didn't really feel like hanging around."

Their eyes met. She folded her arms over her chest, as if that could protect her heart from feeling any empathy for him, because she could see a tiny flash of hurt in his eyes.

Saving her from filling the sudden, veering on awkward, silence, he said, "Well, at least tell me how the date with Harley Davidson went." He took another bite of pie. One more and he'd have the entire thing gobbled up.

"Harley Davidson?"

"He looked the type."

"And that was the best you could come up with? You being a writer and all?"

He shrugged. "I thought it was pretty clever."

"The date was good." What more could she say? She didn't particularly want to open another can of worms.

"Yeah?" he mumbled. "Looked like it was going well." Ethan swallowed down that bite and then popped the remainder into his mouth. "Gonna be another one?"

Her eyes were glued to his mouth as he chewed. She watched the muscles in his jaw munch through every morsel. It wasn't until he cleared his throat that she realized she'd been staring. "Sorry. I missed what you—"

"I asked if there's gonna be another one."

"Don't you think you've had enough pie before dinner?"

"Date," he said. "Another date."

"Oh." She paused and bit her lip. "I think so, yeah."

He wiped his mouth again. She could almost hear the internal debate waging in his head as he eyed the bag of remaining pies, but he opted against eating them. For now. He obviously had a sweet tooth, but you'd never know it to look at him. And look she did, admiring the impressive landscape, from his smoothly muscled shoulders and pecs, to his shockingly ripped abs. Those demanded the most attention. Who knew the writer hid the body of a . . . not-writer?

Glancing at Ethan, she was startled to see his gaze set on her. "Are you done, then? Want some milk to wash it down?"

He smiled, and those devastating dimples appeared. They weren't always visible. Only when his smile was especially deep and delicious, like those abs she kept ogling. "You got any?"

"Yeah, I travel around with a mini-fridge in the back just in case anyone gets a case of calcium deficiency while I'm selling the pies."

He laughed. Oh, that laugh made her tingle from the inside out. There was a husky quality to it, and more than a tinge of mischief. "Might be something to invest in."

She made a point of checking her watch. Best not to let him think she was enjoying this as much as she was. "I didn't realize this would take all day."

At that moment he was righting her bike, but he paused mid-motion. "You have somewhere to be? Is Harley Davidson taking you for a spin on the back of his hog?"

"*Tyler* has plans tonight."

He shook his head. "See, that's the problem with most men. They're never there when you need 'em."

Or they're around so much they become a habit. "Want me to take over with the bike?"

That spurred him into motion again. Slow motion. He shook out the T-shirt draped over his shoulder, pulled it on, and pushed ahead. *What's a girl supposed to gawk at now?* She'd remarked to Gwen before about the mystery man she'd seen running around the town in his dark shades. They'd nicknamed him The Shirtless Wonder. And now The Shirtless Wonder was walking her home.

And seemed to be taking the most indirect route to get there.

She wasn't even going to acknowledge the flippy feeling in her stomach at the thought of him trying so hard to prolong this . . . whatever it was.

A soft summer breeze washed over them, carrying with it the sounds of summer—children's laughter, birds chirping in the trees, and the din of late-afternoon lawn mowers slicing through blades of grass.

Ethan had incredibly nice arms. Well-defined, I-should-be-mowing-the-lawn-shirtless kind of arms. Arms that made a woman wonder how he managed to develop such remarkable muscle tone. "You're in, uh, pretty good shape for someone who writes all day." Okay, so that sounded like she was checking him out. "Do you lift books in your spare time or something?" There, better.

He cocked his head, slowing his steps more, if that were possible. "Well, besides the running, I swim."

Wow. She so did not see that answer coming. Swimmers' bodies were right up there with soccer players and gymnasts, as far as Addie was concerned.

"At the public pool. It's near my place. I live with Carmen Deacon, and—"

"Whoa. Carmen? She's a man-eater. You diggin' for gold?"

"Not like that, you sicko. I'm renting from her. And on the days when I can't squeeze out a single word, I run or swim. Sometimes both. That's often when I get my best ideas. Been getting a lot of workout time lately."

So Ethan was a swimmer, and that combined with the running explained the tan. Not a deep tan. More the natural and even tan of someone who conscientiously applied sunscreen. Her mouth ran dry as she conjured an image of him slicking on his SPF-whatever and plunging into the water. Naked. Cripes, it was all she could do to concentrate on the task of bagging his pies without begging him to take it off, take it alllll off, public indecency be damned.

A few dog-walkers passed them by as they ambled along. There were some kids playing ball hockey on Chestnut Street. Ethan squinted when a patch of sun hit him square in the face, turning his hazel eyes golden. She worried he might put on his sunglasses again and she wouldn't see those crazy-long eyelashes blinking back at her, but the sun hid behind the clouds again before he had the chance.

"I'm not sure I've ever asked you this, but how long have you been living in Kendal?" she asked as they reached Poplar. She could smell the street before she saw it. Mr. Turcott's rosebushes took over half of his corner lot. His roses won first prize nearly every year at the county fair, with good reason. The blooms were full and they had such a sweet fragrance. Whenever she needed a pick-me-up, she detoured to Poplar and took a whiff of the roses.

"A few months. I used to live in the city. My parents—my father, specifically—wanted me to take over the family business, but my heart just wasn't in it. I've always wanted to be a writer. Always. From the time I even knew what it meant. It was either stay in the city and do my own thing with the weight of my family's disapproval hanging over me, or get out, go someplace completely unexpected, and try to find inspiration."

"Wow. That was very brave of you."

He cracked a wry smile. "Before you go thinking I'm some great adventurer, a risk-taker, whatever, you should know that I've been living off a trust fund my grandparents set up for me since I turned twenty-five. Well, the interest, anyway." Ethan ran a hand through his hair and sighed. "Interest isn't what it used to be."

Addie wondered if the pressure from his lack of money was affecting his writing mojo, but she didn't feel comfortable asking. Instead, she decided to open up about her own living situation. "I used to be a waitress at the Country Corner restaurant on Main Street, on top of my side pie business. But then I lost my great-aunt Edna, who left me her house, and my priorities kind of changed."

His eyebrows lifted. "Lucky you. I mean, uh, I'm sorry for your loss, but it's good that you . . . Oh, hell."

Addie chuckled at his stumbling. "It's okay. I get what you're saying, and thank you. You know, I have this dream of opening my own bakery one day . . . ."

They'd stopped moving again. The way he looked at her, like her dream was anything but far-fetched, should have made her heart sing, but instead transported her back to the night of their fight. When his disbelief and derision knocked her down just when she needed to be lifted up. All at once, the humiliation she'd felt came flooding back.

He must have picked up on her change in demeanor because he propped the bike on its stand and moved in front of her, taking her hand in his own. "Listen, I know I screwed up. You're doing things the way that's right for you. Don't ever listen to anyone who tells you that's wrong. And I know you may not believe me when I say this, but, Addie, your pies are incredible. In case you didn't notice me wolfing one down earlier."

Ducking her head, she tried to shake off the heat creeping up her cheeks, but it was no use. Of course she'd noticed. Just like she noticed how small her hand looked in his own. And how safe she felt in his presence.

"In fact," Ethan continued, "I'd say your cherry pie is right up there with the danishes from the coffee shop. Maybe even better."

From him, that was the highest compliment. The man all but lived on them, according to Gwen. "Told ya you'd be back for more," she teased. "You're gonna have to start swimming more laps."

He let go of her hand, and a vague sense of disappointment lodged in her belly. Their feet and the bike began moving again at a pace so sluggish it put their previous leisurely stroll to shame. "Hey," he said, "I'm not usually one to spout out all that 'Reach for your dreams' inspirational crap, but I can see you owning a bakery. You'd have every man, woman, and child from miles around wrapped around your flour-covered finger."

She didn't care about every man. Only the one with the freckles. The surprisingly tall one who wasn't so surly when you got to know him. The one who walked her home, and made her laugh, and had a way of gazing at her that set every nerve ending on fire. *And Tyler*, her brain intruded. *The other tall, handsome man you're supposed to be more interested in. You care about him, too.* "Thank you," she whispered, not even sure if he'd heard her, but he nodded as though he had.

They'd reached her street, two houses away from her own. Should she invite him inside? No, it seemed too forward. Besides, it was late, and she hadn't eaten dinner yet, and she had baking to do. Because a certain person cleaned her out of all her stock. Ethan didn't shy away from sharing his opinion on things, which she'd learned the hard way, so she knew down to her toes that he was being genuine in his complimentary review of her hand pies. Talk like that served as wonderful inspiration for a girl.

And she suspected, especially after his revelation from earlier, that he could use a dose of it, too. "Hemingway? I think if it's your goal to write a bestseller, you'll do it. I really believe that."

He turned to face her, surprise plastered to his face, like he was so unaccustomed to receiving any kind of encouragement. Despite how prickly he could be, he absolutely deserved to hear he was talented.

"What I read of your work that day in the coffee shop? I mean, even the stuff you wanted to throw away was amazing. I can only imagine what you keep."

Ethan blinked several times. She thought he might dismiss her kind words as rubbish, but then he said, "That means a lot, thanks." Nothing more, nothing less. For him, it was as sincere a statement as she'd heard since officially knowing him.

She glanced up in time to see her house number, 1452. The stainless steel plate glimmered when the sunlight caught it at the right angle. She turned to Ethan. "This is my place," she said with a shrug.

"Nice digs."

It was a beautiful home, no question, with its Victorian-style charms and all the rich history that came with it. But it was just so . . . big. So empty. "I can never complain that I don't have enough storage space."

Ethan rested the bike against the white picket fence that outlined her yard. "No, I guess not." He spun around again, and this time stood closer than before. She felt the heat radiating off his body and had to lean her head back to look into his eyes. "Make sure he treats you right."

She tugged nervously on the strap of her tank top. "I will."

His eyes dropped to her chest, where dozens of sparkly red lips, in every shape and size, clung to the fabric of her top. And then, as if they'd tempted him to it, his gaze flew to her mouth.

Her pulse hammered in her throat. He wanted to kiss her. For ten terrifying seconds, she couldn't breathe. He leaned in, or maybe she did. Or maybe she was passing out from lack of oxygen. He planted a warm hand on her hip. She'd been so sure they were wrong for each other. Then why did this feel so right? Being near him, sparring with him, having him walk her to her door. Right, right, and oh-so-right.

A dog barked in the distance, and just like that, the spell was broken. Ethan jerked back, his eyes dark and his cheeks glowing red. "Uh. Sorry. I should . . . ."

"And I've got . . . ." She nodded to her house. "I need to do more baking—"

"Right. Well, uh . . . good night, Addie."

Ethan shoved his hands into his pockets and walked briskly away. He was already two houses down the street before she called to him, "Hey, thank you for the walk!"

His steps slowed but he never turned around. She watched him until he disappeared from sight. Somehow, she found the ability to put one foot in front of the other and climbed the steps to her front door. With a shaking hand, she slid the key into the lock.

She let the weight of the door carry her inside as it swung open, then pressed her back against it when it closed. Taking a deep breath, the first real breath she'd swallowed since he'd almost kissed her, she slowly sank to the floor.

"What am I doing?" she whispered to the silent house. All this time, she'd been waiting for the right sign. Her date with Tyler had been drama-free, laden with chemistry, perfect from beginning to end. There was no point dwelling in whatever feelings her walk with Ethan had engendered, because their path would lead to heartbreak. She knew that all too well.

With Tyler, the tea leaves had said to sleep on it. For how long and how many days, she wasn't sure. But that was tonight's top priority. Get a solid eight hours in. Everything might look different in the morning.

Even if she didn't want things to.

11

Addie baked. And baked. And baked a little more, taking advantage of Maybelline's rare responsiveness. She experimented with flavors, swung from sweet to savory and back again, then cleaned up the epic mess she made, reorganized the fridge and freezer, and carried out about a thousand other chores to keep her mind off the men in her life. When she finally crawled into bed that night, she nearly fell back out again at the sound of her ringing phone.

She grabbed the offending object on her bedside table, about to hurl it out the open window when she saw Tyler's name on the screen. What guy called when texting was all the rage? Why'd this guy have to go and be all different, and sexy, and different? She sat up in bed and ran her fingers through her hair, as though he could see her through the phone . . . the one she hadn't answered yet.

"Hello?" she croaked. *Great. Way to be hot, Addie.*

"Hey, pretty lady." His deep, raspy voice crawled all over her skin, which promptly broke out in gooseflesh. "Hope I'm not calling too late."

She shook her head back and forth a few times before realizing he couldn't see that, either. "Nuh-uh."

"Listen, I won't keep you long. Just wanted to make you an offer you can't refuse. At least, I hope—"

"Yes," she said, her gooseflesh getting gooseflesh at the sound of his husky laughter.

"Don't you want to know the offer?"

"Yes."

Again, his laughter vibrated through the phone. "Tomorrow night, around six o'clock, a guy on a motorcycle will be parked in front of your house, wondering if you'll hop on the back so he can take you to dinner in the city."

She was silent for several seconds, pretending to think it over. Here was this gorgeous man, asking her to skip town with him the next evening so he could take her for a ride on the back of his bike. What girl in her right mind could say no to that? Especially when dinner came with the deal. Food won every time. "Well, you tell this guy that I'll be ready and waiting. And hungry . . . for food, I mean, because the dinner—"

"I'll tell him," Tyler said, chuckling. "Good night, Addie." He spoke her name like it was a blessing, and she had to bite her lip to keep from saying "Amen."

"Night, Tyler."

Setting her phone back on the nightstand, she wiggled into a horizontal position again and sighed. The numbers on her alarm clock glowed a bright 11:45. Quarter to midnight. So much for getting a solid eight hours of sleep, but full beauty potential was still attainable. With that uplifting thought, she switched off the light and closed her eyes.

Unfortunately, her mind stayed wide awake. Had she misread Ethan's intentions? He wasn't really trying to kiss her, was he? His offer to walk her home had just been a friendly gesture. Well, that, and probably to repay her for the pies, even though she'd given them to him as a gift. Sure, he could have slapped some cash into her palm the next time he saw her, but that wasn't his style.

Not that she knew his style. Or his intentions. Why the heck didn't he kiss her? She was kissable, damn it.

Ugh. Grabbing a spare pillow, she smooshed it against her face, trying to suffocate the thinky-thoughts. She counted to thirty, then added an extra ten seconds for safe measure. Satisfied they'd gotten the point, she threw the pillow to the floor, curled onto her side, and relaxed her breathing.

And tossed and turned all night.

The chiming bells as she entered the Cup-A-Cabana the next morning were a blessed relief that temporarily blocked out the sound of her annoying, over-thinking brain. She'd made plans for a quick bite of breakfast with Hannah and Gwen before the workday began, though technically Gwen's workday began the moment she opened the shop. Addie claimed a table near the door, but since Hannah hadn't arrived yet, and Gwen was tending to customers . . . well, she had to entertain herself somehow.

Her gaze traveled to the back of the shop and landed on Ethan. At his corner table. Fully clothed. *Le sigh.* Couldn't blame a girl for hoping for a replay of the sweaty, shirtless, perfectly sculpted Ethan from yesterday. Did any of the other women in town have any idea what he looked like sans shirt? Clearly not, otherwise his table would be swarmed by hormone-crazed groupies clamoring for another glimpse of tantalizing flesh.

Good Lord, get a grip, Addie.

"Hey," she said, all casual-like, when she made her way over to him.

He pushed his laptop aside and indicated for her to have a seat. "Don't usually see you this early in the day."

"I'm trying to shake things up a bit."

"Ahh," he murmured. Then he took a drink of a beverage that looked suspiciously like tea.

"Are you drinking *tea*?"

Ethan returned his cup to its saucer and shrugged. "I've developed a taste for it."

Like that even *began* to answer her questions. How? When? Why? Poised to launch her interrogation, her thoughts were derailed by his next comment.

"I've been thinking about our conversation last night."

She sucked in a breath. "Oh?" *The talking part or the not-talking part?*

"What will you call your bakery, you know, when the day comes?"

A dull ache of disappointment spread through her chest, one she couldn't explain. This was a good, supportive question. From a friend who never kissed her. "I dunno. I haven't really thought about it too much. How about Adelaide's Pies?"

He cocked his head. "Really? That's the best you got? You need something catchy, like, A Slice of Life, or Pie Caramba!, or . . . The Pied Pieper."

"Shut your pie hole."

A shocked laugh tumbled out of him. "And we have a winner, folks." As if in reward for the zinger, he held up his plate and offered her half his danish.

She gave him a sad smile. "I'm joining Gwen and Hannah for breakfast shortly . . . Can I take a rain check?"

He pulled the plate back and curled his arm around it protectively. "No. I already regret offering it to you. One who truly deserves such a special treat would accept it with grace and boundless gratitude."

At once amused and captivated by the teasing light in his hazel eyes, she almost dared to trample over his improvised barricade and take a big bite out of his precious danish, just to see what he'd do. But then Hannah's booming voice announced to the entire world that she'd arrived, so it was time to scoot. "I better get over there. Talk to you later."

He picked away at his leftover danish as she joined the other women at their table by the door. The Cup-A-Cabana wasn't overly busy at that hour, and with his regular training in the skill of eavesdropping, he heard a few words here and there. *Motorcycle. Second date. Leather.* And then their conversation devolved into a giggle-infused discussion on bondage.

Shuddering, he set his laptop in front of him again. She said nothing about late-evening strolls or almost-kisses.

The Girl Who Was Almost Kissed.

He could have just as easily brought up the phantom kiss while she sat at his table, but he'd chosen instead to regale her with cheesy names he'd thought way too hard about for a business she didn't own yet.

Too late now. He'd have to wait this one out. Let her give Harley Davidson another shot and hope the guy screwed up enough that she'd ditch him like the others. Like him.

Maybe he wasn't trying hard enough with Addie. Ironic, since he was trying harder than he ever had before. But she was probably used to guys who flirted shamelessly, leaving absolutely no question as to what they wanted and when. The whole flirting thing never came naturally to him, being an introvert, but he wanted her badly enough to do whatever it took.

He'd caught Addie checking him out the other night. It was nice to know she appreciated his physique, because he sure appreciated hers, and her many, many assets. From the pixie haircut, to the doe eyes, to the legs that went on forever. Don't even get him started on that tea leaf tatt behind her ear. Every time he saw it, he wanted to lick it. One day. He'd lick and suck every inch of her.

He'd told her to give these guys she was dating a chance. He'd challenged her to try to make one last longer than an average sitcom time slot. So she took a chance on Harley Davidson, and they'd passed drama-length and were moving on to mini-series. She'd done what he dared her to do. But why couldn't she give *him* another chance?

At a quarter to six, she heard the unmistakable sound of a revving motorcycle engine. Peeking through the curtains, she watched in sheer womanly appreciation as her date took off his helmet and ran a hand through his hair. Thick, wavy, oh-so-perfect hair. She darted to the mirror in the entryway and checked her own hair and makeup for the eleventy-billionth time.

Would he come to the door, or was the revving a signal to get her ass in gear? Just as she made to open the door, he knocked, causing her to leap a foot in the air. "Okay, breathe. Breathe. Don't scare the pretty biker man," she murmured to herself. Taking a bracing pull of oxygen, she turned the doorknob.

Holy crap. She'd forgotten how tall he was. And how good-looking, especially up close. He wore his leather jacket, a pair of jeans that were really working for him, and dark-tinted aviators. She wore jeans too, as he'd suggested for safety precautions, and a sleeveless red blouse with frills running down the center, because frills were fun, and she was fun, and . . . now would be a good time to say something. It was like every time she came near this guy, she forgot how to put words into sentences. "Hi. Tyler. Hey, Tyler."

A grin broke out on his face. *Guh.* "Addie, you look fantastic." He pulled her into a hug, just as he'd done the first time they met, but this one felt much more intimate. Perhaps because of the placement of his hands. Low on her hips. "C'mon," he said. "Let's get you suited up, then we'll head to the restaurant."

Like a lust-struck puppy, she trailed behind him, somehow managing to lock up the house before she lost all her wits. He tossed her a jacket that lay draped over the back of his bike—a women's leather jacket. That served to snap her to attention again. She wondered how many women had been on the back of this bike, with its sleek red paint and shiny chrome pipes and other . . . bikey parts. She didn't know the names and wasn't good at inventing them. Ethan was the writer, not her.

Tyler helped her zip on the jacket, then he turned and grabbed the extra helmet clipped to the side of his bike. She reached for it, but instead he jerked her forward, catching her with his mouth. On her mouth. His lips moved over hers with a firm pressure that demanded her participation, but he was clearly in the driver's seat. His tongue teased the seam of her lips until she opened for him, and then it went deep. So deep, she gave a moment's thought to the logistics of having sex on a motorcycle. In broad daylight.

Before she could wrap her mind around it, he let her go. She blinked several times, trying to get her bearings.

"I've been waiting all day to do that," he said, his tone husky. Maybe that's what she'd been missing up till now—a man who took charge.

Tyler patted the leather seat and she sprang into motion, climbing onto the bike. It vibrated beneath her, reminding her in terrifying detail that this wasn't the ten-speed she was used to. Admiring a motorcycle from afar was one thing, but being on the back of one? Shit just got real. He pulled the helmet over her head and strapped it on. She couldn't hear a thing after that, save for the pounding of her heart. Once he settled in front of her, she wrapped her arms around him in a vice-like grip. How often did people die on these things? And how many of those people were on dates?

When her fingers became claws, he turned to check on her. "You okay?" Or that's what she thought he said. He gave her the universal thumbs up sign, so she answered with one of her own. Because she would have felt like a complete loser asking him to stop the ride before it even started.

Yeah, riding on the back of a motorcycle sounded fun, even romantic, in theory. The wind whipping through her hair, clutching tightly to the hard-body in front of her, hugging the asphalt with every twist and turn.

He revved the motor again. *Jesus. This thing is a death trap.* When they jerked into motion, she squeezed her eyes shut, prayed to the good Lord above, and held on for dear life.

She supposed he was going a respectable speed, but anything over twenty miles an hour felt like breakneck. How far were they going? Okay, so the vibration between her legs wasn't entirely unpleasant, but she'd get a bigger thrill from her trusty vibrator in the comfort and *safety* of her own home. You could reach the outskirts of Kendal in five minutes, and they'd already been going at least that long. Oh, hell. Would he take the highway? They should have talked about this. Taken her car instead. Or her bike—that beautiful, wonderful, non-motorized bike that didn't require an iron will to ride it. *Back roads*, she silently begged. *Take the back roads.*

Wait. Wiping out on gravel would hurt just as bad, maybe worse. And her clothes would get all dusty. If he went a little faster, they might get pulled over by a cop, and then she could ride in the back of the officer's car to safety. That pleasing visual in mind, she cracked open her eyes and instantly regretted it. He was pulling onto the highway.

Snapping them closed again, she thought about anything other than the swerving motions he made between lanes. Tyler had great hair. His face was a winner. Nice nose—not a feature she'd appreciated on a man before, but his was really well-shaped and pretty much the ideal size for his face. She wondered if any other woman had ever remarked on his nose before. Yeah, because it was the perfect prelude to sex. 'Hey, you look super-great naked, but I'd be remiss if I didn't give a shout-out to that sniffer of yours.'

She giggled at the absurdity of her thoughts, quieting suddenly when she became aware that the ride had stopped. Opening her eyes, she found Tyler staring back at her in concern. He'd taken his helmet off, his still-fabulous hair deserving of an ode. "We're here," he said. She read his lips, which were yet another check in the plus column. Full, firm, commanding—

"Addie?"

—tinged with a hint of her pink lipstick, which oddly made the man look even sexier . . .

"Addie!"

She shook her head to clear it. "What?"

He twisted awkwardly in his seat and unclipped her helmet, gently removing it from her head. Shooting her a sympathetic grin, he said, "You're gonna have to let go of me or we'll never make it inside."

"Oh. Right." She relaxed her grip, cringing at the stiffness in her joints. "Sorry about that."

"I tried to go slow," he said in apology. "First time's always a little scary, but you get used to it."

That was the truth when it came to sex, but there was no way in hell she'd ever get used to riding a motorcycle, and she hoped he planned on plying her with wine, because that's the only way she'd be getting home by the same mode of transport. The only thing that scared her more was the current state of her hair. Too much to hope hers had come out of the battle looking as fresh and flowy as his. She ran her fingers through the limp and lifeless tresses matted to her head. His hair looked like he'd leapt straight out of a shampoo ad. Hers felt like she'd slept on it for forty-thousand years. And she'd taken extra care with the spiking tonight, too.

He held out his arm and helped her off the bike, pressing a possessive hand to her lower back as they walked toward . . . *Specialteas*. She'd heard people talking about this place. They were renowned for their hundreds of unique tea flavors, and they'd also received multiple acclaims for their menu items. All those points he lost for trying to kill her on the way here? He just won, like, a truckload of them back.

Tyler escorted her inside the trendy interior and spoke to the hostess. Within moments, they were seated at a table in a back room of the restaurant, separated by beads that hung from the archway. It felt secluded and intimate, comfortably so. Once they were alone, Tyler was the first to speak. "I remember you said how much you loved tea. Figured this place was a safe bet."

"I've never been," she said, "but I've heard wonderful things."

"Even if it's terrible, which I doubt, we'll make up for it later." He finished the promise with a wink. A very suggestive wink. A "your place or mine?" kind of wink.

She reached for her water glass and drained half of it. Sex on the second date wasn't completely out of the question. Though he hadn't flat-out put the offer on the table, she couldn't help but contemplate the possibility. He was undeniably attractive, confident, smooth—in his mannerisms and his words—and he could kiss a woman so thoroughly that smoke came out of her ears. It was very easy to lust for a man like Tyler.

Three tea lights flickered in the center of the table. She watched as the flames dipped and danced, twirling and bowing for their audience.

Great-Aunt Edna once said, "Lust burns out. You can't truly love someone unless you like them first."

She did like Tyler, but she lusted for him more. Did it really matter if the scale tipped more one way than the other?

"Order anything you like," Tyler said. "Tonight is my treat."

A smile curved her lips as she perused the menu. "I've got my eye on this berry kiwi colada herbal tea."

"Oh, yeah? I'm jealous."

Her smile became a grin, and she met his gaze. "Don't be. These kinds of affairs may start out hot and steamy, but they never last long."

"Order it. I wanna hear you moan when you drink it."

"A little *When Harry Met Sally*, huh? I'll see what I can do."

He relayed their drink orders to the waitress, then sat back and openly stared at her, his chocolate-brown eyes seeming to penetrate right through her. "I still can't believe a woman who looks like you, who bakes insanely delicious pies for a living, which is basically every man's dream come true, is single."

"Yeah. I'm actually not. I've been meaning to tell you . . . ."

His eyes widened. "Oh, wow. I didn't realize—"

"No! No. I'm not . . . I was just kidding. I'm single. I'm as single as a, uh, slice of American cheese." *Oh, jeez.*

By some miracle, Tyler's smile returned. "Good news."

Yes, good. Keep the man smiling. Cut down on the sarcasm. Some guys don't like funny girls.

Ethan appreciated her sense of humor. Well, he'd at least spar with her, and his sarcasm detector synced up with hers . . .

Stop invading my thoughts, Hemingway.

Her tea was delivered, thank goodness. She needed something to grasp in effort to stay grounded. She took a drink, the sweetly smooth liquid trickling down her throat while the man across from her waited expectantly. The barest moan escaped her lips, and his smile stretched even further.

Tyler reached for her free hand and pressed his lips to the center of her palm. "That was the sexiest sound I've ever heard," he whispered against her now-damp skin.

He said all the right things and made all the right moves, like he'd done it a thousand times. Rehearsed without being predictable. Smooth like her tea, and sweet too, but with a hint of wickedness that made her toes curl. She wanted him. It was just a question of whether she could sit through the meal before she climbed him like a tree.

A light summer breeze caused the branches on the trees to sway ever so gently. As if hypnotized by their motion, she swayed into him and sighed a girly sigh when he wrapped his arm snug around her and helped her off the bike.

In the end, the food saved her from making like a monkey in heat, at least for a while. She'd ordered a toasted turkey and brie sandwich. Every last bite melted in her mouth. And by the time her plate was scraped clean, her mind was locked and loaded with dirty, dirty thoughts. She was so sure they'd cap off the night with sex, she hadn't even asked for dessert. He'd ordered it anyway, possibly because he could see her squirming in her seat and it gave him a thrill. But it was she who got the greatest thrill of all when that sinfully rich triple-chocolate mousse torte touched his tongue, because the man's eyes rolled into the back of his head and he groaned—long and low.

She'd relived that groan over and over again on the ride home, when she'd clung to him more out of the desperate need to touch him than self-preservation.

How soon is too soon to invite him in? There was still the matter of him walking her to the door, but, really, why wait? She was past playing coy. In this day and age, surely a woman could tell a man to get his ass in her house and start stripping, especially on a second date. Especially-especially when said man was unzipping her jacket, all slow and suggestive.

If they started the lip lock out here on the street, like before, she knew full well she wouldn't be able to stop it this time. So once she shed the jacket, she took him by the hand and pulled him frantically behind her. They made it as far as the picket fence when she froze mid-stride. Just last night, on that same patch of earth, a very different man had stood there. Swallowing hard, she spun around to face Tyler.

His face registered dismay. "Addie, you okay? You look like you've seen a ghost."

Not a ghost. More like a phantom kiss that apparently still haunted her. No. Ethan would not ruin this for her. He would not screw her out of a good screw. "I'm great! Never been better!"

Too bad she'd never been a good actress, either. The forced enthusiasm deepened the worry lines that bracketed his mouth. "Listen, I'm not sure what spooked you, but—"

"I'm not spooked!"

He smiled and cupped her cheek. "That's a good thing, because I definitely want to see you again."

"You can see me any time you want to see me, like right now, even, but maybe not in this particular spot. There's just some, like, bad juju here."

He laughed at her bizarre—and that was putting it mildly—explanation for her even more bizarre behavior. "Maybe there was something in that tea," he joked.

Oh, yes, the tea. She'd barely glanced at her tea leaves in the restaurant, but it was all coming back to her now. Most of the clumps and clusters were illegible, although one clear symbol caught her eye: a comet. It spoke of a pivotal change or dramatic event soon to be experienced.

Sex could be dramatic. They should totally have some.

"You free Thursday?"

His question jolted her back to the present. "Wha? Yes, but I—"

Tyler closed his mouth over hers, effectively sealing in her protests, kissing her on sacred ground. "Good night, Addie."

Sacred ground? Where the hell had that come from? Maybe there *was* something in her tea. He kissed her once more while her brain tried to puzzle out if she'd been drugged by those nice people at the restaurant. That had to be the explanation, the reason why she let him walk away and get back on his bike fully clothed and un-sexed. He waved to her before he fired up the engine and took off. For several minutes more, her feet were glued to the same spot. The kissy and non-kissy spot.

And the crazy thing was, she hadn't felt quite as much of a thrill from the real thing with Tyler as she had from the almost-kiss with Ethan.

12

Idle hands were good for baking. And since she didn't have anything better to do, thanks to intruding thoughts of Ethan, she trudged into the kitchen and preheated the oven. Her internal oven was at a billion degrees, and her best opportunity for getting laid had just fled the premises. Was she delusional, or had he not been putting out the sex signals all night?

She reached for her copy of *The Art of Reading Tea Leaves,* cracked open the cover, and turned to the glossary to make sure she hadn't misinterpreted the comet symbol. Nope.

Swapping the book for the container of flour, she placed it on the counter, then washed and dried her hands. She grabbed the bag of pre-made dough from the refrigerator, setting it on the counter as well, and sprinkled the surface with a handful of flour. This was her favorite part of the pie-making process: rolling the dough. It helped a girl get out her frustrations. On this night, she had a good many.

She pulled out the individual mounds of dough, one by one, and began rolling them. Her forearms flexed with every press. Her shoulders burned from the exertion. She'd added a splash of apple cider vinegar to her recipe, ensuring the crust would be extra flaky and tender. Now that she knew two guys had their eyes on her pies, she had to up her game.

While the dough rested, she retrieved the container of blackberry/peach filling from the fridge, then prepared an egg wash.

It was probably wrong to resent Ethan. It wasn't his fault she'd missed out on undoubtedly hot sex. She would admit that, but she wouldn't admit to the tremor that shot through her body when referring to sex and Ethan in the same sentence. Because it wasn't a tremor. It was a chill . . . or something.

She brushed the dough with the egg wash, scooped a generous amount of filling onto each circle, then folded them over. Tomorrow was another day. A fresh start.

She finished brushing the outside of the pies with the egg wash, then cut tiny vents into their tops to allow steam to escape. Lastly, she recited the rhyme her grandmother had taught her during the many hours they'd spent in the kitchen together, baking and laughing. "Rise, rise, my beautiful pies," she whispered, then slid her babies into the oven.

Hannah and Gwen nearly trampled her when she entered the coffee shop the next afternoon, anxious for details about her date with Tyler.

"Sooo, how'd it go?!" Hannah asked, her eyes practically bugging out of her head. Her blonde curls were so elaborately coiffed, they should have been featured in a hair magazine.

"It was another really great date. We're going out again on Thursday." Addie laughed as the overenthusiastic pair pulled her behind the counter for some privacy, though Hannah's high-pitched squeals were anything but subtle.

"Oh, this is so fabulous. He's so hot! And so tall. You guys are gonna have the most gorgeous babies!"

Gwen snorted. "It's been two dates, Barker. Let's not start naming their children just yet."

"I think this is a sign. I'm meant to be a matchmaker. You know, I always had a feeling that this was my true calling in life—"

"You already have a job," Gwen cut in. "The Barkery, remember?"

"Yes, but this could be, like, a side gig. Ooh! I could have a doggie dating service, too!"

"I think you've seen *Lady and the Tramp* one too many times."

Gwen's remark reminded Addie of something she'd meant to bring up earlier. "Have you seen that guy putting up those dog leash posters?"

"He's been loitering outside my store all week, harassing my customers. I think *he* needs a leash," Hannah snarled.

"Now, now, retract those claws. Paws for the cause," Addie teased.

Hannah rolled her eyes. "Could he not have come up with a better slogan? Hell, the dogs could have worded it better."

"Easy there, tiger," Gwen said, laughing. "What's your beef with this guy? It's not such a bad cause."

She started to speak but then stopped. "He's just . . . He's all judgy because, well, okay, sometimes I let Muffy, my Labradoodle, off her leash . . . and he kind of saw me do that the other day."

Gwen eyed her suspiciously. "He kind of saw you, or you purposely did it in front of him to set the guy off?"

Hannah shrugged. "Potato, pot-ah-to."

"Barker."

"What? Fine. I'll stop provoking him, but if he tries to put up even one poster on my storefront windows, that man is going to see firsthand that my bark is far worse than my bite."

"You're a kitten and you know it."

"In any case," Addie began, hoping to steer the conversation back to its original track, "I think you may be onto something with your philosophy that men with dogs are the pick of the litter."

"See? I told you!" Hannah pointed a finger at Gwen. "She always underestimates my brilliance. I think I'll write a book."

The mention of books brought a certain author to mind. Addie glanced around the interior, but Ethan wasn't camped out in his usual corner. "Hey, have you guys seen Hemingway?"

"Who?" the other women asked in unison.

"Ethan . . . the writer guy."

Gwen shook her head. "Nope. Haven't seen him yet today."

"Who's Ethan?" Hannah asked. "Is his name seriously Ethan? That's, like, the name reserved for the hottest of hot guys. Is he hot? Please tell me he's hot."

Addie felt like her cheeks had sucked in every ounce of heat in the room. "He's . . . well, he's, uh—"

Inadvertently saving her, Gwen said, "You've probably seen him before. He sits in the corner over there." She gestured to his usual table. "Very serious writer-type. I think he's a cutie. Plus, he tips well, which makes him aces in my books."

Hannah cocked her head inquisitively. "Hey, maybe I should give this Ethan guy a whirl."

"No!" Addie snapped her mouth shut a fraction too late. The emphatic 'no' practically echoed through the coffee shop. Both women gave her the stare-down. "Um, I mean . . . I just really don't think he's your type. You know, you're so upbeat and, um, bubbly, and he's very surly. Not really all that friendly. I don't even think he's looking for anything long-lasting anyway."

Gwen's laser beam stare sharpened, but Hannah perked up, seemingly pleased by her analysis. "Who is, honey? Well, besides you, which I think is adorable and perfectly right for you. But people like Ethan and me . . . we're just looking for a good yank on the ol' chain."

Gwen rolled her eyes. "Says the woman who doesn't even know the guy. There are lots of people looking for long-term relationships, Barker. Ethan could be, too." She spoke the latter part to Addie who was contemplating buying a muzzle for herself. Maybe Hannah could get her a discount.

"You know I enjoy a challenge, Gwen," Hannah said with a gleam in her eyes. "And speaking of challenges, I better get to The Barkery. Princess Prancey Paws is coming in to get her nails trimmed and polished and she won't sit still for anyone but Auntie Hannah."

Both Gwen and Addie giggled as Hannah click-clacked to the door on her way-too-freaking-high heels. The woman had curves for days and she showcased them in form-fitting clothing that hugged her in all the right places. It made Addie wonder, not for the first time, how Tyler had ever looked past Hannah. But then again, Hannah thought dogs should date.

"It's weird when I'm the normal friend," Addie murmured as the bells signaled Hannah's departure.

Gwen smirked. "Says you." She looked like she wanted to say more, but, much to Addie's relief, decided against it.

"Hey, we still on for yoga tonight?" Addie asked.

"Oh! I meant to tell you. Shawn has a rare night off, and we were thinking we could have a date night. Are you cool with switching to Friday this week?"

Gwen taking an extra night off was a rare occurrence, too, so Addie was more than happy to accommodate her friend. "Friday it is! See you then."

"I'll be there, making like a human pretzel."

"I think I'd enjoy it a lot more if we actually got to eat pretzels. And not do the yoga part."

"I'll bring a bag," Gwen said, inspiring another round of giggles.

As he crossed the threshold into the Cup-A-Cabana, his gaze immediately landed on Addie. She and Gwen were beside the counter, both doubled over in a fit of laughter. He made for his usual table, set down his bag, and began unpacking all the essentials of writing—even for pretend writers. That's how he felt anymore. Like he was an imposter, carting around his *stuff*, looking the part, but with absolutely nothing to show for it.

Addie waved at him and started for the door, apparently too busy for a sit-down chat. Disillusioned by her quick retreat, he frowned at his computer screen, knowing today's effort would indeed be futile. How else was he supposed to get the scoop on her latest date with Harley Davidson? Bad enough she'd met the guy somewhere outside of the coffee shop, thwarting any chance he had of snooping.

Shaking his head at himself, he looked to the front of the shop to get one last glimpse of her before she took off, but she was gone. Always in such a hurry.

The Girl Who Rushed Through Life.

He opened a blank document on his laptop. His fingers flew over the keys and a flurry of words appeared on the screen, only to be deleted minutes later. With a huff of frustration, he closed his laptop again. If he thought she wasn't even a little interested, he could let it go. Eventually. He'd get over it and move on. Find a new writing spot in another coffee shop in another town. But the other night, during their walk, there was . . . *something*. A spark. She leaned in first. Or did he? Her lips were begging to be kissed, and he'd intended to, with every fiber of his being. Instead, it became another missed opportunity.

He'd vowed to try harder. If he sat there and let her go on dating all these other guys, he'd have no one to blame but himself. No more waiting around, wondering if she might show up and with whom. He knew where she lived. He could try the old 'I just happened to be in the area' routine. Casual hadn't worked for him up till now, but he doubted she'd find friendly neighborhood stalking a turn-on.

Blowing out a frustrated breath, he rubbed the pads of his fingers against his temples. And so what if he did go to all this effort? Would it all be for naught? Why should he try so hard when she couldn't be bothered to try for him? That completely-opposite-of-zen date they'd had didn't count in his eyes. Besides, they'd never even made it past the stupid cucumber water portion.

He was stirred from his internal rant by the vision of a woman sitting across from him. Unfortunately, it wasn't the woman who took up 90% of his thoughts.

A striking blonde beamed at him, her stark white teeth almost blinding. "You've gotta be Ethan. Quiet, focused guy, sitting at the corner table with a sour look on his face."

"Are you on a scavenger hunt?"

Her smile turned almost predatory. "I'm on the hunt for something."

Ethan waited for her to continue, but she was too busy devouring him with her eyes. He swallowed, not used to this kind of blatant scrutiny.

"I'm Hannah Barker," she said, stretching out her hand. "I own The Barkery down the street."

He shook her hand, startled by the softness of her skin. And by the splotches of gold near her thumb and wrist.

She followed his line of sight and explained with a laugh, "The hazards of painting puppy nails."

Now he'd heard everything. Dogs had their nails painted? "You're joking, right?"

"Not at all! It's one of our biggest cash cows. Princess Prancey Paws always goes for the gold polish. It looks lovely on her, but half of it always ends up on me."

"I'll bet," he said, because he had no freakin' idea what else to say. Hoping she'd get to the reason why she'd taken over the other half of his table, he sat back and crossed his arms.

"You know, I don't think either of those girls did you justice."

"What girls?"

"They never even mentioned the smoldering eyes, the full lips, the mouth-watering bit of stubble. And don't get me started on that thick head of hair. Lord almighty, I wanna run my fingers through it."

Every inch of his skin prickled with heat. "Do you talk like this to all men or just the lucky ones?"

"Only the ones I wanna date. Oh, and he blushes, too!" she cooed.

If she could get her fill of him, then he'd damn well take his fill of her. He started with her hair . . . A bit too blonde for his taste, but he liked the way she piled it on top of her head, little ringlets escaping here and there. She had a knockout body, which she tucked neatly into an outfit that was functional yet form-fitting—as form-fitting as an outfit could be for a woman who spent most of her time with canines. But he couldn't fault anyone who loved dogs the way she clearly did.

When he finally met her gaze again, she grinned ear to ear. "You, me, dinner date. Whaddya say?"

Well, if Addie could date everybody and their brother, why couldn't he? Date their sisters, that is. But, good heavenly God, dating sucked. Dread pooled in the pit of his stomach at the thought of enduring another wacky restaurant with overpriced food.

"I know a great burger joint," she added.

There. The most beautiful six words in the English language. "How's Friday?"

13

On Thursday evening, Tyler pulled up to Addie's place in a car. A beautiful, safe machine with four doors and metal on all sides, comfy seating, and air bags. She could have kissed him for that alone, but the scent of his aftershave, his snug-fitting T-shirt, and flowing hair were enough to do the trick.

He laughed when she enthusiastically grabbed him by the waist and pulled him in nice and close for a kiss on her front porch. His warm lips glided against hers, gentle at first, then all at once demanding. The change came so sudden that she hardly noticed, until his tongue tangled with hers, and his groin joined in the seduction. Addie pulled back, feeling lightheaded from lack of oxygen and the Tyler effect.

Yeah, the man had an effect. Some kind of hypnotic spell he put her under anytime he drew near.

"I was thinking we could hang out at my place tonight, maybe watch a movie. I made brownies," he said, waggling his eyebrows.

"Oh, right, I forgot you said you baked." She reached for his outstretched hand, then paused, a disturbing thought suddenly occurring to her. "These aren't . . . special brownies, are they?"

His broad shoulders shook as a full-bodied laugh rolled through him. "No. You may be dazed and dazzled by the taste, but they won't give you a buzz."

She grinned at his openness, his easiness. He was so relaxed with her, which weirdly made her more nervous. Because this was only their third date, and you weren't supposed to feel so comfortable with someone on your third date, were you? There were still so many things she didn't know about him. She was pretty sure he wasn't a serial killer at this point, but something about Tyler seemed almost too smooth, too perfect.

"Everything okay?" he asked her as they descended her front steps.

"Mmhmm," she lied. "Fine."

His warm palm on her back, he guided her to the passenger side of his jet-black Jaguar, opened the door, and helped her into the vehicle. She moaned as she sank into the buttery-soft leather of the seat. The car smelled new. Or unused. He probably kept it in storage and only let it see the light of day on dates with women who were too chicken to park their butts on the back of his bike. Yeah, well, this ride came with a seatbelt, so chicken or not, she'd get to her destination in a safer and more secure way.

Tyler rounded the hood and slid into the driver's seat. She held her breath, expecting the car to jolt into motion, but instead of reaching for the gear shift, he reached for her hand. "Sure you're okay?"

Addie realized then how tense she was. Releasing the air from her lungs in a whoosh, she turned to him and smiled. "I'm just wondering if you're, like, secretly an alien or something."

He blinked. "I'm sorry?"

"You're too perfect."

The confusion on his face morphed into amused disbelief. He stayed silent, most likely expecting her to elaborate on why that was a bad thing, because she'd said it like an accusation, not a compliment.

"You're tall, obviously attractive, you've got the hair thing going on, and you're always freakishly on time, and you smell good, and you're well-groomed, and, and . . . you bake. Your brownies better suck, otherwise I'm convinced you're an alien."

A gust of laughter burst from his chest, and sheesh, even that was perfect. "I'm tempted to sabotage my brownies before you try them, but that seems a bit like sacrilege."

"No, no, don't even speak of such a thing. That's brownie blasphemy."

Lacing their fingers together, he moved their joined hands to the gear shift and put the car into drive. The tires squealed as he veered out of his parking spot and shot down her side street. Fast. Too fast.

Okay, so not completely perfect. Whew.

When they pulled into Tyler's driveway, Addie wasn't entirely sure how many towns they'd driven through or how many speed limits they'd broken, but she was relieved to be not moving. She opened her door before he had a chance to, curious to see if the house was as big as it looked from inside the car. "Nope. Definitely bigger," she murmured, taking slow steps closer to a contractor's fantasy come true.

Long white columns lined the entryway. A wraparound porch, equipped with a swing that rocked gently in the breeze, spoke of quiet, peaceful evenings watching the sunset. Blue and grey brick detailing along the sides. Huge picture windows. Light, open, oh-so-inviting . . . obviously made for a family.

But her home, Edna's home, that's where she always pictured herself raising children.

Tyler stepped into her field of vision. "Gotta say, I'm a little jealous of the way you're staring at my house."

Addie grinned. "Well, it's a sexy house. Did you build it?"

"With my bare hands," he said, shooting her a wink. "Mighta been a few guys who helped me out, but I drew up the blueprints. Had this design in my head for years. I was just waiting for the right time, the right property. Turned out better than I ever imagined it would."

"That's so cool. I can totally see a family living here. I mean . . . if you want one, that is. You know, whenever. With whoever."

He laughed at her stumbling. "Maybe someday. Not really a priority at the moment. Just enjoying life while I can, you know?"

"Sure." She nodded. "I can hardly wait to see the inside."

His eyes lit up and he grabbed her arm and tugged her toward the steps. "C'mon, I'll show you."

As soon as the front door opened, Max, his schnauzer, dropped at his feet for a belly rub. Addie stooped to scratch at the dog's thick coat of fur, while Tyler obediently rubbed Max's belly. He wiggled and squirmed against the hardwood floor, moaning and groaning in sheer doggy delight.

"Addie, this is Max," Tyler said, continuing his ministrations. "An eighteen-pound bundle of energy, and the ruler of this domain."

She smiled as Tyler signaled for Max to shake a paw in introduction. "I'm honored and humbled to meet you, Master Max."

Tyler bounced back up to a standing position, and Max fell into line beside him. "Hope you don't mind, but we'll probably have a tail for the whole tour."

"I don't mind at all."

Whether on purpose or not, their first stop was Tyler's bedroom—on the main floor with a sliding door that opened to an outdoor inground pool. Very masculine décor. Lots of browns, greys, and rust-colored accents. There were a few family portraits, and several of Max. Not a single trace of a woman—current or former.

Tyler turned to her as though awaiting some kind of response. Had he been talking all this time? "The pool looks nice," she supplied, hoping that's where his one-sided conversation had been headed.

"Wanna go for a swim?"

"I, uh, didn't think to bring my bathing suit . . . ."

His lips curved into a grin, and his eyes took on a devilish gleam. "This is a pretty private lot. Not a lot of neighbors, and the trees are extra tall."

As much as she'd pay big bucks to see him in his birthday suit, there was no way in hell she'd be going skinny-dipping. "Those trees, uh . . . must be great for climbing. So, where to next, Master Max?"

Tyler laughed at the abrupt change in subject. "I think we'll take a detour to the kitchen. I'll make you a cup of tea to go with your brownie and grab a treat for Max. Sound good?"

Tea. In other words, truth serum. So far, the leaves had given her a bed and a comet symbol concerning Tyler. Perhaps, whatever happened here today, or was about to happen, signified the pivotal change or dramatic event the comet alluded to. She turned her attention back to his bed. Well, it was certainly big enough for two. Looked to be quite plush and cozy. Subconsciously, she reached out and stroked the quilted comforter, humming in approval of its soft texture.

Tyler's eyes widened with interest. "Or we could just hang out in here a while longer."

She pulled her hand back, using it to guard her against the man currently stalking toward her like a cat after its prey. "Buh-buh-buh. I believe I was promised a brownie. Don't deny Max and me our treats."

Max stood on his hind legs and pawed at Tyler's thighs in a show of solidarity. "All right," he acquiesced. "I can't fight both of you. Follow me to the room where the extraordinary happens. The *other* room, that is." He darted a meaningful glance in her direction.

Despite the cockiness of his words, despite the smugness in his features, she couldn't help envisioning him hovering over her in his bed, feeding her brownies. Shirtless. And pantsless. And she'd be panting for more. More brownies. More . . .

She paused mid-fantasy, imagining Ethan rolling his eyes at her pathetic attempt at pornographic prose. Jarred by his intrusion into her thoughts, she shook her head and hurried to catch up to Tyler and Max who were already a few steps ahead of her.

The kitchen, like the rest of the house, was both immense and immaculate. Tyler filled a kettle with water and placed it on the stove. She smiled in thanks as he graciously set out three different tea flavors of the leafed variety. *Bonus points for you, Mr. Jameson.* He pulled open a drawer and grabbed a bag of biscuits for Max, rewarding him with two. She wouldn't have thought it possible, but his tiny little tail waggled triple time.

Addie moved to the island counter and studied the different tea flavors, selecting the jasmine apple. Tyler scooted in behind her and waved the cooled pan of brownies under her nose. If she'd had a tail, it'd be making like Max's.

"I hate you for how freaking incredible that smells."

"Aww, you don't really hate me, do you?" He wrapped his free hand around her waist, slipping his pinkie finger beneath the hem of her shirt. She shivered as the dexterous digit tickled her sensitive skin. "Icing or no?"

Her eyes closed, and she half-wondered if he meant on the brownie or her body. "Always," she whispered. "Never skimp on the icing."

He chuckled, the warmth of his breath raising goosebumps on her nape. "Extra icing it is," he said, and then the bastard backed away from her and took his beautiful, talented finger with him. She turned and leaned against the counter, pleased that Tyler heeded her advice and slathered her piece—the corner piece, God bless him—with enough icing to give her a toothache.

Moments later, he presented it to her, on a plate and everything. She accepted the plate, eyeing the brownie with a mixture of curiosity and suspicion. Tyler's gaze never left hers as he waited for her to take a bite. Satisfied that she'd made him sweat it out long enough, she brought the square to her mouth and bit into it. Her teeth sank into the tender center. Sweet, but not too sweet. He'd even snuck some chocolate chips into the batter. The man was either a sorcerer or a culinary genius. Once she'd swallowed the bite, she stared at him long and hard. "You're hiding the Barefoot Contessa in here somewhere."

Laughing, he shook his head. "Nope, although, I've been known to steal a few recipes from some of the chefs and home cooks on the Food Network."

She took another bite as he went about fixing her tea. Cripes, it tasted better than her last bite, not that she'd tell him that. "You sure this isn't Betty Crocker?"

Tyler pressed a hand to his heart. "Though I won't deny Ms. Crocker makes a mean brownie, this is all me."

"You are an evil, evil man, making something so delicious," Addie said as she polished off the last bite. Tyler took her plate and traded it for a cup and saucer.

"Hope you'll forgive me." His chocolate-brown eyes blinked slowly, pinning her to the spot, making her tongue trip all over itself.

"Uh, you could, um . . . Your eyes are like brownies." *Your eyes are like brownies?* Had she just said that? Shaking out of her stupor, she clarified, "I mean, another brownie would help. Me. To forgive you. Put those pieces of a sentence together and they'll probably make a whole one."

Tyler beamed. "Comin' right up."

Addie drank some tea, swishing the hot liquid around in her mouth in attempt to kill any idiotic remarks that remained on her tongue. Tyler served her up another brownie, which he set on the counter next to her, but he had no intention of letting her eat it. Truthfully, she hadn't expected him to. So it didn't come as a surprise when his warm hands landed on her hips and he pulled her flush against him.

"Hello."

Tyler's answering smile made her toes curl. His lips latched on to the pulse beating rapidly at her throat. And then he licked the spot. Traced circles around it. Made her forget her own name. Yeah, she'd heard the expression before and thought it was bonkers, but she seriously couldn't remember her name. *Allison?*

One muscular thigh wedged between hers, and his mouth found her mouth, and she felt the earth move. And it took her brain an uncomfortable amount of time to process that they'd literally moved from the kitchen to the archway leading to his living room.

Andrea? Adrienne?

"Still think I'm evil?" he whispered as he ground against her.

"Yuh-huh," she managed to utter.

Oddly spurred on by her profundity, he took the kiss even deeper. He cupped the back of her head and plundered her mouth, his tongue thrusting against hers in a dance that left no question in her mind as to where this would end. His other hand traced the contours of her body, skimming teasingly close to her breast a half-dozen times before making contact. Her breath hitched as he squeezed the pliant flesh, paying special attention to her nipple that stood proudly at attention. She may not have had a lot to offer in the breastage department, but her nipples more than made up for it.

Tyler gradually dislodged his tongue from her mouth and, while he pinched her nipple between his thumb and index finger, whispered, "Addie?"

Oh! Addie! That was her name!

"Hmm?"

"Stop thinking."

Her cheeks burned with embarrassment. He knew. Of course he knew she'd been distracted, but it's not like he wasn't doing a kick-ass job at the whole seduction thing. "My mind won't shut off. It's like it has a mind of its own . . . which is a terrible joke that I didn't even mean to—"

She shrieked as Tyler picked her up, like she weighed absolutely nothing, threw her over his shoulder, and carried her to the couch. Her squeals of surprise turned to giggles when he unceremoniously tossed her to the cushions and climbed on top. And the couch, too, was plush and perfect, matching everything else in his life.

One arm flopped to the floor as her limbs became looser beneath his weight.

"That's it," he growled. "Just relax."

Sensations swirled inside and outside her body. Heat. Throbbing. Wet. Hand . . . Wet hand. Why was her hand wet?

"Max!" she gasped, jerking upright.

Tyler reached for the back cushion to balance himself, impressively staying astride the bucking bronco she'd transformed into. "Not exactly the name I was hoping you'd cry out."

Rolling her eyes, she nodded to the four-legged voyeur currently licking her fingers. "Is this not weird for you, having an audience?"

He shrugged. "Nothing he hasn't seen before."

"Oh." *Wait.* "What?"

Tyler flashed her an enigmatic smile as he reached over her and grasped one of Max's chew toys. He chucked the thing into the next room, and Max shot like a bullet to retrieve it. Addie assumed he'd be back to play fetch, but apparently this was an act the two had practiced and the pup stayed put.

"Well played," she commended both dog and owner.

Tyler nodded in thanks, then, with her assistance, resumed his previous position. She sighed and closed her eyes as he kissed her neck, blazing a hot, wet trail down to her chest.

Too much. The weight of his body. The press of his mouth. Too soon to be feeling all these feelings—heart-pounding, palms tingling . . .

She gasped as the button on her jeans gave way.

Too fast.

Opening her mouth to speak, she startled when a shrill ringtone beat her to the punch.

Groaning in frustration, Tyler pushed himself up on one hand and reached for the phone in his back pocket. "Shit," he said, glancing at the screen. "I need to take this. One of the guys on my crew."

"Oh, sure. Yeah. Go ahead."

He pecked her forehead as he stood. "I'll just be a minute. Go and have another brownie if you like." With that, Tyler disappeared into the next room.

There was no way she'd be strutting into his kitchen all disheveled-like. She refastened her jeans button and smoothed out all the wrinkles before shuffling in that direction. Instead of dishing up another brownie, she headed straight for her abandoned cup of tea. Nodding resolutely, she tipped back the cup and hastily gulped down the remaining liquid. She blew out a gust of air and replaced the cup on its saucer, allowing the leaves to settle at the bottom.

What would they reveal this time? Their future children? Snorting, she leaned close and studied the shapes and patterns of the leaves. One unmistakable figure caught her eye. A tortoise. She could recall from memory that a tortoise represented the notion of taking it slow. The symbol encouraged a person to push the pause button, take a breather and, if necessary, reassess the path they were following.

Standing in Tyler's tidy kitchen, the scent of freshly baked brownies still lingering, she had to wonder if the tea fairies were playing some kind of sick joke on her. Hot guy, adorable dog, great house . . . what exactly was missing? She lifted her gaze to the ceiling and cried, "Please tell me what isn't perfect about this situation!"

"Sexy woman, pan of brownies, the whole night ahead of us . . . ." Tyler trailed off as he sidled up next to her. "I'm comin' up empty."

"I have to go."

The blunt statement knocked the hopeful smirk straight off his face. "What? Why?"

Addie shook her head, wishing she knew how to explain. "I just . . . ." She grasped his hand, attempting to soothe him as she searched for the right words. "Tyler, I like you. A lot. A scary amount, actually."

When his eyes widened in alarm, she squeezed his hand reassuringly.

"What I mean to say is, I'm not used to feeling this way and it's all happening really fast for me. I just need a little breather."

"Addie," Tyler said, "nothing has to happen. We don't have to do anything you're not comfortable with. Don't you trust me?"

She sighed. "It's not you I don't trust."

"We can watch a movie. I'll sit on a different couch. I won't even come near you."

Addie laughed at his persistence. "That sounds horrible."

"Yeah, it does."

The man who stood beside her looked more like a boy who'd had his puppy stolen. Disappointment dragged the corners of his mouth down. She hated being the cause of it. "Listen, I'll take a rain check on the movie, okay? I'll go home, do some baking, and we'll try this again another night."

She expected him to offer a multitude of reasons for her to stay—a few probably would have done the trick—but he nodded once and said, "Will you at least take some brownies with you?"

Addie smiled, warmed by his easy acceptance and generosity. "Got any Tupperware?"

14

"Here's your tea," Gwen said, dropping off the hot beverage at Ethan's corner table. After his mumbled thanks, she hung around longer than usual. Curious as to why, he peered up to find her grinning at him. "Ready for your big date tonight?"

He stared at her, deadpan.

Her enthusiasm unflagging, Gwen added, "Hannah is pretty excited. She's closing The Barkery early so she can buy shoes. Shockingly, it's not the first time she's done that."

"I'll alert the media."

She leaned on the back of the chair across from him, taking advantage of the mid-morning lull to force him into a conversation he didn't want to have. "If there's anything you'd like to know before tonight, now's the time to ask. Her likes, dislikes, taste in music—"

"Isn't that what a first date's for?" he interrupted. "To find out all these vastly important details? Why would you rob me of the pleasure?"

Gwen raised her hands in concession. "Fine. Go into the lioness's den unprepared. She will eat you alive."

"Yeah, but what a way to go."

"You're impossible," she said as she pivoted on her heel. "Maybe Addie will have more luck with you."

Ethan jolted in his seat. "What?" He turned to the door just as Addie breezed through it, the bells jingling merrily and his heart humming right along with them. Good grief, he had it bad.

She waved to Gwen but otherwise ignored all other patrons in the shop. Except him. The smile on her face wavered only slightly as she looked him up and down. "That what you're wearing on your date?"

How did she know about his date? Hell, by now it was likely on the front page of *The Daily Dispatch*. He gazed down at the graphic T-shirt he wore. The words 'Don't bother me, I'm writing' were scrawled across the front in I'm-not-kidding font. Perhaps the message needed to be bigger, bolder, or written in neon lettering for it to make any difference to her. His accompanying khaki shorts didn't have any stains on them or anything. "I don't normally dress three hours in advance, so no. This is just my plain, old author uniform."

She took a seat opposite Ethan and jumped right back into the interrogation. "Do I get to judge you afterward?"

"Judge me?"

"Tell you everything you did wrong?"

"I hope not. I don't plan on talking about it, and it won't be taking place in the coffee shop for all eyes to see."

"Right, because the rest of us have nothing better to do with our time than eavesdrop on *your* dates."

"You're not happy for me?" he asked, pushing for her to say more, because her tone had passed mocking and came precariously close to something that sounded like jealousy.

Addie's eyes widened and she pressed a hand to her heart. He almost believed she was hurt by the accusation, then she smiled. "I'm *thrilled* for you. Really. In fact, I think you should wear exactly what you have on. Let her know right up front that the snark comes with the package."

"Can we please change the subject?" Talking about dating another woman with the woman he actually wanted to date was enough to give him hives.

She crossed her arms and leaned back in her seat. "My mom's taking me shopping to buy me a new mixer."

"Wow. Now *I'm* jealous."

Cocking her head to the side, she frowned. "Why are you saying it like that?"

"Like what?"

"Like, now *you're* jealous, implying that *I'm* jealous of you going on a date with Hannah. I'm not jealous of your date."

"Okay."

"I have plenty of my own dates."

Ethan fought back his laughter. "Oh, I'm well aware."

"Good."

He nodded, expecting her to continue. When silence prevailed, he swallowed a few sips of tea, then said, "Now that we have that settled, what happened to your old mixer?"

"Oh, Maybelline's dying a slow and agonizing death. I wanted to keep her as long as possible . . . You get attached to these things, you know?"

"Well, sure."

"So I had a friend look at her, even took her into a shop, but the repairs are too costly. Makes more sense to get a new one."

He nodded again and took another drink. Feeling her gaze on him, he glanced up to find her staring as if he were swallowing battery acid. "Something wrong?"

"Uh, no. No. You're just . . . with the tea again."

"Can I buy you a cup?"

She waved him off. "Thanks, but I have to leave soon. My mother's meeting me shortly."

"Right, the great search for Maybelline 2.0. Does your mom live nearby?"

"In the city. She only visits when she's feeling guilty for her parental shortcomings, and then she buys me something new and shiny to make up for it."

Addie fidgeted in her seat, like the topic was an uncomfortable one for her. He could relate. He'd rather talk about his date with Hannah than rehash the many arguments he'd endured with dear old Mom and Dad. Though, to his recollection, his parents had never bought him any writing-related supplies, or felt guilty, so she had him beat there.

"I'm sorry," he said, and he meant it.

"Eh. Most of my kitchen appliances came from her, so . . . ."

He met her cheeky smile with one of his one. "Get the most expensive one with all the magical mixing powers."

"I plan on going top of the line," she said, shooting him a wink. Her phone buzzed on the table. She glanced at the screen, muttered something incoherent, and tucked the phone in her purse. "She's almost at my place. I better go."

"Have fun," Ethan said as she stood.

"I'll try." She walked several steps away, then paused. Turning to face him suddenly, she said, "Enjoy your date, Hemingway."

He smiled. *I'll try.*

Addie spun on her heel and passed by the counter before she left. Gwen skipped out of the kitchen looking almost in a daze, her hair and once-crisply-pressed shirt both a bit rumpled. While the girls engaged in a quick exchange, a guy decked out in a security guard uniform made his exit from the kitchen. Gwen's obvious partner in crime tried to sneak behind them unnoticed, but Addie was sharp as a tack.

"You've got some lipstick on the corner of your mouth, Shawn," she pointed out, smirking.

The man blushed thirty different shades of red as he rubbed at the incriminating mark, then hurried to the door.

"Later, babe," Gwen called after him.

"Byeeeee, Shawwwwn," Addie cooed.

Gwen stared at the exit long after he'd left and let out a gusty sigh. "I could watch that tight ass walk away from me all day long."

Addie laughed. "Speaking of tight asses, I'll see you at yoga tonight. Don't forget the pretzels." She blew Gwen a kiss and headed out the door.

Grabbing the coffee pot from the burner, Gwen circled around the tables, topping up cups. When she passed by Ethan's, he said, "Are you sure that's sanitary?" nodding to the kitchen and what was clearly going on in said kitchen only moments ago.

"It's all above the belt, hon," she said with a grin. "Sure is good to be the boss."

With that, she whisked away, leaving Ethan to ponder. Seemed like just about everyone had someone to kiss. Everyone but him. Hannah gave the impression that she didn't shy away from affection—public or otherwise.

Tonight was a chance. An opportunity not only to kiss and be kissed, but to change his status from single to . . . actively pursuing. To prove that he was available and ready for what the dating world entailed.

If given the chance, he'd kiss her. He would. He'd put every bit of unsolicited advice he'd given to Addie into practice. Hannah deserved a fair shot just as much as he did. Whatever happened, he could go home tonight proud that he'd put himself out there for the taking.

Get ready, Hannah. This will be a night you won't forget.

For the third time that night, Addie lost her balance and wound up in a heap on the floor, earning a none-too-pleased glare from their guest yoga instructor, Evangeline.

"Ya know, for a woman who has the word 'angel' in her name, she's a touch on the demonic side, don'tcha think?" Addie whispered to Gwen.

Gwen chuckled and helped Addie back to her feet. Again. Her chuckle was shushed. Again.

"How can she even hear us?" Gwen murmured. "We're at the back of the room. There has to be, like, twenty-five people in here."

Twenty-five hardly sweaty, freakishly silent, perfectly balanced people. Julian's Yoga Studio drew a healthy crowd of yoga enthusiasts on any night of the week, but tonight's group screamed of Stepford.

"Now, bring your feet together, tighten your core, and prepare to become the king of the birds. The Eagle Pose requires unwavering concentration," Evangeline said, her eyes fixed on Addie and Gwen. "Bend your knees slightly, and, balancing on your right foot, bring your left foot up and cross your left thigh over the right." As she spoke, she effortlessly moved her own body into the correct position to demonstrate. "Hook the top of your left foot behind the lower right calf, remembering all the while to breathe through the nose . . . ."

Gwen managed to twist her torso into something resembling a winged creature. Considering her struggles with even more basic poses tonight, Addie was positive if she attempted to soar like an eagle, she'd wind up flat on the floor again, so she simply admired Gwen's form. "You are the wind beneath my wings," she whispered, causing Gwen to snort.

"If our mouths are closed, I shouldn't be hearing any talking," came Evangeline's sharp rebuke.

Feeling antsy under Evangeline's judging gaze, Addie attempted to contort her body into a magnificent bird, but it was no use. She felt so shaky. Grumbling in frustration, she told Gwen she needed a break and went in search of her water bottle. The hardwood floor squeaked noisily under her feet, because why wouldn't it? You could hear a mouse breathe in that room.

When she found her bright green bottle peeking out of her gym bag, she chugged down a third of it, sighing in relief. Evangeline rattled off more instructions, but Addie was oblivious to them, her focus drawn to the big picture windows that lined the front of the studio, overlooking the street three floors below.

Somewhere out there, Ethan was having dinner. With Hannah. On a date.

But that was fine. Good for them. Her stomach didn't appear to agree, though, forming a tight knot, making her wonder why her inner body could do yoga better than her outer body. *I'm happy for him. Not jealous. He deserves to be happy, too. Yes, TOO. Because I have Tyler, and Tyler is my happy place.*

Coaching herself to think Tyler thoughts, over and over again, Addie shoved her bottle inside her bag and wove her way back to her mat next to Gwen's. Her friend was currently Wonder Woman-ing it in an enviable warrior pose.

Addie locked her gaze on Evangeline as she lunged into position, practically daring the woman to find fault with her glorious form. "I am Diana Prince. I am Xena. I am Joan of Arc," she spoke in a voice just above a whisper. "I am—"

"Going down," Gwen said in alarm as Addie's back leg lost traction and she toppled over. "How do you fall out of warrior pose? Is there vodka in that water bottle?"

"I wish." She sat up on her knees, looking through the rows of Stepford yogis to find Evangeline smirking at her. *Okay, you win this round, Dragon Lady.*

"And now, class, let us return to the lotus position. Sitting up nice and tall . . . ."

"Oooh," Addie said excitedly, turning to Gwen. "A sitting one? I think we're bonding, Cruella and I. Either that or she feels sorry for me."

"Place your feet on the opposing thighs, shoulders back, neck long," Evangeline said. "We're going to do some alternate nostril breathing to help relax and settle our minds and bodies."

Addie cringed, having experienced this technique before with Julian. "I hate this one," she complained to Gwen. "I can't do it."

Gwen arched an eyebrow. "You know it's just breathing, right? I think even *you* have that down."

"I'm fine breathing through my right nostril," Addie explained, "but lefty is the problem. Deviated septum."

The room filled with the sounds of normal noses functioning the way they were intended to. Addie attempted to join in on the inhale . . . and then her nose whistled. Gwen's startled guffaw kicked off the chorus of giggles that spread through the studio like wildfire, and soon the entire class collapsed with laughter. As expected, Addie received the evil eye from their beloved teacher. "Can't wait to see what Cruella will have to say about this."

Ethan arrived outside Burger Bros. with ten minutes to spare. The place was a step up from a hole in the wall, or half a step, really, but the food smelled incredible. He rolled back the sleeves of his dress shirt, took a deep breath, and walked inside. A family stood in line in front of him, so he casually scanned the interior while they waited for a table. He couldn't see Hannah. Should he get a table, then? Or wait by the door? Wait outside? Christ. Maybe he should text her to say he was here and getting them a table. But it might be better to wait until he had a table before he told her he had one so he could tell her exactly which table he had. Hell. He hated texting. He hated dating.

Holtz, snap out of it. Be cool. Be a good dater. This is your chance, so make it count. Just as he finished his internal pep talk, the host greeted him with a friendly smile.

"Welcome to Burger Bros.!" she said, grabbing a menu.

"Thanks. I'll actually need two menus. I'm meeting someone else here."

Her smile widened as she reached for a second menu. "Not a problem at all, sir. Follow me." She directed him to a booth tucked around the corner from the entrance, dropped off the menus, and wished him a wonderful night.

He tapped his fingers on the tabletop, glanced at his watch, then pulled his phone from his pocket to check if she'd texted him. Seven o'clock sharp. No text. No Hannah.

Okay, so not every woman was punctual . . . like Addie. Some preferred to be fashionably late. And Hannah had a business to run, and employees to manage, and certainly a life outside of dating, so there were unlimited reasons why she might be running late. A whole two minutes late now.

Ethan observed the goings on around him. The place buzzed with activity. People of all ages, parties of all sizes. Pop art lined the walls, along with intermittent grease stains. Cleanliness may not have been a top priority, but, judging by the wide eyes and empty plates, they made a damn good burger.

Picking up his phone again, he decided to text her to say he had a table near the entrance. While he was one-finger typing the message, the unmistakable scent of coconut filled his nostrils. His head shot up to find Hannah gazing at him, her eyes crinkled in amusement.

"This seat taken?" she asked with a broad wink.

Tossing his phone . . . somewhere, he slid from the booth and stood next to her and took her in from top to bottom. She wore her hair down in loose ringlets that framed her heart-shaped face. Her makeup was much lighter than he remembered seeing in the coffee shop, showing a younger, softer side of her. The turquoise dress showcased her curves, gave a tantalizing, oh-so-brief glimpse of her breasts, and put her shapely legs on full display. He swallowed hard as he looked up at her. Yes, up. The toothpick heels made her a good inch taller than him, which weirdly turned him on, too.

Not trusting his voice, he guided her with one hand on her lower back to the seat opposite his, then returned to his own. She appeared even more amused by his inability to speak.

"I think we need booze, and lots of it," she said with a nod.

"Yeah. Yes."

Their waiter, having heard the exchange, made his way to them in a hurry. "Hey, folks, I'm Tanner, also known as your personal bartender. What can I getcha?"

"Just bring us the Big League pitcher to start," Hannah said. "You like beer, yes?" she asked Ethan, who nodded.

"One Big League, coming up! Be right back, guys."

When Tanner disappeared, she reached for Ethan's hand, which he'd been unconsciously tapping on the table again. "Were you texting me? Before?"

"Oh, um, yeah. Just to let you know where I was sitting."

"You're a one-finger texter?"

"Well, I mean, I'm used to the bigger keys on my laptop. I don't really use my phone much. Or at all."

She squeezed his hand. "That's so cute!"

"It is?"

He nearly jumped out of his seat as her bare foot made contact with his calf under the table. "You don't date much, do you?"

Before he could choke out a response, the alcohol cavalry came to his rescue. Hannah took the liberty of filling both their glasses to the brim. Ethan drank a third of his.

"Attaboy! Loosen up those lips of yours." She equalled his efforts, then leaned back with a slow, satisfied smile.

Her foot was gone, and he found that he missed the contact. "I hardly ever date," he confessed. "I hate it, to be honest. But I don't hate this. You. What's happening so far . . . You look amazing, by the way. Have I said that yet?" He closed his mouth, wishing he could glue it shut permanently. God, he was acting like an absolute fool. He wouldn't blame her if she left now and let him drown his idiocy in the remaining beer. When he finally summoned the nerve to lift his head, he was astonished to see her grinning like a Cheshire cat.

"Drink some more. It's working."

Laughing, he did as she requested. Hannah had a definite domineering quality about her, which, again, served to turn him on rather than off. She topped up his glass once he'd polished off three quarters of it and signaled their waiter for another pitcher.

"Do you?" he asked. "Date much, I mean."

"Well, I first-date. Lay the groundwork for . . . future encounters, if you catch my drift."

He assumed she meant sexual encounters, but he didn't feel comfortable asking her to clarify. Instead, he redirected. "So you'd describe yourself as a casual dater as opposed to someone who's looking for a relationship, then?"

Hannah chuckled as she fluffed her hair. "Getting to the tough questions already, huh?"

Their waiter stopped by to exchange the empty pitcher for a fresh one, then he took their orders. Hannah ordered a burger with the works and a tower of onion rings. "To share," she said. He had a sneaking suspicion she wouldn't be doing so much sharing, but he loved a woman who wasn't afraid to eat. It showed her confidence. Or appetite. Hannah gave the impression she had a very healthy appetite for more than just food. Ethan ordered a burger as well, then poured them each a tall glass of beer from the new pitcher.

She raised her glass and he clinked his against hers. "Here's to dates in dives!"

He laughed. "I'll drink to that."

While she swallowed down her drink, she kept her eyes trained on him. "To answer your question . . . well, let me put it this way. I've tried the serious stuff. Looking for something real. But, I swear, it's like I'd go on dates with guys—really great dates—and never hear from them again. Sometimes I wondered if the guys I dated, like . . . died or something."

Ethan blinked. "Died?"

She grinned at his reaction. "I know they probably didn't actually die, but it was easier for me to think they did than to accept the fact that they just didn't want to get to know me and couldn't even bother telling me that."

"They call that 'ghosting' now, don't they?"

"Yeah," she said. "And it sucks, big time, if you're the ghostee. The ghost floats away scot-free."

Where were the Ghostbusters when you needed them? Nonsense like this was the very reason he avoided the dating arena. Hannah's theory of her dates' disappearances, though some might find it a tad morbid, was like candy to his writer mind. "How do you think the last guy died?"

She frowned at first but gradually caught his meaning, a smile stretching across her face. "He's a chef—"

"*Was* a chef," Ethan corrected.

"Right!" she said with a laugh. "He was working on a flambé and added a touch too much alcohol."

"*Sacré bleu!*"

"The flames shot up so high they burned his eyes, and without his sight, he couldn't cook, he couldn't gaze upon himself in the mirror . . . so he jumped off the roof of a building." She tipped back her head and drank, perhaps in salute to the lost soul.

Ethan clapped in appreciation of the cleverly woven tale. "You threw me for a twist there at the end."

"Then there was poor Jordan before him. He took me ice skating and shivered the entire time. Big brute of a guy who couldn't handle a bit of cold."

"Did he fall through the ice on his next date? Die from hypothermia?"

"Nope. He tried to show off for the skinny bitch on his arm, but there was this kid who was outskating him. So he challenged the kid to a race, except he lost control just before they reached the end of the rink, and he plowed through the boards . . . and fell off the roof of the building!"

Ethan laughed out loud. "The rink was on top of a building?"

"Yeah, obviously." She giggled along with him. "God rest his soul."

"I'm kinda glad we're on solid ground right now."

"I'm having a lot of fun," she said.

"Me, too." And he was, no question. Things were going much better than he'd thought they would. The laughter, the banter. Reminded him a lot of someone else . . .

15

"I can't believe you got us kicked out of yoga class!"

Gwen gaped at Addie. "Me? That was all your handiwork, Mitchell."

Addie snagged the bag of pretzels from Gwen and grabbed another handful. They'd barely made it down the steps and out the door before Addie'd ripped open the bag. "You're the one who started the giggle fest."

"It just struck me as hilarious. Your whistling septum."

"It's not nice to laugh at another person's breathing problems."

"You're gonna choke and have far worse breathing problems if we don't park our butts down somewhere."

Addie stopped walking and took a three-sixty view of their surroundings. Julian's Yoga Studio was a twenty-minute drive from Kendal, and neither of them were in a hurry to get home. They usually went out for a drink with some of their classmates following the session, but tonight's batch would likely turn up their noses at such a wicked suggestion. "Aren't you glad we got away from the Stepford yogis?"

"There!" Gwen pointed. "Park bench, ten o'clock."

"Oh, good eye!" Addie refrained from eating any more pretzels until they made their way to the bench, which she thought showed excellent restraint on her part. But as soon as her butt hit the metal and she ditched her gym bag, she was back on Snarf Central Time. "See, I really think they should incorporate the pretzels into the class. I bet my balance would improve." She brought both feet onto the bench in a cross-legged position and pressed her free thumb and middle finger together. "Ommmm-nom-nom-nommmm."

Gwen rolled her eyes. "Your balance has never been great, but tonight you seemed way off. What was up with that?"

Addie stopped munching, feeling a dramatic shift in the seriousness of their conversation. "The, uh . . . the poses were hard."

"Evangeline didn't ask us to do anything we haven't done before with Julian. You were in another world."

Putting the bag of pretzels aside, she brought her feet back to the ground and turned to face Gwen. "I was distracted, okay?"

"By?"

"My . . . mother." *Oh, that's good.* Gwen would believe her, too, because her mother was the very reason she started practicing yoga. "We went shopping, as you know. She bought me a fabulous mixer, by the way. The latest model. It has twice as many speeds as Maybelline, and the dough hook is a thing of beauty—"

"Addie," Gwen cut in. "Focus."

"Right, sorry. Anyway, we got to talking about Tyler. I told her things were going really well, and that's pretty much all I told her because we're not into the whole sharing personal details about our lives thing. But I like him a lot. We've had three amazing dates, and for some reason, despite all that, I freaked when he wanted to have sexy times . . . . ."

"Whoa, what?"

". . . And he hasn't texted or called me since, which isn't a big deal, but we've been texting regularly since we started dating, so it just seems a bit off."

"Okay, back up a few hundred steps here. Why did you freak out?"

Addie shrugged, not wanting to disclose everything to Gwen. "I dunno. I guess it all seemed too fast."

"Did you tell him that?"

"Yes, and he was completely fine with it. Not pushy or anything."

"Then that's perfect. Maybe he's trying to give you some space, not wanting to freak you out any more than you already are."

Gwen had a point. She hadn't meant to bring up the subject of Tyler, but she was grateful her mind had steered her in that direction. She'd been quietly stressing about the way she'd left things, but it made sense that he'd give her space after she'd essentially requested exactly that.

"It's still new," Gwen continued. "You're both still feeling each other out. You could text him and tell him about you getting us kicked out of yoga class. Great conversation topic."

Addie elbowed Gwen in the side. "Try again."

"Ow!" She reached over Addie for the bag of pretzels and clutched them to her chest protectively. "No more pretzels for you." Gwen popped a few into her mouth and chewed. "I wonder how Hannah's date is going."

"Hmm? Oh. Yeah. I'm sure it's fine." Addie stared at the street, where a group of runners were assembling for an evening jog. The Stepford yogis were probably folding up their mats now. Hell, some of them might even join the joggers. She was about to share that comment with Gwen when a pretzel hit her cheek, thrown by a woman more twisted than the baked biscuit itself. "What was that for?"

Gwen snorted. "You are so obvious."

"What?"

"Like you don't care how the date is going."

Addie felt her cheeks growing warm, and it had nothing to do with the impromptu pretzel attack. "I don't. It's none of my business."

"Then why'd you get all weird when Hannah asked about dating Ethan at the Cup-A-Cabana?"

She scoffed. "I didn't get *all weird*. I just . . . thought they were an odd match, that's all."

"Uh-huh." Gwen's knowing smirk bugged the crap out of her.

"It's true. They're adults. He's single, she's single. They can date."

"I'm not as oblivious as you think I am." She held up her bag of edible weapons and shook them . . . either enticingly or menacingly. Perhaps a combo of the two. "I'd bet every pretzel in this bag that you were thinking about Ethan in the yoga studio, and he's the reason, more than Tyler, that you couldn't make like a tree."

Addie shook her head but couldn't formulate a retort in time for Gwen not to see through the façade. Her silence didn't help her case, either. "You are extremely annoying sometimes. You know that, right?"

Gwen laughed. "I should have bet something better, like ice cream."

"Oh, man, I could totally go for some ice cream."

"C'mon," Gwen said, pushing off the bench and helping Addie to her feet. "I'm buying."

Three hours and two empty pitchers later, Ethan smiled as Hannah regaled him with yet another story of the high jinks that ensued at The Barkery. "And so little Chester hid behind the counter, but that's where the mouse was, and the poor thing shot ten feet in the air!"

"The mouse or Chester?"

"Chester! Oh, it was hilarious." She shook with laughter, tears forming in the corners of her eyes. Taking several calming breaths, she finally got herself under control again. A rare moment of silence descended. "So, this isn't working, right?"

"What?" he asked cautiously, hoping against all hope they were on the same page.

"This." She gestured between them. "Us."

Relief whooshed from his chest. "Nope."

"You're fun, funny, cute as the dickens, but . . . zero chemistry."

Ethan might have been offended if he weren't in complete agreement. "Thank you for saying it first."

Hannah covered his hand with her own, just like she'd done at the start of the date. "I want you to know that I don't regret tonight. I loved hanging out with you."

"Same here."

"It's so great that we're on the same wavelength. No ghosting necessary! I want us to be friends, okay?"

He sat back and marveled at the situation. A night out with a beautiful woman. He had fun, let loose, had a few beers, and really got to know someone he might not otherwise have had an opportunity to know. He put himself out there, and he didn't hate it. To top it off, he'd made a new friend, something he'd been quietly yearning for since moving to Kendal. Not a bad outcome. "I'd like that," he said, earning a smile from her.

Their waiter circled by to check on them again and dropped off the bill as requested. Ethan automatically reached for it.

"No," Hannah said. "You don't have to."

He waved her off. "I insist."

"But I friend-labeled you before the bill. We should go Dutch treat."

"Nah, it's *my* treat. You can buy me a coffee sometime." And then he winked at her. When in the hell did he become a winker? Is this what dating did to him? Or was it the beer? Shaking off the hideous action, he pulled some cash out of his wallet and stuck it inside the bill folder. That settled, he slid out of the booth and helped her do the same.

They walked together outside and stood for an awkward moment, neither really knowing how to properly end a date that no longer qualified as a romantic one.

"You know," Hannah began, gazing at him in a more-than-friendly way, "the night is still young. If you wanted, we could add some benefits to this friendship thing we got goin' on . . . ."

For a split second, he almost said yes. He was a guy, after all, and he had needs. But, he'd never been *that* guy. One who had sex for the sake of sex, no matter how tempting the invitation. Hannah had so much going for her. Gorgeous face, incredible body, vivacious personality. Most men wouldn't need to look past the first two in order to give her the green light, but he got to see every side of her, every facet of her individuality. And she was worth more to him than an easy lay.

"I get it. You aren't that kind of guy."

He smiled apologetically. "I appreciate the invitation. I just—"

"So cute. So innocent. *So* not my type."

The blunt assessment shook a laugh from him. "Hey, maybe you could ask for that waiter's number. Tanner, right? I saw him checking you out a few times."

Her eyes widened with obvious interest. "Ooh, he was cute!"

"Good night, Hannah." He leaned in and gave her a brief kiss on the cheek.

"Good night, Ethan." She smiled, darted a glance both ways, fluffed her hair, and then marched right back into Burger Bros. again.

He watched her enter like she owned the place, and he rooted for her all the way. Tanner was about to receive the best tip of his adult life. Certain that Cupid would handle the rest, Ethan spun on his heel and headed for his car in the parking lot, an unexpected lightness in his step.

He did it. He dated. Proved to himself—to the world—that he was ready to be a contender.

Now, if only he could prove it to Addie.

Yawning for the umpteenth time that afternoon, Addie ambled along the sidewalk toward The Barkery. She'd taken Gwen's advice and texted Tyler last night, who enthusiastically replied. And back and forth they went with the text-à-text into the wee hours of the morning. He said he'd be busy with his crew trying to finish a big job over the next week, so they'd set a fourth date for the following Saturday, agreeing to meet at the Cup-A-Cabana and go from there. She felt much better about where things stood between them, but that didn't prevent her from wanting the scoop on the Hannah/Ethan date . . . for curiosity's sake.

She considered asking Ethan directly, but he'd already read too much into her interest the day before. So she sought out the next best source.

Gripping the tennis ball-covered door knob, she strode into The Barkery, which was every bit deserving of its name. Tile floors with paw print accents, artwork featuring such classics as 'Dogs Playing Poker,' over-the-counter doggie treats of every size, shape, and color that looked disturbingly appetizing.

"Addie!" Hannah squealed, causing several canines to shudder at the decibel level. She scuttled around the counter and pulled her into a hug.

"Hannah, hey," she said, easing herself from the woman's near-suffocating clinch. "I had a few extra pies left after my loop, so I brought them for you and your staff." She lifted the paper bag in her hand.

"Ooh! People food!" Hannah squished her again, then happily click-clacked behind the counter to disperse the pies to her employees.

While she was occupied, Addie squatted down and made friends with the wiener-dog sniffing her toes. Muffy, Hannah's Labradoodle, seemed more interested in MoJo, the lone cat on the premises. The two eyed each other curiously. MoJo's tail began swaying, the universal cat signal for get-the-hell-away-from-me, but apparently not for this cat. He nuzzled his head against Muffy, then collapsed to the floor and rolled onto his back. Addie followed his hot-pink leash upwards until she spotted his owner, Carmen Deacon, leaning over the counter to select MoJo's favorite biscuits.

Most everyone in town knew Carmen and her beloved pet. She was Kendal's self-appointed one-woman welcoming committee, and MoJo, her far less congenial sidekick . . . except when in the company of dogs. Carmen and Edna had been quite close, sharing a love of spiritual teachings.

Hannah knelt down next to Addie. "It's such a perk being able to take this special little princess to work with me every day." She rubbed and patted Muffy's thick coat. When MoJo shot Hannah a look, she doled the same affection to him, and he purred in appreciation.

"Are you selling cat treats now, too?" Addie asked, nodding to Carmen.

"Um, no." Hannah lowered her voice conspiratorially. "MoJo's going through an 'identity crisis,' so we're just playing along."

"Got it."

"I think the other dogs, the *real* dogs, are starting to believe it, which is the scary part."

"MoJo's just a cat pretending to be a dog, pretending to be a cat."

Hannah snorted, then squeezed Addie's shoulder before pushing to her feet. "Gotta go grab some more kibble from the back. Be out in a jiffy."

Addie stood, too, needing to give her joints a break. A flash of movement outside drew her gaze. There stood a man wielding a stack of paper and a roll of tape. "Dog Leash Dude," she blurted, then smacked her hand over her mouth. God help the guy if Hannah found out he was lurking nearby. But regardless of Hannah's less-than-adoring opinion of him, he seemed decent enough. Addie hadn't interacted with him much, but if his most nefarious plot in life was to keep dogs safe and their owners accountable, that wasn't such a bad thing. Plus, he was kinda cute in his dark-rimmed glasses. Definite Clark Kent vibe happening there.

Their eyes met as he took a step forward, preparing to affix one of the posters to the window. Alarmed, Addie lunged toward the glass, waving her arms frantically. "Go! Get! Shoo!" she mouthed, as if he were a dog himself.

He reared back with a blink, followed by an affronted frown, then slowly but surely he walked away with his tail between his legs. Just in the nick of time, too. She saw Hannah's reflection in the glass, a huge bag of kibble slung over her shoulder. A vision of that bag being thrown through the window at Poster Boy made Addie all the more glad he'd taken the hint and split.

She held the door open as the last of The Barkery customers made off with their merchandise, giving an extra pat to the wiener-dog's head. Only Hannah, another employee, and Carmen remained in the shop, along with Addie. A perturbed meow from the lump of fur at Carmen's feet reminded her of MoJo's presence, too. He wasn't getting the attention he craved from Carmen, who was talking a blue streak to the ceiling.

Addie meandered behind the counter next to Hannah and whispered, "Who's she talking to?"

"Delilah Frost," Hannah replied without missing a beat.

"As in the former owner?"

Hannah nodded.

"The dead one?"

"Yup. She feels her spirit in here."

Carmen turned toward them suddenly and said, "Delilah thinks you're adding too much liver powder to the blue biscuits. And you should bring back the peanut butter balls."

"I will definitely take that into consideration," Hannah said, sounding genuine.

Addie bit back a grin as the two women continued their exchange, like it was completely normal to be having a conversation that involved a woman no longer of this earth. She wondered if these so-called requests Carmen relayed were geared more toward MoJo's desires than her deceased friend's.

When the two women seemed to run out of things to talk about the un-living, Addie cleared her throat and broached the subject of last night's date. "Hey, so, um, how'd it go . . . with Ethan?"

"Oh!" Hannah said, as if only just now remembering she'd been on a date. "It was a blast! He's super-cute, so funny, we drank and laughed and had the best time . . . ."

Blindsided by the revelation, and not sure why, she reached for the counter to steady herself. This was good. She was glad for them. Why shouldn't they have a good time? They deserved to have a good time, and drink, and laugh, and—

"But he's just . . . no. Not for me. I mean, you know I like my guys a little rough around the edges, but Ethan is, like, the polar opposite of rough. He looks like he exfoliates."

"Not that I know of," Carmen cut in. "'Course, I don't know all the boy's grooming habits."

Hannah nodded. "He's a good, clean, honest-to-goodness gentleman. Not at all what I'm looking for."

Addie gripped the counter even tighter, her emotions having been put through the wringer. Her toes tingled with relief, which she'd ignore, for the time being. "So you're not gonna date him again, then?"

"God, no. I'd screw him, but he's not into that."

Addie's eyes widened. "He's not?"

"I mean, I'm sure he's *into* it," she clarified, "but not with the no-strings-attached stuff. See? Too squeaky-clean."

She suddenly found herself wanting to come to his defense, to say, "Don't you know how wonderful that is? To find a guy who wants to know you and not just jump into bed with you? Who actually wants to feel something?" Fortunately, she kept her mouth shut, knowing such a remark would be pounced on faster than a T-bone steak on The Barkery's floor.

And then Hannah turned the tables on her. "How are things going with Tyler?"

"Uh, great! Really great. We're going on our fourth date next Saturday."

"Oh, yay!" Hannah pulled her into another hug and squeezed hard. "That's amazing!"

Addie smiled, despite the near-strangulation. "You did a terrific job matchmaking for me."

"I don't think it's too big a leap to try my magic with dogs, then, do you? I'm thinking some kind of doggie speed-dating event. It would be a hoot!"

"Hmm." Carmen looked pointedly at MoJo. "I just hate to think that some four-legged friends might be excluded from such an event."

Hannah's enthusiasm wavered for only a second. "Of course, MoJo is more than welcome to participate, too. We'll just have to specify that he's looking for a 'friend' and not a 'mating partner' in his profile."

Addie glanced from one woman to the other. *Dating profiles? For pets? Good grief.* Yet, as outrageous as the whole idea was, she couldn't help but contemplate what some of the profiles might say. *Ginger loves long walks in the park, belly rubs, and eau de 'other dogs.' Brutus likes big bones and he cannot lie. Sadie's always submissive to her master. Toby will shake his tail for treats, and he'll let the right girl ride shotgun.* She giggled out loud, earning stares from the other two women. "Right, *I'm* the strange one."

"People often judge a lady by the company she keeps," Carmen said with a wink.

The comment amused Addie for a different reason—the fact that eccentric Carmen shared her residence with Ethan. She'd have to ask him about their interactions next time they saw each other.

"Oh, you've got to be kidding me!" Hannah cried.

Addie winced when she saw Poster Boy loitering near the door again. Hannah threw off her apron and rushed outside to confront him. Addie huddled next to Carmen at the window to watch the action unfold. The Barkery owner dished out the first blow, stealing the stack of posters from her stunned opponent, motioning to rip them in half. He charged at her, but she veered left, then hooked a sharp right down the sidewalk with him hot on her sky-high heels. How the woman could run in those things was anyone's guess.

Carmen tsked. "There's no love lost between those two."

"Nope."

"But oh, those hands. Have you seen his hands? Lord, I'd love to read those palms."

Addie chuckled. "You might get a chance to on 'Palm' Sunday."

"That's right, kitten. I'd love to get a look at yours, too, especially now that I hear you've landed the whale."

"We'll see." The pie business was usually profitable on Sundays in the town square, thanks to hungry churchgoers, Sunday strollers, and the crowd Carmen drew to her purple palm-reading tent. But Addie usually avoided that tent like the plague. Not because she thought it was a lot of rubbish. Quite the opposite.

"All right, honey, you run along. Do the things that young people do. I'll hold down the fort here till Hurricane Hannah returns."

Addie smiled, grateful for the offer. "Thanks, Carmen. Take care. And you too, MoJo." She waved goodbye and walked out the door with an extra spring in her step.

16

Addie spent most of the next week baking, biking, and breaking in her new mixer. She'd decided to let things flow at a more natural pace with Tyler. To live in the moment with him, and, if it felt right, take that next big step. Their texts had gotten much steamier as a result of her newfound freeness . . . Well, *his* had. Hers still contained more emojis than salacious remarks. She'd just never really been the sexting type, but Tyler was a total pro.

After tossing her apron over the back of a kitchen chair, Addie gave an appreciative pat to Maybelline 2.0 for working like a dream. She still kept Maybelline The First, storing her in a place of honor atop her kitchen cabinet—an ever-present reminder of her journey as a novice baker to one who profited from it.

As one might expect, such tireless baking resulted in a depletion of her supplies, namely flour, so on Friday she tidied herself up and dashed to the grocery store to replenish. Her grandmother always told her that the secret to baking was in the flour. The fresher the flour, the sweeter the results. It was the one ingredient she splurged on, but she had to drive two towns over to Essential Ingredients for just the right blend.

While she perused the different brands, she heard a voice say, "Come here often?"

Smirking at the overused pick-up line, she turned to find Matt Tully holding a basket full of baking supplies. Memories of the night he'd paid her a visit to fix her broken mixer and instead had broken down himself trickled through her mind. "You clearly do."

A red blush dotted the larger-than-life man's cheeks. "These are for my mom. She broke her ankle a couple weeks ago. Dad's waiting on her hand and foot at home, so I'm stuck doing her shopping."

Though she couldn't claim to know Matt very well, she could tell he was the sort to offer his help as opposed to being forced into it, but she played along. "You gonna do her baking for her, too?"

"Hell no. Not unless she wants the house burned down in the process."

Addie chuckled. "I'm guessing not."

"Dad's filling in as her backup baker. She watches him like a hawk so he doesn't try to sneak an extra cup of chocolate chips into all her recipes." He set his basket on the floor and shoved his hands into his pockets. "Listen, thanks again for . . . you know."

She nodded. "Thank you, too."

"Did you get a new mixer?"

"I did, actually. Santa came early this year. Cherry-red, just like her sister."

He smiled, and when Matt Tully smiled, she could practically guarantee every woman within a three-mile radius swooned. "Looks like progress on other fronts, too."

"Hmm?"

"I saw him walking you home a week or two ago . . . You and that guy. I mean, I'm assuming it's the guy you were talking about at your place—"

"Oh, Ethan? You saw us?"

"Yeah." He shot her a meaningful look. "Guess you didn't notice me."

Now it was her turn to blush. "That wasn't . . . I mean, we aren't . . . It's not anything serious. We're friends."

"If you say so."

"I *do* say so," she said more defensively than she meant to. "I'll put a little announcement over the PA system in case you think any other shoppers need to know."

Matt laughed, thankfully, saving her from digging herself any deeper into the pit of denial. "Or put up some posters like that dog leash guy. Man, I've seen those stupid things in every town. If only he cared about trees the way he cares about keeping Fido fettered."

"No kidding," she said, relieved for the change in topic.

"I keep ripping 'em down, so I'm probably not helping."

"Eh, depends who you ask."

He bent to scoop up his basket again. "I better go before Mom sends out a search party. Take care."

"You, too."

"Oh, Matt!" she blurted, stopping him in his tracks. He turned back to her and she lowered her voice so only he could hear her next words. "That night you came to my place? I, um, read your tea leaves. It's a thing I do . . . ." Expecting him to share Ethan's reaction to such a revelation, she was pleasantly surprised when Matt listened with keen interest. "I had a vision that things will work out for you and Amy."

"Really?"

The hope written across his face made her heart feel so full. "Yes. Just . . . fight for it. Fight for her."

Matt nodded. He didn't question her. He didn't call her crazy for believing what she saw in the bottom of a cup. "Thank you," he said, his voice gruff.

With another nod, Matt stomped away in his work boots, his shoulders almost as wide as the aisle. She didn't realize she was staring at him until he whirled to face her again. "I really hope you find what you're looking for," he said, and she knew he wasn't referring to the items on the shelves. He gave her a gentle smile and waved with his free hand before turning the corner.

Addie released an audible sigh. Damn him for being taken . . . even if the woman who'd stolen his heart hadn't yet recognized she possessed it. But she would. They'd figure things out.

She stooped to grab four bags of flour, dropping them into her basket, one by one, then grunted her way back to her feet again, basket in hand. As she walked toward the checkout, Matt's words kept echoing in her head. *Looks like progress on other fronts.* What exactly did "progress" look like? And how could a guy who was practically a stranger claim to detect "progress" between two people who were merely walking next to one another?

"That'll be $53.68, ma'am."

Well, it didn't matter what Matt *thought* he saw. There was nothing to see. Besides, the only man who mattered right now was the one she had plans with tomorrow.

"Ma'am?"

Addie jumped. "Oh! Sorry." She had zero recollection of arriving in the checkout line or putting her bags of flour on the conveyor belt, yet, there she was. "How much?"

The woman grinned and repeated the amount owing, waiting patiently as Addie fished out her wallet and paid the tab. An older gentleman offered to help her carry the bags of flour to her car, and she gratefully accepted.

Once the trunk had been loaded, she turned to thank the man, and her jaw promptly fell open. The guy across the street had dark, wavy hair, like Tyler. He was tall. Also like Tyler. He wore a leather jacket and clutched a leash with a schnauzer attached to it. Huh. Tyler had never mentioned having a twin brother before, but that was the only explanation for it. Why else would he be on the sidewalk with another woman. *Kissing* that other woman . . . in a very un-brotherly sort of way.

"Everything all right, ma'am?"

She jolted, forgetting the kind gentleman who'd helped her with her groceries. "No. I mean, yes. It's fine. Thank you so much for your help."

He nodded, then meandered back inside.

Alone once more, Addie stared for an uncomfortable amount of time at the two locking lips, clearly lost in their own little world. She had to stop herself from running through traffic to pry them apart. Perhaps a slight overreaction on her part. She and Tyler weren't exactly exclusive. Addie'd been on dates with many different guys as of late, but there hadn't been any other dates after she started seeing Tyler. And, really, once your tongue was down someone's throat, wasn't that the equivalent of saying, "Hey, we're exclusive now"? But here he was with his tongue jammed down another woman's throat instead.

Well, they were still on for Saturday, and they'd be having a little chit-chat about where and with whom tongues were appropriate.

Fed up with the NC-17-headed heat level of the sidewalk smoochers, she hopped in her car and sped home, making it there in record time. She trudged into the kitchen, the bags of flour landing with a *thunk* on the island counter. Huffing out a breath, she paced the floor. It was stifling in there. She needed to get out. Get some air.

Her bike was her livelihood and a lifesaver in times like these. This ride would be for leisure . . . and a public service. It might prevent her from committing a double homicide. She retrieved her bike from behind the house and set off on a circuit of the town. Peddling fast at first, she slowed as the comforts of home swam into focus. The gazebo in the town square. Puppies pulling their owners into The Barkery. Children and their parents playing in the park, celebrating the end of another work week.

In the distance, she spotted the public pool. *Oh, that's perfect.* She could cool off for a bit, swim a few laps, and get in another form of physical activity. Funny, with all the dates she'd been on in the past few weeks, none had led to anything even remotely physical . . . except for the dates with Tyler.

She was about to head home to grab her bathing suit when movement in the pool caught her attention. Spurring her bike into motion again, she peddled closer.

Water sprayed through the air and splattered the deck as the mystery swimmer canon-balled into the deep end of the pool. The waterlogged youngsters in Mrs. McCallister's care looked on in awe from the other side of the gate. They shouted their approval of his theatrics as their grandmother steered them back to the car, but not before blowing the guy a kiss. Addie chuckled as she rested her bike against the fence. Apparently, everyone was feeling overly amorous today.

Puffing out a breath as he resurfaced, the solo swimmer turned in the direction his admirers had stood moments ago, only to find Addie in their place. Her heart stuttered to a stop when their eyes locked.

Ethan.

He pushed off the edge and shot through the water like a torpedo, swimming harder and faster than she'd ever witnessed anyone swim. Lap two became lap twelve. Drawn to him like a magnet, she opened the safety fence and entered his sanctuary.

He stopped abruptly and reached for the edge. She could feel the heat of his gaze as she navigated the slippery deck with measured steps. The urge to pretend to lose her footing was overwhelming, just to see what Ethan would do . . . and maybe to get in a little foreplay of her own today. What? Everyone else was doing it. The lifeguard, with his nose pressed to the screen of his phone, would likely be none the wiser.

She didn't fake-fall after all. She sat in a lounge chair and stared straight at him, waiting for him to join her on land.

He didn't disappoint. Slapping his palms on the concrete edge, he hoisted himself out of the pool. Excess water dripped from his trunks as he closed the distance that separated them. Her gaze dropped to his chest, then lowered . . . and lingered.

"Lost?"

She jerked as if she'd been splashed by cold water. "Wha?"

He smiled. "Just wondered if you took a wrong turn. You live on the opposite side of town, and I never see you here, so—"

"Thanks for the geography lesson, Hemingway. I've been here before. I swim. Sometimes. Okay, like, twice since they put the pool in, but I—"

"You got a swimsuit on under there?"

She needlessly glanced down at the outfit she wore. "Uh, no."

"Too bad. The water's nice."

Back to ogling his body, she nodded. "It looks nice. The water, I mean." She cleared her throat. "Do you offer lessons?"

He bent down to retrieve the towel on the chair next to hers and started with his hair first, scrubbing his hand through it a few times, leaving delightfully boyish tufts pointing in every direction. Then he patted dry his collarbone, his toned, tanned arms, his torso. "You need some?" She imagined he went through a similar ritual after he showered.

"Uh-huh." Oh, lessons. He meant the lessons. "Er, no, I'm . . . I just . . . You have good form, is all." At his amused expression she was quick to add, "Swimming. I meant with the swimming. God. I need to stop talking." Her head fell forward and she stared at her feet, trying to hide the scorching blush that crept up her neck.

He laughed, and she felt the heat moving into her cheeks. "Thanks, Coach."

She had to get out of there—fast. Away from him and her hormone-y thoughts. She stood, wobbling slightly before regaining her balance. "I'll be at the coffee shop tomorrow. Maybe I'll see you there?"

He hooked the towel around his neck, standing there all cool and pool-ified and . . . Yes, time to go. "I'll be there."

"Good. Well, good. Okay." Ignoring the first safety rule on the list secured to the fence, she hustled for the exit. She wasn't sure what had ever possessed her to walk into the pool area in the first place. The truth was, she'd felt a bit discombobulated ever since she left the baking goods store. And jealous. And unjustifiably hurt.

The kiss she'd witnessed ran on replay in her mind and she just couldn't shake it. One of those cases of being in the wrong place at the right time. Or the right place at the wrong time. It was easy to pretend things were casual before, but now . . . she had to admit that there were real feelings on the line. If she liked Tyler enough to hate what she saw, then it was time to tell him. Or time to dump his sorry ass and move on.

Signaling a right turn, she pulled onto her street and decreased her speed. She tugged at her shorts, which were dangerously close to riding up her ass, and that's when she noticed the splashes of water on them.

Ethan. His strokes were as smooth and flawless as the sculpted muscles of his shoulders and arms. It wasn't the first time she'd seen him without a shirt, but this time those muscles were in glorious motion, and it was one of the most beautiful things she'd ever witnessed. When he'd climbed out of the pool, rivulets of water cascaded down his front, trickling along the grooves of his abdominals. Her throat convulsed as she recalled how erotic the sight had been.

Coasting to a stop, she hopped off her bike and walked it to the back of the house. She grabbed a can of oil and greased the chain so it could soak in before the next ride. *Keep busy. Just keep busy.*

If she kept her mind occupied, she wouldn't have to think about the fact that the man with the killer bod was Ethan. Because she had other things to think about, like her date with Tyler tomorrow.

Two-timing Tyler.

Chastising herself for the moniker, she retreated into the safety of her kitchen, where she could work out her womanly woes with a rolling pin. Great-Aunt Edna used to say, "Don't get so caught up in a man you can't think straight." Trust was a two-way street. If she wanted to pursue things with Tyler exclusively, then she needed to stop the side-dating (and flirting), too. They'd planned to meet tomorrow at the coffee shop for a quick bite, followed by a walk in the park—his suggestion. It was hard to picture a guy who rode a Harley happily hiking along a wooded trail.

A feline smile curved her lips as she envisioned a different trail altogether. A happy trail. Her mind summoned an image of Tyler's handsome face, then took a detour to his shoulders and chest. Her eyes slid shut as she enjoyed every moment of the descent until, somewhere along the way, Tyler's torso became water-slicked and disconcertingly like Ethan's.

Baking. Focus on the baking.

Tonight felt like a s'more kind of night.

When she walked through the door of the Cup-A-Cabana on Saturday, his heart lodged in his throat. He'd thought all night about their encounter at the pool. She'd been flustered. By what, he wasn't sure. He and Addie had flirted before, but there was something different in her looks last night. They'd lingered. And she specifically asked if he'd be here today, so he thought that maybe he'd finally done it. He'd paid his penance and she was ready to give him another chance.

Which also scared the crap out of him.

Oh, Christ. Maybe he could hide. Had she seen him yet?

The very moment he contemplated ducking his head beneath the table, her eyes zoomed in on his, but then quickly darted away. Like she was just as nervous about seeing him. Not good. Definitely not good.

Addie took a seat several tables away from him. Perfect. That wasn't weird at all. She drummed her fingers against the tabletop and tapped her feet to an anxious beat—actions vastly similar to the first time he'd seen her in that very coffee shop. It could only mean one thing. She glanced at her watch, confirming his suspicion.

Addie was meeting someone.

There wasn't any sense torturing himself by watching her watch the door. He opened his laptop instead, for his other favorite form of torture. *The Girl Who Dated the World. Chapter One.* He managed to grind out a few hundred words before looking up again.

She still sat alone. And she seemed more determined than ever to avoid making eye contact with him. He hoped she wasn't meeting someone new for once, because that would feel like a big bucket of salt in the wounds.

Gwen came around with a hot mug of tea for her and what appeared to be a consoling pat on the shoulder. When she darted past his table, he caught her by the elbow and lowered his voice to barely above a whisper. "Is she . . . waiting for someone?" he asked, nodding to Addie.

In a show of sisterly solidarity, Gwen crossed her arms, her eyes narrowing to slits. "She was. Asshole didn't show. And he's not answering his cell."

He wasn't just an asshole, he was a first-class idiot. How could any guy stand her up?

"She's pretty crushed," Gwen continued. "But I'm telling you, if I see that jerk anywhere near here again, I'll be crushing his toes with Hannah's stilettos."

Ethan nodded. Though he would have loved to join in the persecution of the prick, he found it hard not to be grateful to the guy and his clear lack of brain cells. "Listen, grab me a couple danishes," he said as he shoved his work-related equipment aside and stood. "I'm relocating."

Gwen's eyebrow arched in question. "You sure that's a good idea?"

"It's the best one I have."

Fueled by sheer bravado, he took long, deliberate strides toward her table, but once he reached it, he froze. He hadn't a clue what to say.

She raised her head to meet his gaze. "Are you waiting for an invitation?"

Feisty. He could deal with feisty. "*You* never do."

The faintest smile twitched her lips. "Go ahead and sit already."

Gwen brought them each a danish—his second that day—and a tea for him as well. While Addie tore into the pastry, Ethan studied her face. Her eyes glistened with unshed tears, but otherwise she was the same beautiful Addie. "You really liked him, huh?"

He hadn't realized he'd spoken the words aloud until her head popped up. "I, uh . . . liked the idea of him. I mean, he was attractive, ambitious, considerate . . . or so I thought. To be honest, I'm not sure what I would have done had he shown up today. Part of me was ready to skewer him for catching him kissing another woman . . . ."

Kissing another woman? What the hell was the matter with him? Ethan hated the schmuck more than ever. He swallowed some tea to get rid of the bad taste in his mouth.

"I just can't believe that bastard stood me up. It's so . . . it's humiliating, really. Doesn't help that you were here to witness it all." Reaching for her danish, she took another healthy bite of the pastry. "Wow, these *are* good," she murmured through stuffed cheeks.

"I told ya. Want another?"

She washed the mouthful down with a drink of tea. "Nah. I'd better not. I plan on eating my weight in Mexican food for a week straight."

Her comment stirred a memory from a previous conversation they'd had, when he'd named all the places he'd take her to for their not-date. He'd suggested El Camino, his favorite Mexican place. He probably would've had better luck there than at Zen Kitchen, because he knew for a fact they had real food—plenty of it.

"Tyler doesn't like Mexican food, if you can believe that. Who doesn't like Mexican food?"

"Oh, I can believe it." Ethan blew across his cup, cooling the tea. "I guess that makes him a guacamoron."

The comment startled a laugh from her. "Or a quesadorka."

Ethan's brow rose in challenge. "You can do better than that." Biker dumbass deserved every name in the book. Besides, name-calling could be very therapeutic. He was sure he'd read that somewhere.

"Arros con putz."

That earned her a thumbs up. "With pico de gutless on the side."

She smiled so wide he could still see it when she lifted her mug to take a drink. He joined her. A feeling of warmth spread through his body, but it wasn't the hot beverage, he knew. It was the result of seeing her happy and being the reason for it.

"How's the writing going?"

He'd never noticed her fingers before, but they were long and thin. Entirely feminine but strong, too. He could tell by the way she gripped her mug, like the contents inside were precious to her. She wore a silver ring with a half-moon design on her pinkie finger that shone when the light caught it. To him it looked more like a sliver of pie. Apple or berry or cherry—

"Hemingway?"

He jumped. "Yeah? What?"

A knowing smirk crossed her features. Returning her mug to the table, she said, "I asked how your writing was going."

"Oh, well, you know. I think I have a good handle on things now." He took another drink, then rubbed a hand over the back of his neck. "How's the pie business?"

"If I bake them, they will come."

He nodded, as impressed with the reference as he was bemused by her casual shrug. She was as humble as pie.

"Now that you mention it," she carried on, "I might as well make a pie run since I've got some unexpected free time."

"Right. Makes sense." It was cool. It's not like he expected her to use her unexpected time to talk to a guy who had nothing but painfully-expected time on his hands. But, for once, he could at least pretend he had somewhere else to be. Something else to do. "I need to get out of here anyway. Got some plans . . . Busy day for me. So, uh, maybe I'll see you again soon? You know, here? Or wherever."

"Yeah, of course. And thanks . . . for everything."

He stood and dropped some money on the table to cover their food and beverages, including the danish he'd left uneaten. He nearly stumbled as he winded his way back to his own table to grab his gear. Shouldering his bag, he made his way to her table again. When she looked up at him expectantly, he said, "Enjoy your Mexican feast."

17

She cocked her head, watching Ethan as he rushed outside. He seemed to be in such a hurry all of a sudden, and she wondered where he was off to. He mentioned having plans. A date with another woman?

Her stomach twisted at the thought. Dates were highly overrated. She still couldn't believe Tyler had stood her up. *Bet he's off somewhere with that sidewalk floozy.* The more she thought about it, the more convinced she became that the real reason she'd shown up for their date was to tell him off. And she hated that she'd missed the chance to give the prick a piece of her mind.

She had to admit, it was awfully nice of Ethan to try to cheer her up.

Swallowing another gulp of tea, she pushed her empty mug aside. After she sold some pies, she'd have a warm, soothing bubble bath and wash away any remnants of Tyler from her brain. Maybe she'd indulge in a little late-night TV, too.

Rising to her feet, she grabbed her purse hanging over her chair and was about to wave to Gwen when she glimpsed an image in her mug . . . and fell right back into her seat again. Her heart slammed against her ribs. She squeezed her eyes shut and waited a beat or ten before pulling the cup closer. The pattern in the leaves was indisputable. Shaking her head to clear it, she studied the image again. A rainbow.

Her wish would come true. Rainbows represented a path between today and destiny. *Destiny? Whoa.*

It was possible she misinterpreted the leaves. Hell, it'd been a while since she'd read Great-Aunt Edna's tasseography book at length. She might have misread that particular bit about rainbows. She'd have to check. But first—

Addie tried her best not to peek inside Ethan's mug. She really did. But the tug of curiosity proved just too strong. She looked for the briefest moment, viewing the distinct outline of an open book. What did that mean again? Something about a question? Or an answer? She was so nervous she couldn't think straight. Whatever it meant, it was significant. That much she remembered.

This time, there could be no denying that the reading was for him and him alone. He's the only man she'd sat with, talked with, mocked with. *Holy cow.*

She stood on shaky legs and carefully made her way to the door. "Bye, Gwen! Thanks!" she called over her shoulder, not daring to look back. Not prepared to share her findings with anyone.

The pie-peddling would have to wait. She could hardly walk on solid ground, let alone circle about the town selling her baked goods on a bike. She wandered home in a daze, and when she made it at last, she went straight to the kitchen.

Lord, she craved a fortifying cup of tea, but she'd had enough revelations for a lifetime. Instead, she dusted off the coffee maker and prayed it wouldn't start speaking to her, too. The machine burbled and gurgled to life, fraying her already tattered nerves. Using the counter for leverage, she reached for her copy of *The Art of Reading Tea Leaves.*

Addie carried the heavy book to the kitchen table, sat down, and took a deep breath. Then, as though ripping off a bandage, she whipped open the cover and searched the glossary. Within moments, she confirmed what she already knew to be correct: a rainbow signified that her wish would come true. But what did that mean for her? What did she wish for? A partner. A family. Someone to help her fill this big, empty house.

Someone who made her laugh.

Flipping back several pages, she located the book symbol and read the passage. An open book was an answer to a question. In the story of her life, the biggest question that remained was who would play the hero.

The coffee maker shuddered to a stop. Pressing a palm to her chest, she was surprised to find a steady beat. Edna once told her, "The heart wants what it wants, but the gut knows better."

Had she been following the leaves or following her gut? If she'd taken the readings out of the equation entirely, for all her dates, would anything have changed? Would she have granted Houdini a second date, or given Simple Simon another go? Her mouth fell open as the plain truth of it became crashingly clear. *No.* Nor would she have risked a round of double *Jeopardy!* with Trebek's biggest fan. Even if Tyler had bothered to show up for their fourth date, she wouldn't have slept with him, not even for the sake of getting a little action. He'd shattered any hope he had of gaining her trust. He was a man who had a home fit for a family but wasn't truly ready to start one of his own.

And Ethan . . . Without her realizing it, he'd carved himself a nice spot in the corner of her mind. In her life. He was exactly what she'd been looking for, and she'd found him, long before the leaves told her so.

"Coffee," she murmured. "Definitely need coffee." Caffeine always helped her deal with the so-not-ready-to-deal-with-yet stuff.

She stood and retrieved a mug from the cupboard, filling it to the brim with the steaming brew. Her hands shook as she brought it to her lips and took a straight shot of the black sludge. Trading the mug for her book, she moved to replace it on the shelf. Her gaze hovered on the glass container of flour. The urge to bake grew so much stronger when she was nervous, and this particular bout of nerves were a powerful sort.

She clutched the container in her palms and brought it to the counter, then took a brief detour to her laptop set up on the kitchen table. When the search engine appeared on the screen, she typed in "cherry danish recipes."

For him.

And for her bakery.

Ethan paced back and forth along the sidewalk, questioning his sanity for the umpteenth time. He'd talked himself into and out of this enough to make his head spin. When he'd left the coffee shop earlier that day, he'd nearly turned around and marched right back in again. How could he have been so stupid? How could he just walk away without asking her, especially when she'd given him such a perfect opening?

C'mon, Holtz. It's now or never.

With a resolute nod, he climbed the steps to her door. Dusk had fallen. Porch lights glowed on the houses around him. But not Addie's.

She couldn't have gone to bed already, could she? *Knock. Just knock, you idiot.*

Making his hand into a fist, he rapped against the door and held his breath.

Twenty agonizing seconds later, the door opened to his pixie-haired dream girl, smelling like she just stepped out of a bubble bath, wearing ridiculous cupcake slippers, and squinting at him like he was a figment of her imagination.

"Ethan, hey. What are you doing here?"

"Sorry to show up so late . . . ."

"It's okay. I was just watching *Seinfeld* reruns."

"Have dinner with me at El Camino," he blurted.

She blinked. "W-What? When?"

"Monday night?"

She quietly processed the request for longer than was comfortable, shifting from foot to slippered foot, and he braced himself for a rejection. "Why Monday? For the alliteration?"

He frowned in confusion.

"Mexican Monday," she explained with a teasing wink.

"Alliterations are so . . . cutesy."

Addie rolled her eyes. "My apologies, Hemingway."

"Don't apologize. Say yes."

"Yes." She looked even more surprised than he felt as the word slipped out without pause or hesitation. "What time should we meet there?"

There went his idea of picking her up first. "How's six?"

"Six is perfect."

"Good." Their eyes met and held. *Go. Go before you shove your foot in your mouth.* "Well, good night, Addie." He walked down the steps again, trying all the while to mute the voice inside his head telling him, *No. Not good enough. Meeting her there won't make you stand out.*

But he couldn't argue the point, and it was the gentlemanly thing to do, damn it. Plus, driving Addie meant more time with Addie. He spun around, glad she hadn't shut her door yet. "I'd like to pick you up. Okay?"

"Okay," she agreed easily.

He smiled all the way home.

Lazy Sundays didn't exist in the town of Kendal. It seemed to be the day everyone set aside to go out and about, shop, socialize, worship the sun or the Lord, and, of course, have their palms read. "Palm" Sunday had been a hit since its institution three years ago, and people came from miles around to "hand" themselves over to the master.

Addie'd slept surprisingly well the night before, considering the shock of her own readings—the tea leaf variety—and Ethan's unexpected visit. The cosmos was surely speaking to her now. Having circled the town square once already that morning, she'd sold most of her pies, but she hoped to unload the remaining selection on her second time through in the afternoon. As luck would have it, Rebecca Ledgerwood, one of the local schoolteachers, had a hankering for the banana-hazelnut kind.

"I'll take four," she said. "If you've got 'em."

Addie nodded, bagging them up for her. "Having a party?"

Rebecca blushed a red as bright as her sneakers. "Uh, no. It's cheat day."

"Oh," Addie said with a laugh. "Well, I'm honored you chose to cheat with my pies." She passed her the bag, then pocketed the bills Rebecca handed over in exchange.

"I'll have to spend a few extra hours in the gym this week, but it's worth it."

The woman was in perfect shape—a Physical Education teacher who tirelessly practiced what she preached. She probably had abs of steel hidden under her T-shirt that read "It's a Rebecca thing, you wouldn't understand." They might've had more to talk about if Addie was into the whole sportsing thing, but baking, biking, and once-a-week yoga were her favorite—and pretty much only—forms of exercise.

"Enjoy!" she called as Rebecca took off with her treats in a half-sprint. *Crazy active people.*

Addie looped the square one last time, selling her final pie to a little boy who paid for it with his allowance while his amused mother looked on. After completing the transaction, she tucked the bags and napkins safely away, but one rogue napkin slipped off on the breeze. She tracked the stray down just outside of the big purple tent, pitched every Sunday, rain or shine, for Carmen's palm reading practice.

Fully clothed in her palm reader ensemble, complete with rhinestones and a purple cape, Carmen insisted people call her Towanda, her tribute to the movie *Fried Green Tomatoes* which she claimed had been stuck in her VCR for ages. The brave souls who dared to enter Towanda's tent were promised an honest palm reading in exchange for a generous donation to the food bank.

Bending to scoop up the napkin, Addie was pulled into the conversation she easily heard through the thin flaps of the tent.

"You're an old soul, Rebecca. The lines on your hands are deep and the skin is tough. You have the palms of a person who's lived a dozen lives. The best thing for a woman with an old soul is to find a younger man."

Addie had often pondered the merits of dating a younger man. She'd never gone there herself, but the abundant energy of a youthful guy could be exactly what Rebecca needed. Addie leaned a little too far forward and had to step to catch herself, landing directly in Towanda's line of sight.

"Oh, Addie! Come in, come in!" Towanda motioned with her free hand. "I've been trying to read this one's palm for years," she murmured to Rebecca, who seemed relieved to have the focus on someone other than her.

"Thanks for the reading, Ms. Deacon, er, Towanda," Rebecca quickly amended as she stood. "I'll be sure to donate to the food bank."

"Wonderful! Ta-ta, darling! Best of luck!"

As soon as she was out of earshot, Towanda said, "God, I'd kill for that figure."

Addie laughed. "You and me both, sister. I don't know how you got her to park her butt for a few minutes. That girl looks like she lives on a treadmill."

"I can never be entirely sure what draws a person into my tent. In her case, I think it was a combination of curiosity and loneliness. The poor dear is looking for love and doesn't know where to find it."

"Maybe she should try tea leaves," Addie muttered.

Towanda's eyes widened with intrigue. "Oh, my. Sit, dear. Tell me more."

Addie complied, wondering if her confession was a slip of the tongue, or just her needing desperately to tell someone.

"You've been practicing tasseography?" Towanda asked. "Edna must have taught you."

"She did. Back then, I didn't really do much with the skill, but when I made a conscious effort to start dating again, I figured it was worth a shot."

"I always thought it was a lot of hooey, to be honest," said the woman currently taking hold of Addie's palms in her own. "But Edna used to swear by it. She was convinced she found Thomas because of the leaves."

Was it so far-fetched? More far-fetched than a palmist pooh-poohing a tasseographer?

Towanda inhaled and then exhaled, gripped her hands tighter, and closed her eyes. Addie studied her face in the silence. Every line and wrinkle told a story. She wasn't a woman who let life pass her by; she took it by the reins.

Her deep-set blue eyes popped open again and focused on Addie's palms. "Let's start with your life line, dear." She smoothed her index finger over the crease to show Addie its location, beginning near her thumb and travelling in an arc toward her wrist. "I'm delighted to tell you you'll be living well into your ninth decade."

"Great. Now, will I be living with a herd of cats, or with a family of my own?"

Towanda cackled. "Patience, grasshopper. We'll get to the heart line shortly. I want to get a good look at this head line first." She traced the line running through the center of Addie's palm, noting aloud that it ran separately from her life line. *Is that good or bad?* "That's good," she answered the unasked question. "It shows you're adventurous and have an enthusiasm for life."

Addie listened, fascinated, as Towanda explained that a person with a curved, sloping line tended to be more creative and spontaneous, while a straight line indicated a more structured, practical approach to life. She was proud to see hers had a distinct curve to it. *Huh. Maybe this palmistry stuff isn't so off-the-wall after all.*

"Finally, let us visit your heart line." She traced the line that ran below her pinkie finger to her middle finger. "Yours is a shorter line that intersects with your life line. You fall in love easily, but your heart also breaks quite easily. It's fragile. You must be gentle with it."

Yeah, Tyler. Didja hear that? Good thing I never gave you my heart.

"What's your astrological sign?"

"Pisces."

Towanda frowned. "No, that's not a good sign."

Addie stared at her unblinkingly. "Umm . . . I can't change it."

"You'll have to work a little harder to find a deep connection. Be more honest, braver."

Like telling Ethan what the tea leaves read?

"Care to know how many babies you'll have?" the older woman asked with a bawdy wink.

"Ah, well . . . in for a pound, I suppose."

Towanda took her right hand and tilted it sideways, closely inspecting the lines that ran horizontally beneath her pinkie finger. "Oh, lovely. Two strapping boys and a little princess in the middle."

Addie's jaw dropped. "Three? I may need a bigger house."

"Nonsense!" Towanda laughed. "Yours is plenty big enough." Still holding Addie's right hand, she turned it so the back was facing upwards. "One last thing." She traced the shape of the blue veins beneath her pale skin. "I can't make out the first letter, but the second letter is very clear."

"Letters?"

"Initials. Of the man you're going to marry."

Her stomach flipped. "Um . . . wh-what's the second one?"

"An H."

Ethan's last name starts with an H. Holtz. Hemingway. "Wow. Maybe the leaves aren't so crazy."

"What's that, dear?"

"Uh, nothing." Addie shot from her chair. "I should go. Thanks, Carmen. Towanda, I mean . . . This was really great. Very informative. Eye-opening. Scary. Wonderful." She gulped in some air. "I'll donate to the food bank tomorrow." *Before dinner . . . with my future husband?* She fled before Towanda could get a word in edgewise.

Two days, two separate, unrelated readings, and all signs were pointing to Ethan. Addie paced her living room floor, pausing only to insert another spoonful of ice cream into her mouth. Tomorrow was Mexican Monday. Tomorrow was less than five hours away now. Well, the date didn't start at midnight, but the date was tomorrow and tomorrow started at midnight. Was it even a date? She considered it a date, but did he? They'd tried before and hadn't even made it to appetizers, so maybe this was just a friendly gesture . . . that he'd made on her doorstep after walking all the way to her house.

"Welcome to the Sunday Night Freak-Out, starring Addie Mitchell!" she yelled to the empty room.

Unceremoniously dropping the half-eaten pint-sized container of brownie fudge mocha swirl onto the coffee table, she pulled her cell phone from her pocket. What were the odds Ethan's number would magically appear in her contacts by wishful thinking alone? The only person she knew who might have his number was Hannah. She could call Hannah and get Ethan's number and call him and ask him if it was a date and then . . . well, die from humiliation. But at least she'd die knowing for sure.

She found Hannah's number in her recents list and tapped the screen to place a call.

Hannah answered on the second ring. "Addie! Hi! What a nice surprise!"

Forgetting that Hannah's excited voice was a decibel level higher than a whale's, she moved the phone several inches away from her ear. "Hey, Hannah. Sorry to bother you, but I was just wondering if you happen to have Ethan's number."

"Ethan? What did you need his number for?"

Great. Exactly the question she didn't want to answer. "Oh, just . . . it's for this thing that we're doing. And he, you know, he needed me to get back to him before tomorrow, so I—"

"Hang on, someone's at the door." She heard muffled voices in the background, and then the sound of dogs barking. "Sorry, hon. Tobias is here for Muffy's play date so I have to go. You got a pen?"

She bent down to grab the pen and notepad she kept on the corner of the coffee table, and held the phone to her hear with her shoulder. "Yep."

Hannah rattled off a number and she scribbled it down. "I know, Muffykins. Mommy's coming. Have a wonderful night, Addie! Call me anytime!"

She clicked off before Addie could respond, bringing a smile to her face. That couldn't have worked out better. Mission accomplished with as little awkwardness as possible. She returned the pen and notepad to their rightful place, staring at the numbers until they were emblazoned in her brain, finally gathering the courage to punch them into her phone.

Every unanswered ring ratcheted her heartbeat up another notch. Soon, after the fourth ring, she was prompted to leave a message. "Wow, out late, huh?" She laughed, then clamped a hand over her mouth for saying something so entirely ridiculous. "Sorry, this is Addie. Mitchell. I'm sure you're, like, one of those rare people who has a life separate from their cell phone. You may never even get this message, but if you do, I should probably get to the point, so . . . hi. I'm freaking out a bit about tomorrow because I'm not really sure—" An obnoxious beep cut her off mid-tangent. *Oh, shit. Shit.*

"Oh, my God!" she cried to the ceiling. "I have to call back. He's gonna think I'm insane."

Gathering what remained of her dignity, she redialed. Again, she was prompted to leave a message. "Hey there. I'm sorry about the last message. I'll try to be more succinct with this one. It's Addie, by the way, just in case you didn't listen to the last message. As a matter of fact, it's probably better if you didn't. Crap. I'm doing it again. Are we dating? I mean, is tomorrow a date? Was that what you meant about picking me up? I don't know why I need to know—" *Beep!*

"Wait! No!" She crumpled to her knees on the floor. "This cannot be happening." Pounding the table with her fist, she stopped only when she caught sight of the ice cream container she'd abandoned, her spoon now floating in the semi-melted deliciousness. She shovelled as much as she could into her mouth, not trusting her legs to carry her to the kitchen.

Once more. She had to try one last time and pray this message would make sense. Writing out a script might help, but judging by how shaky the spoon was in her hand, a pen wouldn't fare much better.

The spoon fell with a plop back into the container and she hit redial. That old, reliable beep came as expected. "Third time's the charm, right?" She laughed. "It's me again. Addie. Also known as the girl who keeps leaving you long, rambling messages. You could just answer the phone and save me the embarrassment. No? Okay. Call me when you get this. If you get this. Or, better yet, ignore all my messages—" *Beep!*

Tamping down the temptation to call a fourth time simply to say how much she hated his phone and his inability to answer it, she found the will to stand and dragged her feet into the kitchen to toss the remains of her ice cream soup into the trash. There were dishes in the sink. Perfect. No better way to take her mind off . . . whatever the hell just happened in her living room. She rolled up her sleeves and filled the sink with soapy water, sometimes preferring to scrub her pots and pans the old-fashioned way.

Of course, she'd left her phone in the living room. And just as she was elbow-deep in dishwater, that pesky phone decided to ring.

Shaking off the excess water, she sprinted to pick it up and accept the call, not even registering whose number appeared on the screen. "Hello?" she said, huffing out of breath.

"Addie? It's Ethan."

"Oh, God. Hi."

"Are you okay?"

The sweet concern in his voice almost overshadowed her urge to throw up. "You got my messages?"

He chuckled. "I stopped listening after the second one."

She fell back onto the couch with a sigh. "I'm obviously too long-winded for your voicemail setup."

"I just didn't have it set on Addie-mode."

His easy banter helped to relax her jittery nerves. "So, tomorrow—"

"Listen, there's no pressure. We don't have to—"

"Is it a date?"

He was silent for long enough to make her wonder if she'd lost the connection. But then he finally spoke. "Uh, I'm . . . Yes. Is that okay?"

The quaver in his voice proved she wasn't the only one feeling a little on edge. They were in this together, for better or worse. "Yes," she said, flopping onto her back, resting her head on the arm cushion, smiling the biggest smile at the ceiling.

"Okay. I'll pick you up at six?"

"Sure. You know the address."

"I do."

Her eyes rolled shut at his gravelly tone, at the way he was able to add so much meaning to two simple words. "I guess I'll see you tomorrow. Good night, Ethan." Though she couldn't see him, she knew he was smiling. She'd spoken his name, after all.

"Good night, Addie."

She gazed at her phone, lost in a dream, for minutes after they'd disconnected. Tomorrow. Now, she longed for tomorrow. Good thing it was only a night away.

18

MoJo growled as Ethan discarded yet another shirt onto his bed, taking over the cat's pilfered territory. "Right," he shot back. "Because *I'm* the one who's being annoying right now."

He wanted to be dressy, but not too dressy. El Camino certainly wasn't a suit and tie affair, but this date . . . It needed to be perfect.

His gaze landed on the grey blazer in his closet. He could pair it with a navy shirt and some nice jeans. Blue was always a good choice. He looked good in blue, or so he'd been told. "What do you think?" he asked the fur ball, holding up the shirt with the blazer. MoJo blinked, uninterested. "Where's the brotherhood, man? You're supposed to have my back."

He laid the two items on the bed. "Ya know, for a cat named MoJo, you sure haven't given me much luck in the writing department, but I was hoping you'd make up for it in the woman department."

"Woman department?" a feminine voice trilled from the hall. Carmen dropped her laundry basket outside his door and then poked her nosy head into his room. Her eyebrows raised with interest when she saw the clothes decorating his bed. "Going on a date?"

There was no sense in denying it. She'd be able to see right through him. "I'm taking Addie to El Camino."

"Addie," she said, smiling delightedly. "Of course! You're the H."

"Huh?"

"Nothing, dear." She sashayed into his room and surveyed the disaster on his bed. "Hmm, I'd definitely go with the blue."

He waited a beat, expecting an inappropriate remark or two, but that's all she said. "Uh, thank you. I think I will."

She nodded, stroked MoJo's jet-black fur a few times, then danced her way back out of the room. But just before she disappeared from sight, she turned to him and asked, "What's your astrological sign?"

Of all the questions she'd asked him since he moved in, this was one of the least weird, so he didn't mind answering. "Virgo."

"Oh, wonderful!" she cried, clapping her hands. "Pisces and Virgo, a beautiful tale of opposites attract! Be generous with your heart, but don't sacrifice too much. You are the earth, and she is the water. Let her move you with her emotions, while you ground her with your strength and constancy."

Even MoJo looked confused as hell after Carmen finished her spiel. "Okay, well, thanks again. I'll, uh, be sure to lock up when I leave."

She blew him a kiss. "Go get 'em, tiger."

Uncomfortable, yet strangely motivating all the same. He closed his door for some privacy, put his game face on, and dressed to impress the girl of his dreams.

***

Rain splattered against his windshield as he drove the short distance to her house. He'd barely made it to his car before the heavens opened and was grateful he kept an umbrella in the back seat for such occasions.

He'd been waiting so long for this opportunity, he wanted to do everything right. And, no, he couldn't control the weather, but he could certainly shield her from it. He could pick her up, drop her off, and do his damnedest to woo her in between.

Even through the rain, he could see the number: 1452. Parking along the curb, he reached behind him for the umbrella and jumped from his seat. Barely a drop hit his jacket before he managed to cover himself from the onslaught and take long strides toward her door. Addie's door. He was almost giddy enough to pull a Gene Kelly.

He raised his hand to knock, but the door opened before he could make contact. And there she stood, his doe-eyed girl. She ducked under his umbrella as she locked the door, then turned to him with a look of pure awe on her face.

"It's raining," she said. "I can't believe it."

Ethan shrugged guiltily. "I would have stopped it if I could."

"No. It's perfect."

He studied her for a moment. "I bet you were the kid who splashed in every puddle."

She grinned. "Not *every* puddle."

Guiding her by the small of her back, he ensured she was completely covered by the umbrella as they descended the front steps and made the short journey to his car parked along the curb.

She turned to him with a raised eyebrow when he opened the passenger door. "I didn't picture you in a sports car."

"It's a safe, reliable automobile . . . that just so happens to look kinda badass."

Addie smirked as she slid into her seat. "Ready when you are, Vin Diesel."

Rolling his eyes for dramatic effect, he circled the front of the car, folded down the umbrella, and slipped into the driver's seat. He tossed the soggy nylon onto the floor in the back seat, then buckled up. Before starting the car, he glanced at Addie, whose gaze was locked on him. "Hi," he mumbled idiotically.

She giggled. "Hi."

His focus shifted to her legs, inches and inches of bared skin below her skirt, dotted with goosebumps. She shivered, whether from his prolonged stare or to emphasize what her skin was already telling him, he couldn't be sure.

"Sorry, I'll turn the heat on." He cranked the ignition and adjusted the temperature dials.

"It's okay. I always feel cold when it rains, the dampness in the air," she explained. "And when I'm nervous."

Her confession echoing in his head, he put the car in gear and pulled onto the street. Nervous was good. Nervous meant that she cared, that she wasn't taking this lightly. "I'm a little cold, too," he admitted, shooting her a meaningful look as he turned onto the main road.

He drove slowly. She might have assumed the bad weather caused his extra care, but it was really an insurance policy for himself. If the rest of the date went downhill from here, at least they'd have this time together. "I tried to make a reservation, but they don't take reservations on weeknights," he said to fill the silence.

"Shouldn't be too busy with the rain."

"Right."

"I don't have an umbrella," she said suddenly.

Ethan blinked. "Okay. But you know I do."

"Yes, you do. Just like Thomas did."

Thomas? He almost asked her to elaborate but was afraid he'd learn Thomas had been yet another bachelor she'd cut loose. "I have an extra, so it's yours . . . if you want."

The smile on her lips made him forget all about the absent sun. "Thomas was my great-uncle. I'll tell you the story of how he and my great-aunt Edna met sometime."

"I'd like that."

They were two minutes, tops, from reaching their destination. He could practically smell the *chili con queso* in the air, but that didn't stop him from thinking about circling the block a few more times. Having her alone, away from prying eyes, right next to him, breathing the same air as him, he wanted to soak it all in just a little bit longer.

"I'm starving."

Or, he could feed the poor woman and take the long way 'round when it was time to drop her off at home again. El Camino's gaudy sign flashed into view. He drove to the front entrance and put the car in park. "You go on in, and I'll find a parking spot."

She caught his arm just as he reached for his door handle, realizing his intention to help her out of the vehicle. "I've got it. I'll get us a table."

You couldn't blame the guy for hoping he'd glimpse more of her thigh as she shimmied out of her seat. Couldn't blame him for watching her walk away, either. Shaking himself out of his stupor, he set off to find a parking spot in the surprisingly busy lot.

Addie followed the hostess to a table near the rear of the restaurant. She'd managed to keep her nerves at bay for most of the day—that is, until she saw him. Standing outside her door. Holding an umbrella. Great-Aunt Edna would be having a field day over that one.

She skimmed through the menu, antsy and anxious, vaguely aware of the waitress who'd stopped by to pour her a glass of water. She'd barely sat for two minutes before she leapt to her feet in search of the washroom. Having heeded nature's call, she stood in front of the mirror, inspecting her reflection. "Not bad, Mitchell. Not bad at all." Then her heel caught on a crack in the clay tile. Her arms pinwheeled as she tried to find purchase, and by some miracle she caught herself on the edge of the sink before face-planting on the floor.

"I'm much better on two wheels," she said to the startled woman who'd entered in time to see the show.

The woman disappeared into a stall. Moving to a safer spot, Addie re-spiked her hair, reapplied her lipstick, ensured none ended up on her teeth, then casually strolled back into the festively decorated interior of El Camino. The one thing missing was a mariachi band. They only performed on Saturdays—a tidbit she'd read on the back of the menu. Just as she reclaimed her seat, she caught sight of Ethan at the front entrance of the restaurant. Their gazes met and held. Her palms tingled as he made his way to her in dark jeans, a navy shirt, and a grey blazer. She hadn't really had an opportunity to appreciate the whole package until now, but yumm-o.

His eyes narrowed, then widened, his gaze lingering just long enough on her cleavage to convince her she'd selected the perfect top to go with the skirt, and that jackets, even in the rain, were highly overrated. "You look . . . incredible."

She ducked her head, afraid she'd be blushing for days, but when she lifted it again she found a man with two very flushed cheeks staring straight back at her. And he wasn't trying to hide it.

Seizing her water glass, she took a long drink. If he could be brave, so could she. There were things that needed to be said. Confessions to be made. But she needed an appetizer, and maybe a margarita, before she opened the vault. "You look good yourself, Hemingway."

At that compliment, he took a seat across from her, a smile still curving his lips. He'd been smiling a lot more lately, which she preferred over the surly vibe he usually put out. There was no denying the man gave excellent surl.

Their waitress returned then—a beautiful young woman in a sleeveless white tunic with gold, green, and red accents. "I see you now have company." She grinned at Ethan, pouring him a glass of water. "Would either of you like something other than water?"

"I'm assuming she'll want tea," Ethan teased.

"We have lovely tea here," the waitress said.

"No!" Two pairs of eyebrows shot up at her outburst. "Uh, I mean, no, thank you. I think I'll just stick with the water for now. Please."

"I'll stick with water, too," Ethan said.

The waitress nodded, then quickly left.

Ethan angled his head, studying her to the point that she felt like hiding under the table. "Is it poisonous here?"

"What?"

"The tea."

"Oh, no." She waved her hand. "But, you know, when you're eating spicy food, a cold drink seems like the better choice . . . right?"

"They have this amazing thing called iced tea now. Pretty popular in the southern states, I hear."

"Ha. Ha."

The waitress dropped off a bowl of nachos with salsa. "I'll come by to take your order in a few minutes," she said before skittering away again.

Ethan lunged for the chip bowl, nearly knocking over the salsa in the process. Addie bit back a laugh. "It's a little weird whenever we're away from the coffee shop, isn't it?"

He finished chewing the chip in his mouth and took a drink. "Yeah. I doubt I can get a danish in this joint."

This time the laugh broke free. "Funny you should mention that."

"Oh?"

His gaze sharpened on her, and she had to take a moment to just breathe. "I guess I had danishes on the brain the other night." *Or you.* "I spent a couple hours in the kitchen working on my recipe." She played with the cutlery on the table, rearranging her knife and fork three times before looking up again. "I think I've perfected it."

"Actually, the fork should be on the left."

She glared at him. "I meant I've perfected my recipe."

There it was again, that smile. "Does that mean you're, uh, thinking more seriously about your bakery?"

"I don't know. Maybe. I guess."

"Or was this your way of flirting with me?"

She blinked, stunned by his frankness. Ethan dove for the chips again, as if belatedly realizing what he'd said. Her lips twitched at the corners. "Why is dating so hard?" she asked aloud.

"Look who you're talking to. It's funny how everyone who isn't dating thinks they're an expert on the subject . . . like Carmen. You won't believe the advice she gave me."

Addie leaned forward, curious to hear the pearls of wisdom she shared with Ethan. "Do tell."

"She suggested I use a Ouija board to summon love through the spirits. And if that didn't work, she offered to lend me her copy of *The Kama Sutra*."

Addie snorted. "She told me that I have a bad astrological sign."

"It's not like you can change it."

"That's exactly what I said!" Addie drank some water, knowing that she'd left off the most important bits of Carmen's advice. Like the part about Addie needing to work harder to find a love connection, to be honest . . . and brave. Well, there was no time like the present. *Okay. I can do this.* Noticing their fast-approaching waitress out of the corner of her eye, Addie sighed. *You are not ruining this for me, seniorita.* "You ready to order, Hemingway?"

"Uh, sure."

"Perfect. I'll take a burrito grande, extra cheese, extra guac on the side," she said before the woman even pulled out her order pad.

Taking his cue from Addie, Ethan jumped in. "And I'll have the chicken enchiladas."

"Oh. Um . . . okay." The waitress looked between the two of them. "Anything else to drink?"

"No, thanks," they said in unison.

She was gone in a flash, and Addie hoped she'd cop a clue and stay away long enough to let her spill her guts.

"Is this a bad time?" Ethan asked. "Do you have somewhere else you need to be?"

The vulnerability in his voice gave her the final nudge she needed to tell all. "As you know, I've been using tea leaves to help me find love." She waited a beat, not quite certain he wouldn't have something negative to say about the subject again, but he silently nodded his head and leaned forward. "And as much as I thought I was relying solely on the leaves, I think part of me, or a lot of me, has been going with my gut all along . . . which is why what happened Saturday scared me so much."

"What happened?" he asked softly.

Captivated by the warmth in his hazel eyes, she leaned in closer, too, and the tension slowly released from her body. "After you left the coffee shop, I, uh, read my leaves. And yours. Mine showed a rainbow, and yours, an open book."

She held her breath as she waited for his response, but he just stared at her for several seconds. "A rainbow is a sign that your wish will come true, I think, right?" he asked. "And the book . . . something about a question. An answer to a question?"

Addie gaped at him, stunned. "How did you . . . ?"

"I've done some research. Read through a few books on tasseography in my spare time."

Her mind reeled. After everything he'd said that day, she thought he'd never understand her or this part of her life. "Why did you?"

He looked her straight in the eye. "I wanted to know you better."

She shook her head in wonder. From the moment they met, he'd found ways of surprising her. Getting under her skin. Into her heart. With him, things had been so different from the start. He wasn't just some guy from a dating app or a newspaper ad. Ethan was a real, present fixture in her life. He had flaws, sure, but he made up for them with romantic gestures that stole her breath. He swooped in and made her feel things she never thought were possible. "You were right about the symbolism," she finally said. "The leaves were telling me it was you."

"Wow."

"Yeah."

Of course, it was too much to hope for a timely interruption from their waitress, and the odds of the mariachi band making a surprise performance were pretty low. Why was it so damn quiet? The place was bursting at the seams with people—families, couples of all ages—but it felt like they were all tuned in to their conversation.

"What's your gut telling you?"

She whipped her head back to him so fast, her neck stung. She'd asked herself that very question a couple nights ago, but the answer seemed so much clearer now. "My gut's telling me that . . . the leaves might not be wrong."

"Huh." One of those slow-to-start, but deliciously deep, smiles creased his face. Dimples appeared, too, as if there wasn't enough landscape to admire without them. "There might be something to this tasseography stuff after all."

"See? Not so crazy." But she wanted him to know there was so much more to it than tasseography. That he'd been a choice, not simply an outcome. He'd been a contender from the minute she laid eyes on him, tea leaves or not. "While I was out there searching, sometimes I doubted the patterns I saw in the leaves, questioned whether I'd interpreted them correctly, wondered if it was intuition or my own influence that affected my visions. But I never doubted the path I took in response to what I saw—real or imagined. I think I've been leaning toward you long before the leaves did."

His smile faded, and she worried she'd said too much, revealed too much. This was a lot for a guy to process, even one as used to her quirks as Ethan. The silence between them teetered on the edge of becoming uncomfortable when he asked, "Are you, uh . . . disappointed it's me?"

She placed a hand over his fidgeting ones, waiting until he met her gaze to answer him. "No. Not even a little."

Ethan started to respond when their waitress stopped by again to deliver their dinners. Addie jerked her hand back, effectively putting the kibosh on his opportunity to reciprocate.

"Thanks," he murmured when his meal was placed in front of him, though he was anything but thankful. An eternity later, the woman left them alone again, only for them to fall back into that same awkward silence.

"How's your food?" he asked.

"Good. Very good. Yours?"

"Fine." The enchiladas were probably delicious, but he couldn't taste them. All he could think about was touching her again, or being touched by her. "I've been drinking more tea . . . ."

She cracked a smile. "I know. I think you're becoming a be-leaf-er."

He groaned at the pun.

"Sorry. I suppose puns are too 'Shakespeare' for your liking."

She wasn't wrong. About the puns or his belief in her. This woman—this beautiful, vivacious, fascinating woman—opened herself up to him completely. Her bravery astounded him. He couldn't believe he'd been so dismissive of her methods when she'd first told him. He'd said something insensitive at the time, about getting a hold of his shrink. If anyone needed a shrink, he did. The guy who sat at the same table in the same coffee shop, day in and day out, who claimed to be writing the next great American novel, but had nothing to show for it.

For months he'd been in Kendal, trying to figure his life out. There was no magical formula for writing, nor was there one for finding love. Addie recognized her gut had much more to do with it, and he admired her for that. Because, in truth, he'd stopped listening to his gut for far too long. He'd been chasing some romanticized ideal, comparing himself to countless other successful authors and foolishly trying to emulate them.

And what the hell had that gotten him? Nothing but aggravation and thousands of wasted words. He was a thriller author . . . but the thrill was gone. Well, maybe not gone, but in full-on hibernation mode.

Again, Addie drew his gaze. As if sensing his stare, she lifted her head mid-bite. Here was a woman who thrilled him more than words ever could. One who trusted tea leaves to tell her who to love, and he was crazy in love with her.

He sucked in a breath as an unexpected flash of inspiration split through his brain like a lightning bolt. Ethan reached for his paper napkin and pulled out a pen from the inside of his jacket. Frantically, he scribbled on the makeshift notepad, desperate to capture the thought before it vanished. When he finished, he read through the rushed scrawl:

Strip Teas – a story of a femme fatale who drugs men with tea to find out their secrets.

Satisfied with his wording, he shoved the napkin across the table.

"What is this?" she asked after reading it.

"A fresh start." When Addie didn't reply right away, he tried to explain. "I stopped listening to my gut. I told you before that I was struggling, but I didn't want to admit how much. I haven't been selling books like I'd hoped I would. I thought I could rebrand myself, but I've been writing in circles. All this time I've been thinking there was some big secret I was missing, but the only thing I'm missing is the love of writing."

"Well, you can't force love."

"No," he agreed. "And you can't find it in the bottom of a tea cup—"

"Or in a crappy book."

The crooked smile on her face baited one from him. "I can't taste my food," he blurted.

"Oh, I'm sorry. Too bland?"

"No." He shook his head. "I can't concentrate on anything right now because I want to kiss you so badly."

"Ethan," she breathed.

His heartbeat thrummed in his ears. Had he just said that? Out loud? *Shit.* He glanced at the other patrons, wondering how many of the guys were thinking he was a pathetic sap, and how many of the women were stifling their laughter at his lame attempt to express his innermost desires.

"Ethan . . . I want you to kiss me."

He raised his head and stared straight into her wide brown eyes that were blinking rapidly. At her porcelain cheeks that glowed red and her full pink lips that parted before she spoke the most beautiful sentence he'd ever heard. "I wanted you to kiss me outside my house that night."

"I should have. I thought about it that whole night. Kicked my own ass a thousand times for chickening out."

"How about a do-over?"

"How about I ask for the check?"

She grinned. "Mexican food tastes better the day after, anyway."

He'd driven so slowly to the restaurant, but now, he tested his car's limits, driving as fast as he could safely do through the quiet streets. The rain had stopped, the skies had cleared, and the man was obviously on a mission.

Once in her driveway, he'd barely parked before he stood at her door, pulling her from the car, and then pressing her against it.

"Are you sure this is what you want?" he asked, his breathing ragged.

"I want *you*, Ethan."

His eyes clouded with desire. "Say it again."

"I want you."

This time there was no hesitation. No distractions. Nothing but the two of them and his mouth moving ever closer to hers. When their lips touched, she sighed. Actually sighed. He kissed her like she was every romance novel hero's dream. Or something . . . Oh, God, she couldn't think. Her lips parted on a gasp as his tongue sought entrance, teasing, tasting, teaching her everything she never knew about how a woman should be kissed.

His hips moved against hers, and she grew dizzy with need. "Ethan," she whispered. "Inside."

He blinked. "What?" The shock on his face made her realize he'd misconstrued her meaning, and she couldn't help but laugh.

"Slow down, Speedy. My house," she said. "I meant inside my house."

"Right. Of course."

She bumped him with her hips. "That means you're gonna have to move."

"Right." Keeping one hand planted firmly on her waist, he eased his weight off of her. "How's that?"

A smile teasing her lips, she slipped around him, grabbed his hand, and dragged him up the steps to the front door.

And then she froze.

Now that he was so close to being in her home, things suddenly felt real. Scary real.

Without a word, Ethan took the key from her trembling hand and slipped it into the lock. She should have known it would be like this. That they'd trade off nerves like they traded wits and barbs. "You okay?" he asked before twisting the knob.

"Yes." She was. Mostly. If she ignored the sweaty palms and the lightheaded sensation. Both were side effects, she suspected, of being kissed by a man who could have written a book on the subject.

Ethan ushered her inside, pausing in the foyer while she collected herself. "This is a beautiful home," he said with his back to her.

"Thanks."

He turned to face her. "Thanks for inviting me in."

They both knew how significant the statement was. "Thanks for . . . uh, coming. In." He took a step closer. "For wanting to come in."

Two steps more. Her back hit the door before she even noticed her own feet moving. His eyes darkened, his chest rising and falling in time with her own.

"Did I tell you that I loved your idea? The Strip Teas story? Because I do. I think it's a very, very good idea. It'll be huge. A bestseller for sure."

"Yeah?" He placed his hands on either side of her, trapping her against the door. "I might need your help with it."

"Well, I can help. I'm a helpful person. I obviously know a lot about tea, and tea is a big part of the story, so—" Her eyes clamped shut when he leaned forward and pressed his lips to the throbbing pulse in her neck.

"You talk extra fast when you're nervous."

"I'm not nervous," she lied, a noticeable quaver in her voice.

He pulled back, and when she opened her eyes at the loss of contact, Ethan smiled at her—an annoyingly smug kind of smile. "No?"

Cocking his head, he kissed the tender skin behind her ear lobe. A shudder raced through her body. He licked the same patch of skin, and she convulsed a second time. Her knees almost gave out entirely when he bit the spot. Yep, it was *the* spot. The new most erogenous zone on her body. How? Why? What sort of sorcery was this man capable of with his lips, teeth, and tongue?

She blinked and he was back in her field of vision again. "Oh, hello."

"I've been wanting to do that since I first discovered it."

"Discovered what?"

"Your tattoo."

The goofy grin on his face made her laugh. "Turns you on, huh?"

"You have no idea."

Pressing into her again, he brought his mouth to her ear, his hot, moist breath driving her mad with lust. "I wanna know the story behind it." He bit her earlobe. Hard. "I wanna know all your stories. Everything there is to know about you." Another bite, and she moaned. "But most of all . . . ."

"Yes?" she panted.

"Most of all, I wanna know when I get to try your danishes." He punctuated the statement by dipping his head and kissing the vee between her breasts.

Good Lord, he felt so good. Almost good enough that she could forgive him for thinking about food at a time like this. "You have to earn those danishes, buddy."

"Well, I might need a little edible energy for what I have planned."

"'A man who is a master of patience is a master of everything else,' or so my great-aunt Edna used to say. Come to think of it, I suspect she was mainly referring to bedroom activities."

"Smart woman," Ethan said, peppering her chest and throat with hungry, hurried nips and pecks.

"God, yes." Jolts of desire ricocheted through her body as he left his mark on nearly every patch of exposed skin. "I want you to kiss me. On my mouth."

"So demanding."

Her eyes popped open, and she shot him a sassy grin. "I want you to dedicate your book to me, too."

"For the biggest tea-se I know, Addie Mitchell."

Her giggles were cut short by his hot, perfect mouth covering hers. *Taking* hers. Proving his earlier kisses were merely a warm-up to the main event. Oh, but it was so easy to give herself to him. He belonged here. In her life, in her house. Her heart. But they had plenty of time. Days and months and years, she hoped, to make memories together.

She pushed lightly on his shoulders and he brought the kiss to a crushing halt. "Hey," she said, smoothing a hand down his rumpled shirt. "How about I take you on a tour of the rest of the place, including my kitchen, where the real magic happens?"

His eyes lit up. Pulling her from the door, he kissed her softly. "I thought you'd never ask."

EPILOGUE

Ethan took a drink of tea, opened the lid of his laptop, cracked his knuckles, and typed.

And typed.

And typed.

The words flowed freely as he delved even deeper into his latest project. His publisher had demanded a sequel to *Strip Teas* before it even hit the shelves, which was astounding enough, but the real shock came when the release went over like gangbusters. He hadn't landed on the bestsellers list, not yet anyway, but he'd become a town celebrity almost overnight.

Addie, unbeknownst to him, had planned a surprise release party down at Sam's bowling alley. She'd pre-ordered dozens of copies of his book—or, really, *their* book—for people to be able to purchase on the spot. And they did. Every last one of them. His wrist hurt from signing so many autographs, and his mouth hurt from smiling so much.

Mrs. McCallister had purchased six copies, claiming she was giving them away to friends, though he suspected she was trying to one-up Carmen Deacon, who'd bought several for her book club. Never would he ever have imagined enjoying the spotlight, but it felt like . . . redemption. Like everything he'd given up, and all the sacrifices he'd made along the way, were worth it. He'd gained so much more than he lost. More than he ever thought possible.

And what he'd lost . . . well, perhaps it wasn't so lost after all.

Ethan paused mid-typing and took another drink of his tea, recalling the conversation he'd had with his mother a few weeks ago. She'd called him. For the first time in more than a year. Just when he'd been about to write his family off altogether, she'd reached out and said hello. A lump of emotion clogged his throat as the words she'd whispered over the line reverberated in his mind. *I hope you'll stop by sometime to sign my copy of your book.*

He couldn't have been happier if he'd sold ten thousand copies. One copy ruled them all.

His father hadn't participated in the call, not that he'd expected him to, but maybe, just maybe, he'd come around eventually. Ethan had taken a stand and chosen a career he was passionate about instead of selling out and settling for what was right in front of him, easy for the taking. Most people would applaud him for that, particularly now, when he finally had the numbers to back up his decision. But true success wasn't measured by sales alone.

Almost as if it had fallen from heaven itself, a freshly baked danish appeared on the corner of his table. He lifted his head in time to catch the smile on his pastry angel's face. "You are a vision."

"You talking to me or the danish?"

"The danish."

She rolled her eyes, smacking him with the tea towel she yanked from her shoulder.

Ethan gazed up at her, the pixie-haired beauty who'd stolen his heart. Addie believed in him and supported him without question. She kept his ego in check, and didn't let him get too smug in his new-found stardom. But her radiant smiles whenever he gave her a preview of his latest work proved she was his biggest fan of all.

"You're staring," she said, unable to hide her grin.

"You're pretty."

Her grin widened exponentially. "Ya know, Gwen still hasn't forgiven me for stealing her best customer."

"Yeah, well, Gwen doesn't come with the added benefits."

Addie quirked her brow. "Oh, so it's just about the sex, huh?"

"No," he said, looking at her like he always did, like she was the last perfect thing he'd ever see. "Not hardly."

She ducked her head, a furious blush creeping up her neck and blotching her cheeks. He loved the effect he had on her, but he didn't dare tell her the power she held over him. No. He just sat there at the same table every day, drinking her tea, eating her danishes, and writing words she inspired.

"Have I told you how proud I am of you?" He glanced around the interior of her new bakery, warming with pleasure to see the customers lined up out the door, like they'd been from the moment she'd opened the place . . . or re-opened it, in a sense. She'd bought the building outright from Fritz and Frank and transformed it into a baked goods oasis—The Apple of My Pie. Even her mother stopped by on a semi-regular basis. Addie'd kept most of the tables and seating space. His was the corner table, right by the window. She'd carved 'Hemingway' on its underside.

"Yeah, a few hundred times."

"Good. There's a few hundred and one."

Addie laughed. "Thank you. How's the story going?"

He leaned back in his chair and folded his arms. "I took your advice yesterday and ramped up the chemistry between the hero and heroine."

"Has she drugged him yet?"

"Not yet."

"Okay. Don't make it too easy. She's the one in control here, so she can draw it out. Make him sweat. Get him right where she wants him, then . . . pow! Right in the kisser!"

"Funny. That's how I remember it being with you, too."

She winked, then bent down and brushed a quick kiss across his lips. "Gotta go check on my tarts, babe. Enjoy the danish, and happy writing."

He watched her walk away, admiring the way her ass moved in her skintight jeans. He *was* happy. Deliriously happy, all because of her. They'd fallen into a comfortable routine since the night he finally kissed her. Eventually, she'd even convinced him to ditch his seventy-five-year-old roommate and shack up with a hot, young pie-pusher instead. When he wasn't writing, he'd spent every spare moment helping her get her business off the ground. And she'd spent every night thanking him. Over and over again.

Ethan peered at the counter, where people in line admired the baked delights on display. Addie burst through the kitchen door carrying a tray of tarts, beaming at the 'oohs' and 'ahhs' that came from the crowd. She caught his gaze from across the room and blew him a kiss. He groaned, his usual reaction to her theatrics, and she laughed right on cue.

Yep, he was pretty much wrapped around her pastry-making finger.

He checked the time on his laptop, then shifted his focus to the door. Today marked exactly one year since the first time they met in the Cup-A-Cabana. Not that he was counting. He wasn't a romantic fool.

The bells above the door jingled and in walked Gwen, ducking out of view so as not to attract any attention from Addie, though their idea to meet there in the first place was anything but discreet. She snagged a seat across from Ethan, smiling politely. "I know you're nuts about the girl and all, as you should be, but would it kill you to visit my place of business for a change? My tips are suffering."

"I have my very own table here. A table that's dedicated to me and only me."

She rolled her eyes. "I'll name a drink after you."

"Nah."

"Two danishes for the price of one?"

He considered the offer for a moment, then shook his head. "Addie's are better."

"Addie supplies the danishes we sell at the Cup-A-Cabana now, for your information. I get the friend discount."

"They taste better here, then."

"Man, you've got it bad. All right, let's get this over with. I've got customers who haven't been blinded by love to serve."

"You'll get everything set up?"

"Yes, before seven." She reached in her apron pocket and grabbed a key, which she slid across the table to him. "Don't make a mess, don't defile any of the tables, and lock up when you're done."

"Defiling tables wasn't in the game plan, but thanks for the idea."

"Oh, and you owe me big time for this."

"I'll be a better customer from now on. One visit a week."

Gwen rose from her seat and rested a hand on his shoulder. "Hey, best of luck, but I don't think you'll need it."

He was about to respond when Addie took notice of the pair and darted over. "What's going on?" she asked, eyeing them curiously.

"Gotta run! See ya!" Gwen was out the door before either of them had a chance to intervene.

That meant Addie's full focus landed on him. "Since when are you two best buddies? She slipping you danishes on the side, buster?"

"Uh . . . well, um, she wanted to borrow something. A book. From me. Not one of *my* books, but another book, and so I gave it to her . . . just now. And that was what we were doing."

She stared at him for ten whole seconds, almost made him believe he'd duped her, but then her face split into a wide smile. "You are the worst liar. How is it that a guy who makes up stories for a living can't lie to save his life? You're up to something, Holtz, and I'm gonna find out what it is . . . or I'm withholding."

"Withholding?" he asked leadingly.

"Everything—including the danishes."

"Well, that's a bit harsh—"

Addie's phone chirped, cutting him off. "Ooh, my mint chocolate chip cookies are done!" She started toward the kitchen, and without looking back she said, "Don't even think of asking for one until you spill the beans."

You'll find out soon enough.

That evening, Ethan escorted Addie to the Cup-A-Cabana. It was barely after seven o'clock, but all the interior lights had been shut off.

She glanced up at him in surprise. "That's odd. Gwen normally doesn't close before ten."

Ethan pulled out a key from his pocket, the one Gwen had given him earlier, and slid it into the lock. Like magic, the tumblers clicked into position and the door swung open.

"Holtz, you've got some 'splaining to do."

He smirked, ushering her inside and flipping on the lights. Wordlessly, he directed her to the table Gwen had specifically arranged for them, with the flowers he'd purchased from Mr. Turcott in a vase at its center. Pink roses, the same shade as Addie's lips.

"Ethan," she whispered in awe as he helped her get seated. She fingered the petals on one of the roses and took a long whiff. While she was distracted, he tiptoed behind the counter to find the rest of the provisions Gwen had organized. Two cups of freshly poured tea, and a bag of food from El Camino. There was a note stapled to the outside of the bag from Miguel, the owner, who told him their dinner was on the house.

Predictably, Addie's gaze locked on him, but she stayed seated as he'd hoped she would. "I'm not even gonna ask what you're doing back there because I'm sure there's a perfectly logical explanation as to why it smells like El Camino in the Cup-A-Cabana."

"Perfectly logical," he echoed. Using the two plates Gwen had left out, he started assembling their meals. They'd have the place all to themselves tonight, the coffee shop where they met, eating the food they'd enjoyed on their first proper date, the night everything changed.

For the better. He dipped his hand into his pocket and played with the ring buried inside.

"I keep waiting for a mariachi band to march through the door. Are you finished yet? I'm starving."

Chuckling, he gathered her cup of tea and plate of food and delivered both to her without error. He then joined her at the table with his own food and beverage. He lifted his cup, waiting for her to do the same, and clinked them together. "Here's to us. Here's to dreams fulfilled."

"Is that all?"

"What do you mean?" he asked, taking a bite of enchilada.

"Am I missing something? An anniversary?" She cut off a piece of her cheese-smothered burrito and popped it into her mouth. "Are you leaving me for our waitress at El Camino?" she asked through stuffed cheeks. "Our original waitress, I mean. She was pretty. Actually, I'm not sure she even works there anymore—"

"No, I'm leaving you because you talk with your mouth full."

She smiled, swallowing her bite and washing it down with a gulp of tea. "Aww, I love you, too."

His heart beat rapidly throughout their meal. But it wasn't nerves or doubts or any kind of insecurity, it was pure excitement. Adrenaline. He'd been waiting months for this day, because he'd known she was the one right from the start.

At long last, Addie got up to use the restroom, and he had his opening. He fished for the ring in his pocket and dropped it into her nearly empty teacup. Perhaps not a grand gesture to some, but Addie would appreciate it . . . as long as she didn't accidentally swallow it, that is. He'd heard horror stories of women choking on their engagement rings hidden inside various food items. *Oh, Christ. What a horrible idea.*

He was seconds away from retrieving the ring and rethinking the entire idiotic plan when Addie returned, eyeing him speculatively as she took her seat.

Instead of waiting for the interrogation, he launched into his speech. "A year ago today, a struggling author met a woman in this coffee shop who fascinated him, mystified him, inspired him in countless ways. A woman who believed wholeheartedly that she'd find love in the bottom of her teacup."

"And look how that turned out," she whispered, nodding to him.

He smiled. "Read your leaves."

Addie obediently lowered her gaze and a surprised gasp escaped her throat. "Oh, my God." She freed the ring and patted it dry on her napkin, gasping for a second time when he dropped down on one knee next to her chair. "Oh, Ethan. So cliché," she teased as tears pooled in her eyes.

"Will you just let me do this?"

"Sorry. Continue."

He took the ring from the napkin and held it in his hand, the gemstone sparkling almost as much as her eyes. Man, he was a sap. "The struggling author wasn't sure if she'd ever notice him in a . . . romantic sort of way. Until the night he walked her home, and—"

"They almost kissed," Addie supplied.

"And he knew she could finally see him. Even so, it took those knuckleheads two more weeks before they figured it out. But after their date at El Camino, when he kissed her for real, he realized she'd been well worth the wait."

"And he wasn't bad, either."

"So the dating became a routine, things got serious, and they moved in together. Every morning he'd wake up to her beautiful face and think, 'How did I ever get so lucky?' He couldn't imagine his life without her in it, but there was only one way he could guarantee she'd be his forever."

Ethan reached for her trembling hand, poised to slip the ring on her slender finger. "He asked her to marry him, hoping, praying she'd say yes, and then he waited with bated breath for her to answer . . . ."

"Yes," she choked out.

"Yes?"

"Yes," she repeated, more clearly this time, laughing at his dumbfounded expression.

Shaking, he placed the ring on her finger, and they both stared for countless seconds at the emerald stone. She pulled him into her arms and hugged him tightly, wiping away the stray tear trickling down his cheek that neither of them would ever talk about.

"This is perfect. Everything. I can't believe you did all this," she whispered against his neck.

Ethan leaned back, prepared to give props to all his helpers, when a commotion at the window caught his eye. "Wonder what the peanut gallery thinks," he said, nodding to their onlookers.

She followed his gesture, beaming as she saw the nosy townspeople with their faces pressed to the glass. "Should we let them in?"

"Do we have to?"

"Yes! I have to show off my ring and tell them all about my schmoopy guy's proposal."

He rolled his eyes, though he didn't really mind one bit if it made her happy.

Addie leapt to her feet and tugged him up with her. "Look all the people who're rooting for us. Man, we're so popular. We're like celebrities. They'll need to give us one of those supercouple nicknames, like Ethie or Addethan."

"Is it too late to back out now?"

Giggling, she held his face between her palms and spoke his new favorite sentence in the Addie sentence hall of fame: "I can't wait to marry you." Then she kissed him and danced her way to the door, inviting the rest of the townspeople inside the shop, inside their lives, and he had to finally admit it felt like home.

Some stories really did have happy endings.

The End

JULIE EVELYN JOYCE

Keep reading for a sneak peek of the next book in the *Make Me a Match* series . . .

Learning to Love

"Why does it smell like a damn pumpkin patch in here?"

Rebecca Ledgerwood tore her gaze from the computer screen and turned toward the door. Pete's burly frame barely squeezed through the opening of their shared office. He raised the collar of his shirt over his nose as he stomped over to his desk, as if he preferred his own body odor to the warm, inviting smell of autumn.

Shrugging, she finally answered, "Pumpkin spice air freshener."

He rolled his eyes. "This is a sickness. You know that, right?"

"Hey, it's better than the sweaty gym socks alternative." She was used to the usual unpleasant aromas that came with working in the Phys. Ed. department at Kendal High School, but the boys this semester were a particularly ripe bunch.

"Got my student teacher coming in today. He's meeting me and the kids before he starts next week, just to get a feel for the place." Opening the mini fridge, he grabbed the grocery bag inside containing his lunch, which usually consisted of at least three courses.

"Oh yeah, I forgot about that. Hey, grab mine, too," she said before he'd shut the fridge door.

He obliged, nosily poking his head inside her lunch bag. "What is that, a veggie wrap?"

"Roasted red pepper, eggplant, and hummus."

Shuddering, he tossed her the bag and took a seat at the desk opposite hers. "Now you're gonna have garlic breath all afternoon, Ledgey."

"Exactly, and I'll threaten to breathe on the little punks if they don't do as I ask."

"Harsh. I like it."

She smiled as she bit into her wrap, chewing as quickly as she could before her lunchtime supervision in the gym started. "So, what's his story?" she asked. "The student teacher."

"Columbia grad, used to work at some big ad agency in New York. Can't believe he quit to become a teacher."

"Our lives are so glamorous. Everybody thinks so."

He snorted as he poured dressing over his salad. "Gotta be some B.S. Probably had a nervous breakdown."

Rebecca rolled her eyes, but it was hard not to speculate. For a guy to take such a 180 in the career sphere . . . must have been something major that spurred on the decision. She couldn't deny her curiosity. Checking her watch, she chomped into her wrap again, because she couldn't deny the students their gym time at lunch, either.

A steady knock at the door stole her attention. Normally, they'd battle it out with a game of rock, paper, scissors to decide who'd have to answer it, but Pete was already on his feet.

She was trying to slurp down a long string of red pepper when the door opened. Sadly, there wasn't an impatient kid on the other side. There was a man. A brown-haired, blue-eyed, knee-wobblingly delicious specimen of a man, one of the finest she'd ever seen.

He was clearly a mirage. Or maybe she was having a stroke.

"William, I take it?" Pete asked, effectively killing the moment. At the other man's nod, he stretched out his hand to properly introduce himself. "Pete Derenberger. Welcome to Kendal High."

While the men exchanged pleasantries, she swallowed down the wily red pepper, set her remaining lunch aside, and sat up straighter. She glanced again at William, noting that although he appeared to be calm and in control, his shifting feet spoke a different story. Couldn't blame the guy. Walking into a high school for the first time on the opposite side of the authority line was unnerving to say the least.

Pete turned to her then to make the introductions. "This is Rebecca Ledgerwood, fellow Phys. Ed. teacher, and the only person I know who can throw a better spiral than me."

William gave her an appreciative smile as he gripped her palm in his own. "Will Whitney, former quarterback."

Warm tingles radiated through her palm, zapped down her arm, and fired sparks to the rest of her body. Touching the man's freaking hand did that to her. Just his hand. Totally normal. "Good to . . . um, nice to meet you."

"C'mon and I'll show you around the school," Pete said, and she was grateful for the interruption because she hadn't breathed a full breath since Will laid those wicked blue eyes on her. "Ledgey has a supervision in the gym." He nudged her shoulder. "Remember?"

"Yes, I remember," she said, shooting daggers at him.

He opened the door for Will to step out, then turned back to Rebecca and spoke in a lowered voice. "You've got hummus on the corner of your mouth."

"Jesus." Her cheeks burned furiously as she searched for something to wipe her face.

"And a spot of drool on your chin," he added with a smirk.

"Shut it, Berg," she fired back, along with a box of tissues. Straight at his big, fat, know-it-all head.

He dodged the flying object at the last second, laughing as he closed the door behind him. The box fell to the floor with a *thunk*, and then the room was blanketed in silence, save for the rapid thrum of her heart.

Rebecca wiped her mouth, horrified by the gob of hummus the tissue collected. She might have noticed she was wearing half her lunch on her face if *he* hadn't come in there looking all . . . older than she expected. He had to be in his late twenties. Maybe even early thirties. Tall. Insanely handsome. Soon to be working in very close quarters with her for the next fifteen weeks.

And completely off-limits.

Sighing in frustration, she collected the remains of her lunch and threw it in the fridge, grabbed her whistle, and headed for the gym.

Acknowledgements

I was blessed to be raised by the most incredible parents on the planet. Their love, support, and unwavering belief in me has allowed me to realize so many dreams, including writing this book. I only wish my mom were here to see it. I miss her more than I could ever say, but Dad and I have become even closer in her absence. He reminds me every day what it means to be strong.

I wouldn't be writing an acknowledgements section at all if it weren't for my critique partner and BFF, Margaret Ethridge. Not only did she inspire me with the idea for this story, she was there every step of the way to help me see it through to completion. Whether I required pushing, prodding, nagging, begging, or cajoling, she always delivered. It's because of her that I can finally call myself a romance novelist. She's the toast to my peanut butter, and now I'm toasting her for being the greatest friend a girl could ever ask for! Thank you, my Bunny, from the bottom of my heart.

An extra special shout-out goes to Hannah Moore for letting me borrow the Pie-Cycle (her brainchild) for my book. Addie thanks you, too!

I need to give props to my Super Cool Party People. We've been on countless adventures together, and through all the good and the bad, they've always got my back. Thank you for being my friends.

I'd also like to shower my wonderful friend Kristan Higgins with kisses of gratitude. Kristan reached out to me during my darkest hours and showed me so much kindness and compassion. Thanks to her invaluable guidance, I managed to find a way to turn what would have been a standalone novel into a series that I can't wait to share with you!

Next in line to receive my undying appreciation is my supremely talented editor, Sarah Pesce. Her enthusiasm, cheerleading, and kickass editing skills quite simply have made me a better writer. And, best of all, she's become a cherished friend of mine, too.

Lastly, I want to thank you, sweet readers, for buying my book and be-leafing in me. :)

About the Author

Julie Evelyn Joyce *is a loud and proud Canuck. When she's not writing quirky and witty romances, she spends her time molding young minds, playing sports, singing karaoke, juggling, and dancing like there's no tomorrow. Sometimes simultaneously. She's also in hot pursuit of her own happily ever after, and anxiously awaits the day serial dating becomes an Olympic event. Last but not least, she worships peanut butter and wants to have its delicious babies. And that's Julie in a nutshell!*

CPSIA information can be obtained
at www.ICGtesting.com
Printed in the USA
LVHW111058090719
623549LV00001B/71/P